HOSTILE ENCOUNTER

Moving with i........................lf
crawled to the low............................re
he had left his rifle..........................ll
singing. Pulling hi...........................o
take a step, slipped,.........................e
Indian girl began sc.......ng. She snatched her dress off
the bush and held it so that it covered her. Matt tried
to calm the girl by making the sign for "friend," "white
man," and "peace," while urgently saying: *Ta-ba-bone,*
you understand? *Suyapo!* I went to sleep, you see, and
had no idea you were around . . ."

Suddenly her screaming stopped. Not because of his
words or hand signs, Matt feared, but because of the
appearance of an Indian man who had pushed through
the bushes and now stood beside her. His dark brown
eyes blazed with anger. Drawing a glittering knife out
of its sheath, he motioned for the girl to step aside, and
moved toward Matt menacingly.

Backing away, Matt thought frantically: *Captain Clark
is not going to like this at all. And if that Indian does what
it looks like he means to do with that knife I'm not going
to like it either . . .*

NORTHWEST DESTINY
Volume One: DISTANT TRAILS
Volume Two: GATHERING STORM
(available December 1992)
Volume Three: RIVER'S END
(available March 1993)

SPECIAL PREVIEW!
***Turn to the back of this book for an exciting look
at Volume 2 in this epic trilogy . . .***

NORTHWEST DESTINY
*. . . the sprawling saga of brotherhood, pride and rage
on the American frontier.*

Jove titles by Bill Gulick

NORTHWEST DESTINY

VOLUME 1: DISTANT TRAILS

Coming in December 1992

VOLUME 2: GATHERING STORM

NORTHWEST DESTINY

VOLUME ONE

Distant Trails

BILL GULICK

JOVE BOOKS, NEW YORK

This Jove Book contains the complete
text of the original hardcover edition.
It has been completely reset in a typeface
designed for easy reading and was printed
from new film.

NORTHWEST DESTINY VOLUME 1: DISTANT TRAILS

A Jove Book / published by arrangement with
the author

PRINTING HISTORY
Jove edition / September 1992

ISBN: 0-515-10863-4

Jove Books are published by The Berkley Publishing Group,
200 Madison Avenue, New York, New York 10016.
The name "JOVE" and the "J" logo
are trademarks belonging to Jove Publications, Inc.

PRINTED IN THE UNITED STATES OF AMERICA

10 9 8 7 6 5 4 3 2 1

A Note About the Vocabulary

Because the Nez Perce Indians had no written language before the white man came, at least three classes of whites have attempted to devise one for them: the early explorers and fur trappers, who were of several nationalities and tongues, and were bad spellers in all; Protestant and Catholic missionaries, the former American, the latter European; and scientific anthropologists, who did not arrive until the language was almost gone.

In the 1830s, a Presbyterian missionary, Asa Smith, who was something of a linguist, worked with Chief Lawyer to simplify the written language, using the Pickering alphabet developed for the Sandwich Islanders (Hawaiians), which included twelve letters—"a, e, i, o, u, h, k, l, m, n, p," and "w"—plus the additional letters "s" and "t." The letters "b, d, f, g, r, v," and "z" were used only in foreign words.

In 1895, the Catholic Society of Jesus at St. Ignatius Mission, in Montana, put together a *Dictionary of the Nez Perce Language*, which an elderly Nez Perce told me "is as good as anything ever published . . . ," a photocopy of which I have acquired and used.

In the late 1960s, a Japanese linguist from the University of California, Haruo Aoki, began a serious attempt to save and preserve the language by spending time with the few older Indians who still understood it. Among other things, he has recorded some nine different versions of Chief Joseph's surrender speech.

During the thirty-five years I have known and worked with these Indians, I have put together my own vocabulary of sorts, working on the not-very-scientific basis of asking "How do you say so-and-so?" and then, when told, persisting with "How do you spell it?" Because there are at least seventeen separate bands in the Nez Perce tribe, there are many ways to pronounce or spell a word.

I have tried to simplify as much as possible. Listed below are a few examples of word usage in the book.

Pg. No.
   3   *George Drewyer*. A French-Canadian with the Lewis and Clark party, his last name is also spelled Drouillard.
   4   *Bitter Root Mountains*. Though modern-day mapmakers condense the first two words into Bitterroot, writers and maps of the day always separated Bitter and Root.
   4   *Shoshone*. Later writers use the word Shoshoni for both the singular and plural. But in that place and time, it was always written Shoshone or Shoshones. For some strange reason their neighbors and relatives to the east were called Northern Shoshoni. I have done the same.
   5   *Nez Perce*. Though of French derivation, the name of the tribe long ago was Americanized and the accent mark on the final "e" dropped. It is pronounced "Nezz Purse." The plural is Nez Perces.
   8   *Traveler's Rest*. Singular possessive.
   12   *Tab-ba-bone*. Shoshone for white man.
   12   *Suyapo*. The Nez Perce word for white man. It refers to the whites as "the crowned ones" for the hats they wore.
   17   *Nimipu*. What the Nez Perces called themselves—"The People."
   19   *Tepee*. Not teepee or tipi.
   24   *Speelyi*. Nez Perce name for the Coyote Spirit that made their world.

33 *Sacajawea*. The Shoshone woman guide for the Lewis and Clark party. Recently the Lewis and Clark Historical Society decided that the name should be spelled Sacagawea. I don't agree.

35 *Koos-koos-kee*, Clearwater; and *Ki-moo-e-nim*, Snake. As in many Nez Perce words, I separate the syllables for ease of reading and pronunciation, but there is no hard and fast rule for this.

59 *Tin-nach-e-moo-toolt*. Chief Broken Arm. Same reasoning.

59 *Kouse*. An edible root. Lewis and Clark spelled it "cows."

PART I

RED SON,
WHITE SON

1805-1809

1

For the last hundred yards of the stalk, neither man had spoken—not even in whispers—but communicated by signs as they always did when hunting meat to fill hungry bellies. Two steps ahead, George Drewyer, the man recognized to be the best hunter in the Lewis and Clark party, sank down on his right knee, froze, and peered intently through the glistening wet bushes and dangling evergreen tree limbs toward the animal grazing in the clearing. Identifying it, he turned, using his hands swiftly and graphically to tell the younger, less experienced hunter, Matt Crane, the nature of the animal he had seen and how he meant to approach and kill it.

Not a deer, his hands said. Not an elk. Just a stray Indian horse—with no Indians in sight. He'd move up on it from downwind, his hands said, until he got into sure-kill range, then he'd put a ball from his long rifle into its head. What he expected Matt to do was follow a couple of steps behind and a few feet off to the right, stopping when he stopped, aiming when he aimed, but firing only if the actions of the horse clearly showed that Drewyer's ball had missed.

Matt signed that he understood. Turning back toward the clearing, George Drewyer began his final stalk.

Underfoot, the leaf mold and fallen pine needles formed a yielding carpet beneath the scattered clumps of bushes

3

and thick stands of pines, which here on the western slope of the Bitter Root Mountains were broader in girth and taller than the skinny lodgepole and larch found on the higher reaches of the Lolo Trail. Half a day's travel behind, the other thirty-two members of the party still were struggling in foot-deep snow over slick rocks, steep slides, and tangles of down timber treacherous as logjams, as they sought the headwaters of the Columbia and the final segment of their journey to the Pacific Ocean.

It had been four days since the men had eaten meat, Matt knew, being forced to sustain themselves on the detested army ration called "portable soup," a grayish brown jelly that looked like a mixture of pulverized wood duff and dried dung, tasted like iron filings, and even when flavored with meat drippings and dissolved in hot water satisfied the belly no more than a swallow of air. Nor had the last solid food been much, for the foal butchered at Colt-Killed Creek had been dropped by its dam only a few months ago; though its meat was tender enough, most of its growth had gone into muscle and bone, its immature carcass making skimpy portions when distributed among such a large party of famished men.

With September only half gone, winter had already come to the seven-thousand-foot-high backbone of the continent a week's travel behind. All the game that the old Shoshone guide, Toby, had told them usually was to be found in the high meadows at this time of year had moved down to lower levels. Desperate for food, Captain William Clark had sent George Drewyer and Matt Crane scouting ahead for meat, judging that two men traveling afoot and unencumbered would stand a much better chance of finding game than the main party with its thirty-odd men and twenty-nine heavily laden horses. As he usually did, Drewyer had found game of a sort, weighed the risk of rousing the hostility of its Indian owner against the need of the party for food, and decided that hunger recognized no property rights.

In the drizzling cold rain, the coat of the grazing horse

glistened like polished metal. It would be around four years old, Matt guessed, a brown and white paint, well muscled, sleek, alert. If this were a typical Nez Perce horse, he could well believe what the Shoshone chief, Cameahwait, had told Captain Clark—that the finest horses to be found in this part of the country were those raised by the Shoshones' mortal enemies, the Nez Perces. Viewing such a handsome animal cropping bluegrass on a Missouri hillside eighteen months ago, Matt Crane would have itched to rope, saddle, and ride it, testing its speed, wind, and spirit. Now all he itched to do was kill and eat it.

Twenty paces away from the horse, which still was grazing placidly, George Drewyer stopped, knelt behind a fallen tree, soundlessly rested the barrel of his long rifle on its trunk, and took careful aim. Two steps to his right, Matt Crane did the same. After what seemed an agonizingly long period of time, during which Matt held his breath, Drewyer's rifle barked. Without movement or sound, the paint horse sank to the ground, dead—Matt was sure—before its body touched the sodden earth.

"Watch it!" Drewyer murmured, swiftly reversing his rifle, swabbing out its barrel with the ramrod, expertly reloading it with patched and greased lead ball, wiping flint and firing hammer clean, then opening the pan and pouring in a carefully measured charge while he protected it from the drizzle with the tree trunk and his body.

Keeping his own rifle sighted on the fallen horse, Matt held his position without moving or speaking, as George Drewyer had taught him to do, until the swarthy, dark-eyed hunter had reloaded his weapon and risen to one knee. Peering first at the still animal, then moving his searching gaze around the clearing, Drewyer tested the immediate environment with all his senses—sight, sound, smell, and his innate hunter's instinct—for a full minute before he at last nodded in satisfaction.

"A bunch-quitter, likely. Least there's no herd nor herders around. Think you can skin it, preacher boy?"

"Sure. You want it quartered, with the innards saved in the hide?"

"Just like we'd do with an elk. Save everything but the hoofs and whinny. Get at it, while I snoop around for Injun sign. The Nez Perces will be friendly, the captains say, but I'd as soon not meet the Injun that owned that horse till its head and hide are out of sight."

While George Drewyer circled the clearing and prowled through the timber beyond, Matt Crane went to the dead horse, unsheathed his butcher knife, skillfully made the cuts needed to strip off the hide, and gutted and dissected the animal. Returning from his scout, Drewyer hunkered down beside him, quickly boned out as large a packet of choice cuts as he could conveniently carry, wrapped them in a piece of hide, and loaded the still-warm meat into the empty canvas backpack he had brought along for that purpose.

"It ain't likely the men'll get this far by dark," he said, "so I'll take 'em a taste to ease their bellies for the night. Can you make out alone till tomorrow noon?"

"Yes."

"From what I seen, the timber thins out a mile or so ahead. Seems to be a kind of open, marshy prairie beyond, which is where the Nez Perces come this time of year to dig roots, Toby says. Drag the head and hide back in the bushes out of sight. Cut the meat up into pieces you can spit and broil, then build a fire and start it cooking. If the smoke and smell brings Injun company, give 'em the peace sign, invite 'em to sit and eat, and tell 'em a big party of white men will be coming down the trail tomorrow. You got all that, preacher boy?"

"Yes."

"Good. Give me a hand with this pack and I'll be on my way." Slipping his arms through the straps and securing the pad that transferred a portion of the weight to his forehead, Drewyer got to his feet while Matt Crane eased the load. Grinning, Drewyer squeezed his shoulder. "Remind me to quit calling you preacher boy, will you, Matt? You've learned a lot since you left home."

"I've had a good teacher."

"That you have! Take care."

Left alone in the whispering silence of the forest and the cold, mist-like rain, Matt Crane dragged the severed head and hide into a clump of nearby bushes. Taking his hatchet, he searched for and found enough resinous wood, bark, and dry duff to catch the spark from his flint and steel. As the fire grew in the narrow trench he had dug for it, he cut forked sticks, placed pieces of green aspen limbs horizontally across them, sliced the meat into strips, and started it to broiling. The smell of juice dripping into the fire made his belly churn with hunger, tempting him to do what Touissant Charbonneau, the party's French-Canadian interpreter, did when fresh-killed game was brought into camp—seize a hunk and gobble it down hot, raw, and bloody. But he did not, preferring to endure the piercing hunger pangs just a little longer in exchange for the greater pleasure of savoring his first bite of well-cooked meat.

Cutting more wood for the fire, he hoped George Drewyer would stop calling him "preacher boy." Since at twenty he was one of the youngest members of the party and his father, the Reverend Peter Crane, was a Presbyterian minister in St. Louis, it had been natural enough for the older men to call him "the preacher's boy" at first. Among a less disciplined band, he would have been forced to endure a good deal of hoorawing and would have been the butt of many practical jokes. But the no-nonsense military leadership of the two captains put strict limits on that sort of thing.

Why Drewyer—who'd been raised a Catholic, could barely read and write, and had no peer as an outdoorsman—should have made Matt his protégé, Matt himself could not guess. Maybe because he was malleable, did what he was told to do, and never backed off from hard work. Maybe because he listened more than he talked. Or maybe because he was having the adventure of his

life and showed it. Whatever the reason, their relationship
was good. It would be even better, Matt mused, if Drewyer
would drop the "preacher boy" thing and simply call him
by name.

While butchering the horse, Matt noticed that it had been
gelded as a colt. According to George Drewyer, the Nez
Perces were one of the few Western Indian tribes that
practiced selective breeding, thus the high quality of their
horses. From the way Chief Cameahwait had acted, a state
of war existed between the Shoshones and the Nez Perces,
so the first contact between the Lewis and Clark party—
which had passed through Shoshone country—and the Nez
Perces was going to be fraught with danger. Aware of the
fact that he might make the first contact, Matt Crane felt both
uneasy and proud. Leaving him alone in this area showed the
confidence Drewyer had in him. But his aloneness made him
feel a little spooky.

With the afternoon only half gone and nothing to do but
tend the fire, Matt stashed his blanket roll under a tree out
of the wet, picked up his rifle, and curiously studied the
surrounding forest. There was no discernible wind, but
vagrant currents of air stirred, bringing to his nostrils the
smell of wood smoke, of crushed pine needles, of damp
leaf mold, of burnt black powder. As he moved across the
clearing toward a three-foot-wide stream gurgling down the
slope, he scowled, suddenly realizing that the burnt black
powder smell could not have lingered behind this long. Nor
would it have gotten stronger, as this smell was doing the
nearer he came to the stream. Now he identified it beyond
question.

Sulfur! There must be a mineral-impregnated hot spring
nearby, similar to the hot springs near Traveler's Rest at the
eastern foot of Lolo Pass, where the cold, weary members of
the party had eased their aches and pains in warm, soothing
pools. What he wouldn't give for a hot bath right now!

At the edge of the stream, he knelt, dipping his hand into
the water. It was warm. Cupping his palm, he tasted it,

finding it strongly sulfurous. If this were like the stream on the other side of the mountains, he mused, there would be one or more scalding, heavily impregnated springs issuing from old volcanic rocks higher up the slope, their waters diluted by colder side rivulets joining the main stream, making it simply a matter of exploration to find water temperature and a chemical content best suited to the needs of a cold, tired body. The prospect intrigued him.

Visually checking the meat broiling over the fire, he judged it could do without tending for an hour or so. Thick though the forest cover was along the sides of the stream, he would run no risk of getting lost, for following the stream downhill would bring him back to the clearing. Time enough then to cut limbs for a lean-to and rig a shelter for the night.

Sometimes wading in the increasingly warm waters of the stream, sometimes on its bush-bordered bank, he followed its windings uphill for half a mile before he found what he was looking for: a pool ten feet long and half as wide, eroded in smooth basalt, ranging in depth from one to four feet. Testing the temperature of its water, he found it just right—hot but not unbearably so, the sulfur smell strong but not unpleasant. Leaning his rifle against a tree trunk, he took off his limp, shapeless red felt hat, pulled his thin moccasins off his bruised and swollen feet, waded into the pool, and gasped with sensual pleasure as the heat of the water spread upward.

Since his fringed buckskin jacket and woolen trousers already were soaking wet from the cold rain, he kept them on as he first sank to a sitting position, then stretched out full length on his back, with only his head above water. After a time, he roused himself long enough to strip the jacket off over his head and pull the trousers down over his ankles. Tossing them into a clump of bushes near his rifle, hat, and moccasins, he lay back in the soothing water, naked, warm, and comfortable for the first time since Traveler's Rest.

Drowsily, his eyes closed. He slept . . .

• • •

The sound that awakened him some time later could have been made by a deer moving down to drink from the pool just upstream from where he lay. It could have been made by a beaver searching for a choice willow sapling to cut down. It could have been made by a bob-cat, a bear, or a cougar. But as consciousness returned to him, as he heard the sound and attempted to identify it, his intelligence rejected each possibility that occurred to him the moment it crossed his mind—for one lucid reason.

Animals did not sing. And whatever this intruder into his state of tranquillity might be, it was singing.

Though the words were not recognizable, they had an Indian sound, unmistakably conveying the message that the singer was at peace with the world, not self-conscious, and about to indulge in a very enjoyable act. Turning over on his belly, Matt crawled to the upper end of the pool, peering through the screening bushes in the direction from which the singing sound was coming. The light was poor. Even so, it was good enough for him to make out the figure of a girl, standing in profile not ten feet away, reaching down to the hem of her buckskin skirt, lifting it, and pulling it up over her head.

As she tossed the garment aside, she turned, momentarily facing him. His first thought was *My God, she's beautiful!* His second: *She's naked!* His third: *How can I get away from here without being seen?*

That she was not aware of his presence was made clear enough by the fact that she still was crooning her bath-taking song, her gaze intent on her footing as she stepped gingerly into a pool just a few yards upstream from the one in which he lay. Though he had stopped breathing for fear she would hear the sound, he could not justify leaving his eyes open for fear she would hear the lids closing. Morally wrong though he knew it was to stare at her, he could not even blink or look away.

She would be around sixteen years old, he judged, her skin light copper in color, her mouth wide and generous, with dimples indenting both cheeks. Her breasts were full but not heavy; her waist was slim, her stomach softly rounded, her hips beginning to broaden with maturity, her legs long and graceful. Watching her sink slowly into the water until only the tips of her breasts and her head were exposed, Matt felt no guilt for continuing to stare at her. Instead he mused, *So that's what a naked woman looks like! Why should I be ashamed to admire such beauty?*

He began breathing again, careful to make no sound. Since the two pools were no more than a dozen feet apart, separated by a thin screen of bushes and a short length of stream, which here made only a faint gurgling noise, he knew that getting out of the water, retrieving his clothes and rifle, and then withdrawing from the vicinity without revealing his presence would require utmost caution. But the attempt must be made, for if one young Indian woman knew of this bathing spot, others must know of it, too, and in all likelihood soon would be coming here to join her.

He could well imagine his treatment at their hands, if found. Time and again recently the two captains had warned members of the party that Western Indians such as the Shoshones, Flatheads, and Nez Perces had a far higher standard of morality than did the Mandans, with whom the party had wintered, who would gladly sell the favor of wives and daughters for a handful of beads, a piece of bright cloth, or a cheap trade knife, and cheerfully provide shelter and bed for the act.

Moving with infinite care, he half floated, half crawled to the lower right-hand edge of the pool, where he had left his rifle and clothes. The Indian girl still was singing. The bank was steep and slick. Standing up, he took hold of a sturdy-feeling, thumb-thick sapling rooted near the edge of the bank, cautiously tested it, and judged it secure. Pulling himself out of the pool, he started to take a step, slipped, and tried to save himself by grabbing the sapling with both hands.

The full weight of his body proved too much for its root system. Torn out of the wet earth, it no longer supported him. As he fell backward into the pool, he gave an involuntary cry of disgust.

"Oh, shit!"

Underwater, his mouth, nose, and eyes filled as he struggled to turn over and regain his footing. When he did so, he immediately became aware of the fact that the girl had stopped singing. Choking, coughing up water, half-blinded, and completely disoriented, he floundered out of the pool toward where he thought his clothes and rifle were. Seeing a garment draped over a bush, he grabbed it, realized it was not his, hastily turned away, and blundered squarely into a wet, naked body.

To save themselves from falling, both he and the Indian girl clung to each other momentarily. She began screaming. Hastily he let her go. Still screaming and staring at him with terror-stricken eyes, she snatched her dress off the bush and held it so that it covered her. Finding his own clothes, he held them in front of his body, trying to calm the girl by making the sign for "friend," "white man," and "peace," while urgently saying:

"*Ta-ba-bone,* you understand? *Suyapo!* I went to sleep, you see, and had no idea you were around . . ."

Suddenly her screaming stopped. Not because of his words or hand signs, Matt feared, but because of the appearance of an Indian man who had pushed through the bushes and now stood beside her. He was dressed in beaded, fringed buckskins, was stocky, slightly bowlegged, a few inches shorter than Matt but more muscular and heavier, a man in his middle twenties, with high cheekbones and a firm jawline. He shot a guttural question at the girl, to which she replied in a rapid babble of words. His dark brown eyes blazed with anger. Drawing a glittering knife out of its sheath, he motioned the girl to step aside, and moved toward Matt menacingly.

Backing away, Matt thought frantically, *Captain Clark is not going to like this at all. And if that Indian does what it looks like he means to do with that knife, I'm not going to like it, either* . . .

2

Knowing George Drewyer to be the best linguist in the party, Matt Crane had spent a great deal of time with him during the party's journey up the Missouri River and across the Shining Mountains, endeavoring to acquire a knowledge of Indian words helpful in communicating with the various tribes. *Ta-ba-bone* meant "white man" in the Shoshone tongue, Drewyer said, while *Suyapo* meant "crowned ones" in Nez Perce, the "crowned" signifying the hats worn by white men. Of course, it always was wise to use hand signs as well as words, Drewyer said, for though local dialects might vary widely, sign language was clear, graphic, and universally understood among the plains and mountain tribes that used it.

Trouble was, Matt thought desperately as he backed away from the knife and tried to cover his nakedness by putting on his soaking-wet trousers, the lessons given him by George Drewyer so far had not taught him how to clasp his hands together in front of his chest in the sign for "peace" while those same hands were busy at knee level pulling up his pants.

Explaining himself seemed far less important at this moment than covering his private parts. In assessing the risks of crossing the continent through hostile country, he had accepted the possibility that he might be killed by an Indian arrow, spear, or rifle ball. But to be caught wrestling bare-assed with a naked Indian girl by an aggrieved Indian man and lose his manhood, his life, or both—Matt shuddered. What would the captains tell his father?

More nimble-fingered than he, the Indian girl already had slipped her buckskin dress over her head, put her hands through the armholes, and pulled its hem down below her knees. As Matt worked his trousers up to his waist, she spoke sharply to the Indian man. Halting his advance, he answered without removing his gaze from Matt's face. He asked her a question. She answered hysterically. He asked another. Her answer this time was more composed. Deciding that he had done all he could to convince them that he was peaceable and friendly, Matt stopped trying to communicate by word and sign, put on his jacket, moccasins, and hat, but was careful to make no move toward his rifle, which was leaning against a nearby tree.

Shaking her head in reply to another question, the Indian girl giggled. Pointing a finger first at Matt, then at herself, she burst into a torrent of words, broken by *"Eeyahs!"* and *"Aayahs!"*, illustrated with expressive hand gestures that appeared to be describing what had happened.

Even though he could not understand her words, the movement of her hands, the mimicry of her facial muscles, and the lights and shadows that came and went in her eyes all made her meaning perfectly clear to Matt. Pointing downstream in the direction from which he had come, she did an apt imitation of a white man's walk, with shuffling feet and swinging arms, without moving a step. She showed how he had discovered the pool, removed his clothes, lay down in the warm water, and fallen asleep. Mimicking the walk of an Indian girl, she showed how she had approached the pool just upstream, covering her eyes as she pointed at Matt to indicate that she had not seen him.

Going through the motions of undressing, she touched her lips and opened her mouth as if singing, then gestured toward Matt and touched her ears to show how he had become aware of her presence. With remarkable insight, she pantomimed his surprise and alarm, then made tiptoeing gestures with the first two fingers of her right hand to indicate how he had tried to slip away without being discovered. Listening to her intently, the Indian man let the knife fall to his side. The anger left his eyes, replaced by a glint of amusement.

Again doing the foot-shuffling and arm-swinging act in mimicry of a white man, the girl reached out and up, stiffened, appeared to slip, threw her arms wide as if falling backward, then gave an accurate imitation of his disgusted cry.

"Ohh-shee! Ohh-shee!"

At this the Indian man hooted with laughter. Sheathing the knife, he bent over, hugged himself, and exclaimed, *"Ahh taats! Ahh taats!"*

Needing no interpreter to translate the expression as *"Very good! Very good!"* Matt sheepishly wondered if the Indian girl and man knew what *his* exclamation had meant.

Smiling broadly now, the Indian man linked his index fingers in the sign for "friend." Matt responded in kind. Raising his open right hand to shoulder level, palm toward Matt to show that it held no weapon, the Indian man shook it from side to side, querying, "Who are you?"

"Suyapo—white man." Matt returned the query. "Who are you?"

"Nimipu," the Indian said, passing the index finger of his right hand just under his nose, as if thrusting a skewer of dentalium through the septum. "Nez Perce."

Most Western Indian tribes called themselves by one name, George Drewyer said; their neighbors called them by another; while the French-Canadian explorers who had first made contact with them fifty years ago identified them with casually applied names that were more rough translations of their visual tribal identification signs than accurate descriptions of their appearance or character traits. Never mind that the Blackfeets' feet were red, that the Gros Ventres' bellies were no bigger than any other Indians', that the Flatheads had normal craniums, and that the Nez Perces seldom if ever pierced their noses—the French-Canadians had named them, and that was that.

Again the Nez Perce made the querying gesture, following it with a more specific question, tapping Matt's chest, asking him his name.

"Crane," Matt said. "Matt Crane." Finding no way to translate his first name into sign language, he attempted to signify his last name by making the sign for a pair of very long legs wading in water, then flapping his arms slowly to signify a large bird flying. "Crane," he repeated. "Matt Crane."

"Ahh!" the Indian said, his dark eyes glowing with sudden understanding. *"Moki!"* Repeating the long-legged, wading mime, then the slow-flying act in much more realistic fashion than Matt had managed, he made it clear that he was well acquainted with the bird after whom Matt's family was named. *"Moki Hih-hih."*

Tapping the Indian's chest, Matt queried him as to his name.

"We-wu-kye Ilp-ilp," the Nez Perce said. Placing his hands beside his ears with the fingers extended upward to resemble a large rack of horns, he lowered his head and pawed the ground in a perfect imitation of a bull elk. Matt nodded that he understood.

"Ilp-ilp." The Nez Perce man rubbed the palm of his right hand against his cheek, as if applying paint, then pointed at the sky. The first gesture indicated a color, Matt knew; the second meant that the color was red.

"Red elk," Matt said. *"We-wu-kye Ilp-ilp.* Red Elk."

"Moki Hih-hih," the Indian said. "Matt Crane. *Moki Hih-hih."*

Aware that the Indian girl was watching intently, Matt queried, "Who is she?"

Red Elk frowned as he pondered the question for a moment. Normally women were not introduced, but this was not a normal meeting. Pointing to the girl, he held his hands in front of his shoulders, palms outward, fingers up, then moved them away from and across his body in a fluttering gesture, at the same time saying, "*Hattia!*"

"Wind?" Matt hazarded a guess.

Now Red Elk pointed up at the sky in the direction where the sun would be, if it were visible, immediately following this gesture by moving his hands horizontally across one another, as if drawing a blanket of darkness over the earth. Western Indians used the same sign for sun and moon, Drewyer said, making the blanket of darkness gesture when they wished to indicate the "night-sun," or moon.

"*Hattia!*" Red Elk said. "*Isemtuks!*"

"Moon Wind," Matt said. He smiled at her. "What a beautiful name!"

As befit an Indian girl in the presence of men, the young lady lowered her eyes and gazed shyly at the ground. Suddenly she stole a look at him and giggled. Red Elk scolded her, apparently telling her to mind her manners. Her head jerked up, her eyes blazed with sudden fury, and she lashed out at him in a volley of words that made him recoil in embarrassment. Though Matt understood nothing she said, her gestures at Red Elk, at herself, and at Matt indicated she was highly displeased with the way she had been introduced to the *Suyapo* and that she wanted Red Elk to make proper amends.

Grinning sheepishly, Red Elk tried. Pointing first at himself, then at her, he made the man-sign and the woman-sign and the graphically explicit sign for what male and female did when they were married. Then he firmly shook his head, spreading his hands far apart in a gesture indicating that theirs was not a man-wife relationship. He walked over to the girl, put an arm around her shoulders, and then made a circular motion to indicate a tepee. Putting two fingers together, he sucked one, pointed at her, then sucked the other. Watching him, the girl nodded and repeated the gesture.

"I understand," Matt said. "You're brother and sister."

Now that it had been established that they were meeting as friends, the exchange of information went with surprising speed and clarity. A large band of his people was camped not far away, Red Elk said, digging and cooking camas bulbs in a marshy area called Weippe Prairie. The Nez Perces had heard that a party of white men was on its way up the Big Muddy and across the Bitter Root Mountains and were prepared to welcome the crowned ones with open hearts. If Matt Crane would come with Red Elk and Moon Wind to their father's lodge, he would be given food, drink, warmth, and shelter.

Later he would be pleased to accept their hospitality, Matt said, but for now he must decline. Explaining that the main body of the Lewis and Clark party was a day's travel behind, he related their sufferings from cold and hunger, told how he and another man had been sent ahead to find game, and described the type of animal they had found and killed. Only the fact that the men were desperate for meat had induced them to kill the horse, Matt said, and as soon as the two captains met the Nez Perce leaders they would pay the owner of the horse a fair price for it.

A small matter, Red Elk said. The Nez Perces had many horses. He would send Moon Wind to the Nez Perce camp, where she would tell her father that a party of white men would meet with the bands led by Twisted Hair and *Tetoharsky* tomorrow afternoon. Meanwhile, he would return with his new friend to the clearing where the meat was being cooked and would remain with him there to make sure no harm came to him. As soon as Moon Wind had delivered her message, she would fill a parfleche with cooked camas and dried salmon and bring it to the clearing. Signing that she understood, the Indian girl gave Matt a shy smile, then was gone.

To protect his rifle from the dampness, Matt had put it in its waterproof buckskin case soon after the horse had been killed. As he picked it up now, Red Elk touched his arm and motioned at the case and then at himself, clearly asking if he might be permitted to examine it.

"Sure," Matt said. "Help yourself."

Watching him closely to make sure that he did not discharge the rifle accidentally, Matt noted the care with which Red Elk removed the cover and the respect with which he examined it. Without pulling its hammer back, the Nez Perce fitted its stock to his right shoulder, supported its long barrel with his extended left hand, sank to his right knee, and aimed at an imaginary target with a rock-steady stance. After simulating firing, he rose, stroked the rifle admiringly, and then smiled at Matt.

"Ahh taats! Ahh taats!"

While Matt put the rifle back in its case, Red Elk moved into a nearby clump of bushes, returning in a few moments with a quiver of arrows and a bow, which he apparently had discarded upon hearing his sister's scream. Handing the bow to Matt, he signed that he wanted him to examine it. Matt did so, with curiosity.

It was made of horn, rather than wood, and despite the fact that it was only three feet long, it had the feeling of great tensile strength. Apparently the animal horns had been straightened by steaming, cut into two-inch-wide strips, then laminated and glued together to form several layers, making a bow of tremendous power that, because of its short length, could be used with dexterity by a mounted man. No doubt this was one of the famed Nez Perce bighorn sheep bows, Matt mused, the best made by Western Indians, a weapon that had possessed a high trade value in the buffalo country before firearms became available. But like all the Indians the Lewis and Clark party had encountered on its western trek, Red Elk would prefer to own a gun.

Handing back the bow, Matt made the walking sign, the short-distance sign, and the sign for eating. Together, he and Red Elk moved down the stream toward the clearing . . .

3

During the twenty-four hours that passed between the time George Drewyer shot the horse and the time the main body of the Lewis and Clark party came straggling down the trail, Matt Crane basked in anticipation of the praise he would be given by Captain Meriwether Lewis and Captain William Clark for the way he had conducted himself. Had he not made the first contact with the Nez Perces? Had he not kept it peaceful under trying circumstances? With an evening, night, and morning in which to converse with Red Elk and Moon Wind—who had brought food from her father's lodge and set up a small tepee to shelter the three of them from the rain—had he not gained a great deal of information that would be extremely useful to the two captains?

Indeed he had. But because of a slight error in judgment, he was in no condition to greet the party when it arrived shortly after noon, next day. Instead, he was squatting in a clump of bushes off to one side of the trail with his trousers down, groaning in agony as his bowels reacted violently to last night's supper of steamed camas and dried salmon.

His error in judgment, he now realized, had been his politeness in abstaining from eating horse meat when he learned that Red Elk would not touch it. By signs, the Nez Perce made it clear that his people had a taboo against eating horses because the animals served them so well in traveling, hunting, and war. Nor would they eat dogs, he said, for these animals were their children's playmates and friends, as well as being related to *Speelyi,* the Coyote Spirit who had created the Nez Perce world, and must not be offended. As yet another food taboo, Red Elk said, the Nez Perces never ate the flesh of the grizzly bear, even though killing one of the monsters was regarded a deed of great valor, for grizzlies had the bad reputation of devouring dead Indians; eating the flesh of one would be an act of cannibalism.

"These are Nez Perce tribal taboos," Red Elk said. "But the crowned ones live by different taboos. Eat the horse meat if you like. I will not be offended."

"I cannot eat while you go hungry."

"I will not go hungry long," Red Elk said with a laugh. "Moon Wind will bring food."

"Then I will wait."

"Good!" Red Elk said, looking pleased. "When she comes, we will eat together."

Since the sweet-tasting, mushy camas was the first fresh vegetable Matt had eaten for a long while, he partook of several helpings. Soaked in boiling water to moisten it, the dried salmon tasted delicious, too, and he made up for all the solid food he had missed the past few days by eating until his stomach was comfortably full.

Feeling drowsy a couple of hours after darkness fell, he said good night to Red Elk and Moon Wind, pulled up his blanket, and went to sleep, lulled by the warmth of the fire Moon Wind was carefully tending, and soothed by the patter of raindrops on the waterproof skin tepee, which was a much cozier shelter than any he could have improvised.

At first, he slept well. Then his stomach began to growl, he began to toss and turn in discomfort, and he wakened to find his abdomen so swollen and tight that he could hardly breathe. Sitting up, he groaned and clutched his stomach.

Why hadn't he eaten the horse meat instead of the unaccustomed foods? Why had he wolfed down that third bowl of camas? Why had he let Moon Wind give him that fourth piece of fish? Oh, dear God, why didn't his belly just burst like an overinflated balloon and give him relief from this cramping pain?

Mumbling an apology to Red Elk and Moon Wind for disturbing their rest, he crawled out of the tepee on his hands and knees, staggered a few steps, lowered his trousers barely in time, squatted, and voided his bowels in an explosive liquid movement. Somewhat relieved, he returned to the tepee, lay down, and tried to sleep. Within minutes, the stuffed feeling returned, followed by cramps and another overpowering urge to evacuate. Again he stumbled out into the cold, rainy dark. For the rest of the night and half the next day the flux continued, draining him of strength. Since neither Red Elk nor Moon Wind, who had eaten the same food, was affected, his ailment had to be caused by the change in diet, he knew—but knowing brought little comfort or cure.

In midmorning the rain stopped, the sky cleared, and sunshine warmed the clearing. Well aware of his condition, Red Elk rebuilt the fire under the strips of horse meat, which the rain had extinguished during the night, filled a bowl with water from the creek, and told him to drink. Moon Wind disappeared for a time, then returned carrying a pouch full of dark-colored bark. Heating several small stones in the fire, she put some of the bark and water into a bowl, picked up the stones with two pieces of wood, dropped them into the water, and brewed a concoction that looked like tea.

"Eat," Red Elk said, handing Matt a small piece of broiled horse meat.

"Drink," Moon Wind said, steadying the bowl for him as she raised it to his lips.

He tried. But one bite of the meat and two sips of the bitter-tasting tea were all that were required to set off another rebellion in his tortured digestive tract.

"Out of the way!" he groaned, rising and heading for the bushes. "I gotta go again!"

By noon, the acute attacks of cramps had eased off, but he was so weak he could barely stand. A dozen or so Nez Perces curious to meet the crowned ones had come to the clearing from their nearby camp, among them an older couple whom Red Elk introduced as his father and mother. Rubbing her stomach and grimacing, the mother made it clear that she was familiar with his complaint and sympathized with his pains. When Moon Wind showed her the concoction she had brewed, the mother tasted it, nodded, and indicated that if he continued taking his medicine he would soon feel much better.

Less frequent though his trips into the bushes had become, he again was on one when he heard horses moving down the trail, followed by George Drewyer's hearty greeting.

"Hey, Matt! Where are you?"

Staggering weakly out into the clearing, Matt muttered, "Here, George," then sagged weakly to the ground.

"My God, boy! What happened?"

"I ate some food that didn't agree with me."

"Horse meat?"

"No—roots and fish. Red Elk and Moon Wind gave it to me. But I don't blame them. They were just being friendly."

Nodding to the two Indians, Drewyer helped Moon Wind as she eased Matt to a supine position and put a folded blanket under his head. Drewyer called, "Captain Clark!"

"Yes?"

"Got a real sick man here. Can you take a look at him?"

Summoning all the strength he could muster, Matt tried to sit up and tell Captain Clark all the interesting things he had learned about the Nez Perces. Brusquely, the captain silenced him.

"Lie down, son. You're looking poorly."

"It was the food, sir—"

Taking his pulse with one hand, then feeling his forehead for temperature with the other, Captain Clark grunted: "I know! I know! Too much fresh horse meat eaten on an empty stomach was bound to give you the colic. But a couple of Dr. Rush's Bilious Pills and a dose of Glauber's salts will flush you out. Once we get the morbid poisons out of your system, you'll be as good as new. Bring me my medical kit, George."

4

Before leaving the East, Meriwether Lewis had studied for six weeks with the most renowned physician in the country, Dr. Benjamin Rush of Philadelphia, learning the skills he would need during the journey across the continent. As a matter of course, he had passed on this acquired knowledge to the man destined to share the command of the expedition, William Clark. More suited by nature to diagnose ailments and administer remedies than the quick-tempered, impatient Lewis, the practical-minded, self-contained Clark soon was doing most of the doctoring for the party's members.

It was Dr. Rush's firm belief that diseases were caused by morbid elements invading the body. If in the circulatory system, these morbidities could be drained and the patient cured by opening a vein and bleeding. If in the digestive tract, they could be cleansed by dosing and purging. Though Captain Clark did not bleed now and then, he had found Dr. Rush's Bilious Pills—each of which contained ten grains of calomel and ten grains of jalap—most effective when treating digestive tract problems, particularly if reinforced with a generous dose of Glauber's salts.

It was a tribute to Matt Crane's physical condition that he managed to survive both his complaint and Captain Clark's cure.

Since the horse meat was soon gone and the genial Nez Perces freely shared their camas and dried salmon

with the crowned ones, every member of the party partook
heartily of the unaccustomed food, despite Matt's feeble
attempt to warn them of its dangers. And for the next
several days, every member of the party came down with
a violent case of the flux—including the two captains.
For all, the same medicine was prescribed and administered.

As the first person stricken, Matt was the first to recover.
By the time the two captains felt well enough to engage in
negotiations with the Nez Percé leaders regarding cutting
down trees, building canoes, and arranging to leave their
horses in the care of the Indians while the whites proceeded on to the mouth of the Columbia River, Matt had
established good communications with Red Elk and his
family.

The first thing he learned was that the two bands of
Indians now camped here were made up mostly of old
men, women, and children. Four days ago, several hundred seasoned warriors and young men eager to distinguish
themselves in battle had ridden south toward the land of
the Shoshones to make war on the neighboring tribe. Led
by Chief Broken Arm of the Kamiah band, the war party's
success was assured, Red Elk told Matt, for a delegation
sent east a few months ago to the Hidatsa country with
several fine Nez Percé horses had traded them for six good
rifles and a supply of powder and lead. Since the Shoshones
possessed no firearms, they would be bound to suffer heavy
casualties if they could be tricked into a fight on grounds
of Chief Broken Arm's choosing, for he was a great war
leader.

"Are you always at war with the Shoshones?" Matt asked.

"No. Just this past summer we offered them the peace
pipe. But they would not smoke with us."

"Why did you try to make peace?"

Red Elk was silent for a time as he considered how
to explain a complicated intertribal relationship in sign
language and the few Nez Percé words Matt understood.

"In the land of the Shoshones," he began, "as in the land of the Nez Perces, there are no buffalo. So each summer many hunters from both tribes cross the mountains by the same trails you took and spend several months on the plains near the Big Muddy River killing and curing meat. This country east of the mountains is claimed by the Blackfeet, Crows, and Sioux. They can have it, so far as we are concerned, for it is a cold, windy country of no account except for its grass. But the buffalo, as you have seen, are so numerous they cannot be counted. We are entitled to our share. Until a few years ago, we took our share without difficulty because we are able to hold our own against any enemy that opposed us. But that has changed."

"How?"

"Now the Blackfeet have guns. Many guns."

"Where did they get them?"

"From the King George men."

Last winter in the Mandan villages, Matt knew, the rivalry between Great Britain and the United States for the fur trade of the Far West had been a frequent topic of discussion between Lewis and Clark. Ever since the Louisiana Purchase two years ago, President Jefferson had made no secret of his intent to channel the trade of the Columbia River country eastward across the Continental Divide, then down the Missouri River by way of St. Louis. Just as openly, Canada had made it clear that its fur companies meant to capture and channel the trade of the region eastward to Montreal by way of the Red River settlements. Geographically, American traders had equal, if not better, access to the Sioux and Crows, so could hope to gain their loyalty. But the Blackfeet, whose lands lay on the upper Missouri and north across the as yet ill-defined border, fell within the British sphere of influence. When they demanded firearms in exchange for their trade, the King George men had responded favorably.

"The Blackfeet are greedy," Red Elk said. "They refuse to share the buffalo with their neighbors to the south and west. Last year, they drove both the Nez Perces and the Shoshones back across the mountains with their guns. In council, our leaders decided we must do two things. First, we would trade horses for guns of our own. Second, we would send a delegation to the Shoshones, proposing that we make peace with each other so that together we could fight the Blackfeet."

"They refused?"

"They spoke with forked tongues. 'Yes, let us have a smoke,' they said. So we sent three of our wisest men to them, carrying a peace pipe. But instead of smoking, the Shoshones killed them."

"Why would they do a thing like that?" Matt exclaimed, horrified.

"Because they are cowardly dogs!" Red Elk answered angrily. "Because they do not know the meaning of honor. But Chief Broken Arm will teach them a lesson."

It was a matter of deep regret that he was not a member of the war party, Red Elk said. The domain of his band, which was called Wallowa, was located four sleeps west and south of Weippe Prairie. It was a beautiful land of high, snow-capped mountains, grass-covered valleys, sparkling blue lakes, and streams full of fish. To this "Land of the Winding Waters," as his people called it, Nez Perces living to the east, north, and west journeyed each summer to catch salmon and visit relatives and friends, just as other bands came here in early September to dig camas and enjoy the company of people they saw only two or three times a year.

When the Wallowa band reached Weippe Prairie, Chief Broken Arm and his warriors had departed just two days before, Red Elk said. Knowing the route they would follow, he had planned to ride south and overtake them, but Twisted Hair and *Tetoharsky*, who had just heard that a large body of well-armed white men was headed this way, urged him to stay and help protect his people.

"We think that the crowned ones will be friendly," Twisted Hair had said, "but we cannot be sure until we meet them.

You must stay with us, Red Elk, until we know they will
be friendly."

Now that he did know that, he had lost all interest in
joining the war party, Red Elk said, for he found his new
white brother, *Moki Hih-hih*, and the party of crowned ones
much more interesting than fighting Shoshones. For that
matter, if he wanted to kill Shoshones, he could do that
right here, for the Shoshone guide, Toby, was too old to
put up much of a fight, while his son, who had accompanied
him, was too young to be a problem. But the truth was, he
told Matt, neither scalp appealed to him as much as the
long, shiny black braids of the young Shoshone woman,
Sacajawea.

"Her hair is a prize I would be proud to have in my
lodge," he said solemnly. "Perhaps I will go after it."

"You would kill a woman?" Matt exclaimed.

"Not for a while. First I would try her out and see what
she was good for." His eyes twinkled, making Matt realize
that he was joking. "If she was good enough, I would still
keep her hair in my lodge. But she would be wearing it
under my blanket."

More than any tribe of Indians yet encountered by the
Lewis and Clark party, Matt discovered, the Nez Perces
had a sense of humor, loving nothing better than a well-told
funny story. Certainly the one told time and again by Red
Elk, relating how his sister had trapped a white beaver she
had found bathing in her pool, gave the father and mother,
relatives, and friends many a chuckle as he told it with
gestures when Matt visited their lodge. Even Moon Wind
enjoyed the story, for she would give Matt a sidelong glance
to make sure he was not offended, then, when he shook his
head and muttered an embarrassed denial, would favor him
with a shy, warm smile.

During the two weeks that the party stayed with the Nez
Perces while the dugout canoes were being made, Matt spent
most nights sleeping in the tepee with Moon Wind and her
family. In some unspoken way, the Indians came to assume

that she belonged to him and he to her. Though Captain Clark had repeatedly warned the men to give no offense to Indian fathers, husbands, and brothers by unwanted familiarities with their women, Matt's acceptance by the family was so complete that both Lewis and Clark came to regard the association as an asset rather than a danger.

"Face it, Captain, the best way to make friends with Indians is to move in and become part of the family," George Drewyer told Captain Clark. "The more they trust Matt, the more they'll trust us. Matt's good at hand talk and real sharp at learning their lingo. But he'll be even better after he eats and sleeps with them for a spell. Take it from me, Captain, he'll be a lot more help to us as an interpreter than the Shoshone squaw."

As Captain Clark freely admitted, the only value Sacajawea had for them now was that her presence with the party assured potential hostile Indians that the intentions of the whites were peaceful, for when Indians went to war they never took women along. Little more than a child when the loutish, ignorant French-Canadian Touissant Charbonneau had taken her for a wife, she knew nothing about the country west of the land of the Shoshones, spoke only her own tongue and the bastardized French her husband had taught her, and was so frightened of him and so awed by the strange adventure into which she had been thrust that her worth as an interpreter was practically nothing.

In addition to having a retentive memory and a keen sensitivity for the nuances of pronunciation, Matt read faces as well as he read hands. Emotions such as fear, hate, affection, and love could be expressed instantly and without any chance of misinterpretation without a word being said, he learned. Where the desire to understand existed—as it did between Red Elk, Moon Wind, and himself—a way could be found to communicate.

That the Nez Perces were a well-traveled people with a wide-ranging knowledge of geography became evident to Matt as he questioned Red Elk regarding how feasible it would be for the party to leave its horses here and continue its journey to the Pacific Ocean by boat. Draining the mountainous eastern portion of Nez Perce country were three forks of a river called the *Koos-koos-kee*, Red Elk said, a word Matt gathered meant "Clearwater." Where the forks came together, the *Koos-koos-kee* became navigable for dugout canoes, and Ponderosa pine trees out of which the boats could be made grew nearby.

A day's travel to the west, the *Koos-koos-kee* joined a northward-flowing river twice its size, called by the Nez Perces *Ki-moo-e-nim*. Probably this was the same river Captain Clark had seen in the Shoshone country to the southeast; finding it too wild and rapids-filled to be navigated, he had abandoned following it, writing in his diary that " . . . in all justice it should be called 'Lewis's River' in honor of the first white man ever to view this branch of the Columbia."

After flowing north for a short distance, Red Elk indicated as he squatted on his heels and drew a map on a bleached white buckskin hide with a piece of charcoal, the *Ki-moo-e-nim* swung west in a long arc through an open, hilly country devoid of timber and at this time of year brown and dry. With care exercised passing through occasional rapids along the way, four days' travel by dugout canoe would take the crowned ones to the juncture of the *Ki-moo-e-nim* with the Columbia, down which they then could float to the "Great Stinking Water," the Pacific Ocean.

"The best I can gather, the Nez Perces pretty much control the country between the Bitter Root Mountains and the mouth of Lewis's River," Matt told the two captains as he and George Drewyer conferred with them. "West of there, Red Elk says, the tribes are fish-eaters and canoe people. He calls them Celilos."

"Are they friendly to the Nez Perces?" Captain Clark asked.

"They're traders, not fighters, Red Elk says. Since they control the best fishery on the Columbia River, Celilo Falls, the tribes that go there usually keep the peace. West of Nez

Perce country, none of the Indians know hand talk, he says, but they do have a simple trade language called Chinook jargon that they use to talk to one another. The Nez Perces know it, too, and use it when they go downriver to trade."

"Will the Nez Perces take care of our horses and supply us with guides?"

"For two rifles and a hundred rounds of ammunition apiece, Twisted Hair and *Tetoharsky* will go along with us as far as Celilo Falls, Red Elk says, and they'll take good care of the horses until we come back next spring. But they're peace chiefs, not war chiefs, he says. They're afraid Chief Broken Arm will be angry when he comes back from his war against the Shoshones and finds that you've promised them gifts but have left no gifts for him."

"Tell them that we have no intention of slighting Chief Broken Arm," Captain Lewis said. "As presents, we're leaving him one of the large medals authorized by President Jefferson and a big American flag. When we return next spring, we hope to see the flag flying in front of his lodge as a sign that his campaign against the Shoshones has been successful."

"He will be pleased," Red Elk said.

By now the whites and most of the Nez Perces had moved down from Weippe Prairie, which was two thousand feet higher in elevation, to the spot where the dugout canoes were being fashioned. After the horses had been relieved of their packs, half a dozen ten- to twelve-year-old boys belonging to Twisted Hair's band were instructed by the old chief to take the animals to a nearby meadow where there was good grass, loose-herd them there, and see to it that they were given the best of care. Watching one of the boys knot a length of hair rope around the lower jaw of a feisty black stallion that had made trouble by kicking and biting the other horses ever since its purchase from the Shoshones, then leap aboard its back and force it into a snorting, sidewinding run up the steep hill, Red Elk shook his head.

"He ought to be cut, that one, before he hurts somebody."

"The boy?" Matt said. "Or the horse?"

"Our girls are too nimble to be caught and hurt by our boys, unless they want to be," Red Elk said with a laugh. "But a mean stallion cannot be broken to carry a pack when mares and other stallions are in the band. That black ought to be cut."

Though Moon Wind, a maiden, still lived with her father and mother, Red Elk, who was married to a plump, jolly woman named Doe Eyes, lived with his wife and their two young children in a tepee pitched next to that of his parents. It was there that Matt and Moon Wind first made love. He had known it was going to happen ever since Red Elk had called him "brother" and the mother and father had welcomed him to their lodge as a member of the family. That she had known no man, just as he had known no woman, caused no strain or embarrassed fumbling. After meeting in the strange way they had, each silently accepted the fact that they were meant to join hearts and bodies—and did so with no shame.

It had been arranged simply enough by Red Elk. After he and his family had eaten with his sister and Matt in his parents' lodge one evening, he had gotten to his feet and motioned for Matt to follow him outside.

"You are my brother," he said simply. "To my father and mother, you are a son. My sister looks upon you with favor. How do you feel about her?"

"She has my heart," Matt said.

"Good. Treat her well. Go to my lodge, brother. She will come to you. You will not be disturbed tonight."

Nor were they. In the world he had left behind eighteen months ago, this was called sin; so Matt knew in a dim, uncaring part of his mind, but in this different, simpler world, all that mattered was warm, eager, willing flesh, the need of a man for a woman, the need of a woman for a man, and the wonder of fresh young love . . .

Before launching the dugout canoes at the forks of the Clearwater, the two captains had caches dug along the banks of the river in which were buried the saddles, canisters of extra lead and powder, and other equipment not needed during the journey to the Pacific Ocean. As a precaution against theft, the digging crews chose secluded spots, worked only when no Indians were around, and carefully covered the caches so as to leave no evidence as to their location.

At this time of year, the river was at its lowest stage, running crystal-clear over the light-colored sand and gravel of its granite-strewn bed; still, the occasional shoals and rapids were troublesome to the crude, awkward, flat-bottomed dugout canoes. True to their promise, Twisted Hair and *Tetoharsky* joined the party in the dugouts, though after seeing a couple of upsets in swift water, with packets of goods thrown out and men who could not swim clinging like half-drowned rats to the boats as they bounced bottoms-up through the rapids, the two old chiefs prudently chose to go ashore and join the mounted Nez Perce boys and men who were keeping pace on horseback along the shore, jubilantly cheering the boats that successfully negotiated the white-water hazards, quickly dismounting, wading into the river, and helping recover the human and material debris strewn into the water by frequent mishaps.

In camp on the flat, sandy shore where the Clearwater joined Lewis's River, Red Elk told Matt that he must part with his brother here. The band of Wallowa Indians to which his family belonged spent the cold months of winter in a low-lying, sheltered canyon on the west side of the river a day's travel to the south. He must help his family get settled there. Three sleeps to the south, in much higher country, lay the lakes, streams, and mountains called the Wallowa Valley—to him the most beautiful land on earth—where his people lived during the late spring, summer, and early autumn months.

"When you come back next spring, I will take you there," Red Elk said. "Moon Wind will be waiting . . ."

5

During the long, rainy winter spent on the Oregon Coast, Matt Crane occupied his spare time recording in a journal everything he had learned about the Nez Perce language, customs, domain, and relationships with bordering tribes. The main purpose of the expedition, he knew, was to establish the validity of the United States' claim to the Pacific Northwest by a land traverse from the contiguous territory to the east before Great Britain, the world's foremost sea power, could explore and lay claim to the region by approaching it from the west.

Exploration was only a first step, of course, for sovereignty could not be established without occupation and trade. Once the physical configuration, the peoples, the flora and fauna of the region were made known to President Jefferson and other farsighted leaders who visualized a nation stretching from sea to sea, decisions could be reached regarding the key locations in which forts and trading posts must be placed in order to control the country. From what he had seen and learned since leaving St. Louis a year and a half ago, Matt was firmly convinced that in the heart of the Nez Perce domain—probably where the Clearwater joined Lewis's River—a strategically important post would be established. He was just as firmly convinced that he would play a key role in the management of that establishment. Not at first, perhaps, for his youth and low rank would preclude his being made commandant if the nature of the post were military. If it were commercial, which seemed more likely, an older, more experienced manager no doubt would be put in charge at the outset. But if getting along with the people native to the area had any value—which he felt it certainly would have—his chances for swift advancement would be good.

Shortly after noon Sunday, March 23, 1806, the party loaded the canoes and left Fort Clatsop on the homeward-bound journey. No one regretted departing from the sodden, miserable, flea-infested post, at which Captain Clark laconically wrote in his journal:

> . . . we had wintered and remained from the 7th of Decr. 1805 to this day, and have lived as well as we had any right to expect, and we can say that we were never one day without 3 meals of some kind a day either pore Elk meat or roots, notwithstanding the repeated fall of rain which has fallen almost constantly since we passed the long narrows . . .

Located two hundred miles east of the mouth of the Columbia, the "long narrows" was a fourteen-mile stretch of constricted channel in which the mighty river literally turned on edge as it began to slash its way through the ten-thousand-foot-high Cascade Mountains. Massive, flat-topped spills of lava were strewn through the narrows, where the current raced as swiftly as thirty miles an hour, causing the French-Canadian traders—the first to view it—to name it "The Dalles," or "Stepping Stones." At the upriver end of the narrows, the entire flow of the Columbia poured over a series of twelve-to fifteen-foot-high basalt ledges called Celilo Falls.

It was here, Matt learned, that two distinctive zones of climate and two vastly different ways of Indian life met. Westward lay rainy, thickly timbered country, whose native inhabitants used dugout canoes for transportation and lived mostly on fish. Eastward lay dry, open sagebrush and grass country, whose wide-ranging denizens owned thousands of horses and laid claim to a share of the buffalo east of the Continental Divide, as well as to the game, roots, and fish of their own domain.

Reaching The Dalles in mid-April and finding the strength of the current impossible to overcome, the captains agreed that the two large wooden canoes must be abandoned and enough horses purchased to transport their supplies back to the land of the Nez Perces. The few horses owned by the Celilo Falls Indians were poor in quality and overpriced, but after a good deal of dickering seven animals were obtained. During the bargaining, Captain Clark became so exasperated with the greed of the Indians, and their refusal to accept the two large canoes as part of a deal, that he ordered the dugouts chopped up and burned as firewood rather than let them the fall into the Celilos' avaricious hands without their giving something of value in return.

"Seven packhorses won't be enough," Clark said wearily. "We'll portage the two small dugouts around the narrows, make as many trips as we have to with the horses, then split the load between the horses and the dugouts. It'll be slow going against the current, but we can't waste any more time here in this den of thieves. Maybe the Walla Walla Indians, farther upriver, will sell us some horses."

As it turned out, it was a Nez Perce who solved the party's transportation problem. Identifying himself as a member of Chief Broken Arm's band, a tall, handsome Indian came riding into camp early one morning, found Matt Crane, and asked to be taken to the party's leaders, for whom he had a present and a message. Matt took him to Captain Clark. With a smile, the Indian placed a bag of gunpowder and leaden balls at the captain's feet.

"He found this where we lost it on the portage trail," Matt said. "He thinks we might want it back."

"With that kind of honesty, he can't be a local Indian."

"He's not. His name is Bear Claw, he says, and he's from the Kamiah band of Nez Perces. Chief Broken Arm sent him to meet us, to act as a guide and help us in any way he can."

"Tell him we're grateful. Can he get us more horses?"

"He has two of his own we're welcome to use. There's a Nez Perce family that's been spending the winter at the falls, he says, that has quite a few horses, which they might hire out if you'll let them travel with us."

"Meaning we'd have to feed the whole lot," Captain Clark muttered. "Well, maybe we can strike a deal."

After a session of amiable bargaining, Bear Claw's Nez Perce friend agreed to sell the party three horses and hire out three more for a modest amount of trade goods and the pleasure of traveling upriver with the crowned ones.

Under the able guidance of Bear Claw, the party reached the arid, sandy, sagebrush-covered plain where the Columbia River passed between high basaltic bluffs, then swung to the north some twelve miles below the mouth of Lewis's River. This was the land of his brothers, the Walla Wallas, Bear Claw told Matt, who by now had learned that in Indian usage a "brother" could be as far removed in blood relationship as a third cousin, just as a "father" or a "mother" could be an uncle or an aunt. Like Red Elk, Bear Claw had a comprehensive knowledge of the country, and he was pleased when Matt asked him to delineate its features with charcoal on bleached buckskin.

Here at the great bend of the Columbia lay the land of the Walla Wallas, who were to the Nez Perce tribe like a little finger to an arm. Half a day's ride to the east were the Cayuse Indians, a small tribe, while to the south of the Cayuses lived a third small tribe, called the Umatillas. Bear Claw said all three were friendly with the Nez Perces, traded, visited, and intermarried with them, and spoke virtually the same language. Because the crowned ones had horses now, they need not ascend the Columbia and Lewis's River; he would take the party directly east through the land of the Walla Wallas by a shorter, easier route that would save two sleeps.

On May 4 in cold, blustery weather the party reached the south bank of Lewis's River seven miles below the mouth of the Clearwater. Here it was met by *Tetoharsky*, one of the two old chiefs with whom the horses had been left last October. Here also was Red Elk, genial and friendly as ever, embracing Matt with a bear hug that clearly expressed his affection. Representing a band of Nez Perces living on the North Fork of the Clearwater, *Tetoharsky* said it would be best for the crowned ones to cross Lewis's River to the north bank here—using the canoes he had arranged to transport the baggage while the horses swam free—thence eastward over an easy trail. Representing the Wallowa band, Red Elk wanted Matt to ride southeast with him, first to his band's winter village on the lower Grande Ronde, then to its summer domain three sleeps to the south, the high Wallowa Valley.

"How long will that take?" Captain Clark asked.

"Three weeks, he says."

"Which means you won't be rejoining us until the first of June," Clark said, scowling. "I don't think we can spare you that long, Matt. Sure, I'd like for you to see that part of the country and bring back all the information on it you can get. But by the first of June the snow should be melted and the trail clear across Lolo Pass. We'll be heading east by then. Ask Red Elk if two weeks will do."

When Matt relayed Clark's statement and question to the Nez Perce, Red Elk shook his head vigorously, made the signs for two double-handfuls of sleeps, two moons yes, one moon no, snow higher than a man on a tall horse within one moon, while within two moons the snow would be gone and the grass starting to grow.

"He says a month from now the snowdrifts in Lolo Pass still will be too deep to travel," Matt translated. "In two months the trail will be clear. Two weeks will not be enough

time for me to see much of the Wallowa country. Since you
won't be able to travel for at least two months, he says you
should give me three weeks with him."

"What does *Tetoharsky* think about when Lolo Pass will
be clear, George?" Clark asked Drewyer.

Watching Drewyer confer with the elderly chief, there
was no doubt in Matt's mind that *Tetoharsky* understood
the question, for to the far-ranging Nez Perces—whose
horses must have sustenance while traveling—the melting
of snowdrifts in the high country, the availability of grass,
and the falling of flood-swollen mountain streams which
must be crossed were vital matters. Reading the vigorous
hand signs and interpreting the graphic words of the old
chief, Matt was pleased to hear George Drewyer confirm
the information Red Elk had given him.

"He says the snowdrifts are deeper than usual this year.
A month from now, it will take a horse seven days to travel
from the new grass on the western slope to the new grass on
the eastern slope. Horses can't stand more than two days on
snow without grass, he says, so they would die. But in two
months Lolo Pass will be clear enough to travel. We must
wait until then, he says."

"Good Lord, that'll be the first of July!" Clark said.
"Surely we won't have to wait that long!" Turning to
Matt, he nodded. "All right, you can have three weeks.
Four, if need be. When you've made your tour, join us
near the place where we made the canoes. We should be
camped in the low country not far from there."

In anticipation of his reunion with Red Elk, Matt had
obtained a rifle for him, along with a few flints and a
small supply of powder and lead, by signing a ten-dollar
note to the party's gunsmith, Private John Shields. The
gun was a battered but serviceable flintlock rifle Shields
had brought along as a spare but seldom used. Made by
J. Doll of York, Pennsylvania, the .50 caliber, 1792 mod-
el flintlock had been issued to four battalions of rifle-
men by President Washington, Private Shields said, at a

cost of ten dollars each, one of several "Kentucky" rifles made by J. Doll, and still highly favored by frontiersmen.

"Reason the barrel is only thirty-three inches long and the muzzle is recessed," Private Shields said, "it originally took a bayonet, which somehow got lost—"

"Seems like you'd ought to knock off a dollar or two for that," Matt said.

"What do you need a bayonet for out here?" Shields snorted. "It's a good rifle and well worth the price—particularly when you're giving me a note instead of cash and I'm throwing in flints, powder, and lead."

Even though ten dollars was twice his five-dollar-a-month wage, Matt did not press the argument. To the Nez Perces, a firearm of any kind was worth its weight in gold, and Red Elk's joy when given the rifle was a pleasure to behold. Caressing the weapon as if it were his first born son, the stocky Nez Perce beamed at Matt.

"This will bring meat to my family for as long as I live, beloved brother. Whenever I shoot it, I will remember you."

"Before you do any shooting," Matt said, "you must learn how to take care of a rifle."

"Tell me how. I will learn."

Unlike the lower Missouri River Indians Matt had known in the St. Louis area, whose easy access to firearms and food made them indifferent marksmen lax in gun care, Red Elk had hunted buffalo and fought Blackfeet under circumstances where a faulty bow or a badly aimed arrow resulted in no meat for one's family or the loss of one's own life, so he proved to be a good student. Once he grasped the simple rule of keeping the rifle clean and dry, of charging it properly, of learning its sure-kill range, and of never wasting powder or lead, he was ready to master the technique of aiming and firing from a firm, locked stance, and of training his horses not to shy or bolt at the sound of gunfire.

All five of the horses Red Elk had brought with him were geldings, for at this time of year the mares had just foaled and were nursing colts, while the stallions that had bred them stood watch against predators. Though at first glance the horses appeared to be narrow-chested and undersized, they were remarkably surefooted and sturdy, Matt discovered, with an easy gait and good disposition. Two were sorrels, one was a chestnut, while the other two were bluish gray in color, their hind-quarters splotched with what looked to be blobs of black paint but which on closer inspection proved to be natural hair coloring.

"Do you breed for those markings?" Matt asked.

Red Elk shook his head. "In olden times, so the grand-father tales say, the Nez Perces painted markings on their horses to show the number of buffalo they had killed, the coups they had counted, and the enemies they had slain. When *Speelyi*, the Coyote Spirit who made the world, saw the paintings, he was so intrigued he did some of his own, using naturally colored hair. He still does this now and then, as you see. But only on Nez Perce horses."

"Why should he favor your tribe over the others?"

"We are his chosen people, created with the heart's blood of the monster *Speelyi* killed the day after he made the world." Red Elk smiled. "I was not there that day, you understand. But the grandfather tales tell us it happened."

"Why do you call them 'grandfather tales'?"

"Because this is the way stories of our people are passed on from generation to generation. Fathers are too busy hunting, fishing, and fighting to tell their sons stories. But when the sons are young, they are eager to listen and remember what the grandfathers tell them of olden times."

"How many horses do you own?"

Opening and closing both hands several times, then making a gesture Matt knew meant "more than," Red Elk laughed and said as he patted the neck of the sorrel he was riding, "If I rode a different horse each day, I would not ride this one again until snowfall."

Guessing that this meant two hundred or so, Matt judged that the Nez Perces possessed more horses per family than any Indian tribe in the nation. Certainly the tall, green, nutritious bunchgrass waving as far as the eye could see across the valleys, hills, and uplands over which he and Red Elk had been riding all day could furnish nourishment for vast herds. So far as quality was concerned, he had heard Captain Lewis say that the lines, speed, and stamina of the Nez Perce mounts equaled that of any horses he had ever seen back home in Virginia.

From what Red Elk told him, the Wallowa band of Nez Perces now was living in its winter village in the lower valley of a river called the Grande Ronde, a short day's ride southeast of where the two men had separated from the main party. If their dwellings were like those Matt had seen along the Clearwater the previous fall, they would be set on canyon sandbars sheltered from wind and weather, with V-shaped frameworks of poles covered by grass or tule mats rising from oval or oblong pits dug down five feet or so in the soft white sand. Open at the top so that smoke from fires built every ten or twelve feet along the bottom of the pit could escape, the dwellings would be up to fifty feet in diameter, if circular, or twenty feet wide by a hundred feet long, if rectangular, capable of accommodating a dozen or more families.

Unlike the longhouses of the lower Columbia River Indians, who lived in them year round and accepted fish smells, fleas, and filth as natural living conditions, the winter dwellings of the Nez Perces were surprisingly well aired and clean. From childhood to old age, these people loved their daily bath, Matt had learned, using hot springs when available, building sweat lodges near their villages or camps, and then plunging into streams, rivers, or lakes no matter how cold the water or air.

Though the longhouses looked solid, moving from the winter village to the summer camp was simply a matter of stripping and rolling the mats and packing them on horses, leaving the frameworks in place. When shelter was needed en route, a tepee could be erected by the women in a surprisingly short time, using poles brought along for that purpose or poles previously cut, peeled, and stored at traditional campsites along the way. Though mats could be and were used as covering for these temporary shelters, many of the Nez Perces of recent years had adopted the practice of the buffalo-country Indians, the Blackfeet, Crows, and Sioux, who scraped hides smooth and thin, sewed them together with waterproofed stitches, and made coverings for the tepee poles that could be raised with little trouble and did a much better job of keeping out wind, rain, heat, and cold than did the sectional mats.

Changing horses to rest a mount that had been ridden for a couple of hours, which Red Elk insisted be done, was a simple procedure, Matt learned. The horses were ridden bareback. Around each animal's neck a braided rawhide rope ten or twelve feet long was looped, its free end trailing on the ground. To switch from one mount to another, Red Elk dismounted, untied the rope secured around the lower jaw of the horse he had been riding, caught the fresh horse by its trailing neck rope, choked it down, forced its mouth open, tied the single rein by which he would control it around its lower jaw, then mounted it.

Though Matt tried to imitate the action in making the second change of the day, he could not control the black-spotted gray into whose mouth he was attempting to force the rawhide rein. As it reared, he tried to choke it down, shouting, "Whoa, boy! Whoa!"

Rolling its eyes and squealing, the gelding pawed at him. In an instant, Red Elk was on the ground at his side, picking up the trailing end of the rope, popping it with stinging force against the horse's flank, then jerking the gelding sharply to the ground. Trembling, the chastened horse stood meekly while the Indian secured the line around its lower jaw. Grinning, Red Elk handed Matt the rein.

"Like a woman, a horse must be taught who is master. Take him. He will behave now."

Though the pace set by Red Elk had been a moderate one and the frequent change in mounts kept the horses easy-gaited, the unaccustomed riding chafed Matt's legs raw and pounded his bottom into painful soreness in the forty miles or so he estimated they traveled during the day. Late in the afternoon, they paused on an elevated bench from which the land fell sharply away to the southeast toward the wide, deep canyon of the Grande Ronde, which here flowed into Lewis's River. Dismounting, Matt moved about with such obvious discomfort that Red Elk eyed him with concern.

"Are you unwell, brother?"

"No. Just rump-sprung and sore. It's been a while since I've ridden a horse."

"A sweat bath will make you feel better. We will take one together. Then Moon Wind will rub the soreness out of your legs and buttocks and warm you with a salve made of pine tar and bear grease."

"I'll be glad to see her. How is she?"

"Well and happy and looking forward to seeing you again." Red Elk fell silent for a moment, then gave Matt a sly sidelong glance. "She would not want me to tell you this, but I think you should know. Ever since you left, she has been preparing a present for you."

"What sort of a present?"

"That is for her to tell you, when she is ready. Truth is, it is not quite finished yet. But I am sure you will be pleased with it, when it is done."

More than that, Red Elk would not reveal. But soon after they rode into the village and dismounted in front of the longhouse in which Red Elk and his clan lived, Moon Wind herself wordlessly disclosed the nature of the present as she greeted Matt with a shy smile. Dropping her gaze to the ground, she patted her swollen abdomen with both hands, then made a palms-open gesture toward him whose meaning was crystal-clear.

She was seven months pregnant. And he was the father of the child she soon would bear . . .

6

Guilt was a feeling Matt Crane had never experienced before to any great degree. Though stricken sharply with it now, he was surprised to learn that it could not be long be self-sustained. Having a child out of wedlock was a mortal sin, he had been taught, with the father as guilty as the mother, and with the child branded a bastard all its life unless the sin were atoned for by the immediate marriage of the man and woman responsible for bringing an unwanted baby into the world. If this had happened back in St. Louis, there would have been no lack of accusatory pointing fingers, disapproving eyes, and scathing tongues. But here there were no accusers. Since Moon Wind, Red Elk, and their parents seemed unaware that a sin had been committed, accusations of guilt could come only from within himself. And with so much new country to see, he had little time for moral self-flagellation.

This band of Nez Perces numbered two hundred or so, Matt estimated, with fifty of them men of warrior age. Three rectangular longhouses served as living quarters for families; nearby, two smaller structures were dormitories for teenage boys and young men who had not yet married; farther removed, several sweat lodges—in which many of the people bathed daily—served the village; still farther away, and not to be approached nearer than fifty paces by any male, were the small dwellings in which women isolated themselves

51

during their menstrual periods and when giving birth.

Though the weather had moderated and turned warm in this sheltered canyon, it still would be several weeks before the reed mats were stripped off the longhouses and families packed up for the move south to the high country of the Wallowas, Red Elk said. In order to show Matt as much of the area as possible in the time allotted by Captain Clark, only the two of them would go on this trip.

"Without women, we will eat poorer and sleep colder," Red Elk said with a smile. "But Moon Wind does not need you now. She can finish her present alone."

"Will she be alone when the baby is born?" Matt asked with concern.

"Of course. Why should anybody be with her?"

"In the white world, the father likes to be close by when the baby is born. I'd feel bad if anything happened to her."

"There is nothing you can do."

"I know—and that troubles me. Likely I'll be gone by the time it's born. Can she raise it alone?"

"Why should she need to? I will be here."

"But I'm the father."

"She is my sister and you are my brother. We share its blood. The child will be mine as well as yours, *Moki Hih-hih.* It will not lack for care no matter how far away you are. But why must you go? You say you like our land and want to trade with us. We like you and we want to trade. So why don't you stay?"

Matt shook his head. With his limited knowledge of the Nez Perce language and Red Elk's ignorance of the white man's world, he knew there was no way he could explain the complexities of establishing a trading post in this part of the Pacific Northwest. In time it would come, he was sure of that. But the logistics involved in obtaining governmental and commercial support would take a year or two to activate, he knew, and the first step would be the return of the expedition to St. Louis.

"Not this year, *We-wu-kye Ilp-ilp*. But someday I'll come back—I promise you that. Now show me this country you think is so wonderful."

For the next three weeks, Red Elk did just that. Though he carried no instruments with him other than a small pocket compass with which he checked the direction of their daily travels, Matt had observed enough of the barometric readings—taken for the purpose of ascertaining altitude—on the way west to make reasonably accurate estimates of variations in the terrain. They were spectacular. From the lower valley of the Grande Ronde, whose elevation he knew to be less than a thousand feet, to the snowcapped, jagged peaks of the Wallowa Mountains in the south, which he estimated to be ten thousand feet high, he and Red Elk traveled from early summer to spring to winter in only three days. At the lower levels, stirrup-high bunchgrass covered the treeless plains and benchlands, giving sustenance to thousands of grazing horses without showing any signs of depletion. Mingling with the horses at twilight and for a short while after dawn were large numbers of white-tailed deer and a scattering of elk, a convenient source of meat which careful Nez Perce hunters slaughtered only as needed without spooking the rest of the browsing animals.

No wheeled vehicle had ever traversed this country, Matt knew, and he doubted one ever would, for the coiling, switchback trail leading up from river level to the plateau three thousand feet above was incredibly steep, narrow, and rocky, underlaid with such slick, hard basalt that he marveled at how their unshod horses could negotiate the terrain without having their feet slashed to ribbons. Following Red Elk's example of checking his mount's feet at every halt for stone bruises or pebbles caught in a hoof, Matt noted that the bony growth forming the hoofs was layered, as if laminated, appearing to be harder and far more durable than the hoofs of horses he had known back home. Certainly these were the best mountain horses he ever had ridden, surefooted, nimble, and possessing amazing endurance.

Watching Red Elk handle his horse, Matt had to agree with Captain Lewis, who had said last fall, "Nobody asks as much—and gets as much—out of a horse as the Nez Perces do. They seem to know the ultimate limit of what a horse can do when pressed—and they make him do it or die trying. Maybe that's why their horses are superior to those of any other tribe of Indians. I've never seen them abuse a good horse. But if it's a bad one, they'll push it till it collapses, then watch it die without a qualm. So far as they're concerned, only the strong deserve to survive."

Each day Matt filled several pages of his notebook with carefully drawn maps of the country covered, supplemented by descriptions given to him by Red Elk of the way rivers flowed, mountains rose, or trails led beyond the area he had seen. The beauty and variety of the high meadows, the thick-timbered slopes, the deep canyons, the streams, the lakes, and, most striking of all, the alpine peaks rising a vertical mile above the surface of the four-mile-long, mirrorlike, deep blue lake that gave the country its mellifluous name, *Wallowa*, impressed him all the more as he realized that in all probability he was the first white man ever to see it.

In camp one evening, he asked Red Elk where he thought a trading post should be established in order to best serve the Nez Perces and their neighboring tribes. After meditating on the question for some time, Red Elk picked up a stick and drew a map on the ground.

"Here, where the *Koos-koos-kee* joins the *Ki-moo-e-nim*, would be a good place. The climate is mild, grass is plentiful, game is nearby, and the rivers teem with fish. Since olden times, my people have gathered at this spot for councils among the various bands and with other tribes. Here we always have talked and traded in peace."

"When the whites do establish a trading post in your country, what will your people want most?"

"Guns and ammunition. Steel knives and hatchets. Iron and brass kettles. Blankets. Beads."

"What will you trade in return?"

"Horses—as we did with your party."

Matt shook his head. "Horses won't be what the traders will want, brother. They'll want beaver."

"What is the value of a beaver?" Red Elk asked scornfully, "compared to the worth of a horse?"

Again Matt faced the difficulty of explaining the workings of an economic system based on the profit motif to an unlettered savage whose system was rooted in simple consumption. To Red Elk and his people, the only things that mattered were food, shelter, transportation, and protection from enemy tribes. They had never seen a city or a ship and knew nothing of the three-cornered British-American-Asian trade built on rum, fur, and tea. That corporate fortunes were being made and national boundaries expanded because of North America's wealth in beaver, which were trapped by natives and traded for manufactured products, were facts he knew Red Elk could never comprehend.

"In the white man's world, beaver fur is made into hats, coats, and many other useful things. White men pay well for beaver and will take as many pelts as you can get."

"Why should we hunt beaver?" Red Elk said indifferently. "Our country is full of deer, elk, and mountain sheep, with buffalo to be taken in great numbers on the plains beyond the mountains. Except for the tail, beaver meat is poor food. Beaver cannot be hunted in daylight, for they are a night animal. Often when one is shot with an arrow, it falls into a pond or stream and cannot be found without much wading in icy water. In winter, when the fur is best and beaver hole up in their lodges, the mud with which they coat the tops is frozen so hard it cannot be chopped through. No, *Moki Hih-hih*, if beaver is what the white traders want, they will have to hunt it for themselves."

"We don't hunt beaver, *We-wu-kye Ilp-ilp*. We trap it."

"Ho-ho! What nonsense you talk! No rawhide snare or trap of woven of willow shoots will hold a beaver for more than two breaths. Not with his sharp teeth!"

"The traps we use are made of steel."

"These I have not seen," Red Elk said thoughtfully. "But the nose of a beaver is keen and his fear of a trap great. I cannot believe you will catch many in our country."

For the present, Matt pressed the subject no further. Like the Iroquois and other eastern tribes, the Nez Perces would have to be taught trapping as a commercial pursuit, with the pelts to be accumulated and traded for manufactured goods, rather than used by the natives themselves. Of course, the Nez Perces lived in a different environment from that of the Iroquois. They were far more mobile and wide-ranging, with a domain covering not only the mountains, valleys, and rivers of their own area but reaching westward to the culture of the coastal tribes and eastward to that of the Plains Indians. In a country abundant in game, with the rivers full of salmon, with vast numbers of buffalo available beyond the mountains to the east, and with their thousands of horses, it might well be that the Nez Perces would not adapt to the cold, nasty, smelly work of trapping beaver as readily as Eastern natives had done. Time alone would tell . . .

7

Earlier that month, the main party had made camp near Chief Broken Arm's village in the Kamiah Valley sixteen miles up the *Koos-koos-kee* from the spot where the dugout canoes had been built last fall. Keeping his promise to Captain Clark, Matt joined it there on the twenty-sixth day of May 1806. With him were Moon Wind, and Red Elk and Doe Eyes with their two children, the family having chosen not to make the early summer move from the lower Grande Ronde to the high Wallowa country with their band; they preferred to stay with him until the final day of his departure from their world.

For the most part, relations between the whites and the Nez Perces still were on friendly terms, George Drewyer told Matt. Sure, Captain Lewis—who had a low boiling point—had threatened to tomahawk a boisterous Nez Perce buck who had made a contemptuous remark about white men eating dogs and then tossed a live puppy in his plate while he was dining. And Twisted Hair and *Tetoharsky,* who had been so friendly last fall, had greeted the captains coolly and had been evasive about the horses left in their care. Even with the help of Sacajawea and a young Shoshone boy who could speak Nez Perce, unraveling that misunderstanding had proved to be a problem.

"Best I could make out, some of the young-uns went hunting on half a dozen of our horses last fall, abusing

57

them pretty bad, as young-uns will do. Twisted Hair and *Tetoharsky* were gone at the time, so it wasn't really their fault. But when Chief Broken Arm and his war party got home—"

"How did their campaign against the Shoshones go?" Matt interrupted.

"Like shooting fish in a barrel. In the first battle, forty-two Shoshones were killed, while only three Nez Perces went under. Chief Broken Arm came home covered with glory."

"I see he's flying the flag we gave him in front of his longhouse."

"Yeah, he's proud to be our friend. But for a while after he got back, he was real jealous of Twisted Hair and *Tetoharsky*. When he heard we'd left our horses in their care, he sent one of his sub-chiefs, an Injun named Cut Nose, to check on them. Cut Nose found out about the young-uns abusing the horses, went back and told Chief Broken Arm, who said that from then on *he* would look after the horses. Which he did. Naturally, this upset Twisted Hair and *Tetoharsky*, who'd been promised rifles for taking care of the horses. They got into a hell of a fuss with Cut Nose, with the captains not able to make heads nor tails of what it was all about."

"Couldn't you figure it out?"

"When it first happened, I was gone hunting. For interpreters, the captains were using Sacajawea, Charbonneau, and a captured Shoshone boy who could speak Nez Perce, but they were getting nowhere. The louder and madder Cut Nose, Twisted Hair, and *Tetoharsky* argued with each other, the tighter the Shoshone boy clammed up. This was a disagreement between chiefs, he said, and he wanted nothing to do with it. Sacajawea was a woman, he said, who had no business hearing and interpreting man talk. When I got there, everybody was yelling in different tongues, with nobody understanding anybody. Finally Captain Clark shooed them all away, told me to go talk to the Injuns one at a time in sign language, until I understood what the problem was. Which is what I did."

"It's all straightened out, then?"

"Yeah, we're all good friends now. Twisted Hair and *Tetoharsky* got their rifles. Except for a couple of lame and sore-backed horses, which weren't much good to begin with, we got all our horses back fat and sassy. But make no mistake about it—Chief Broken Arm is the big man in Nez Perce country right now. It's him the captains will have to sell their peace and trade policy to."

As Captain Lewis and Captain Clark had pointed out many times, there could be no trade between Americans and the natives of the upper Missouri and Columbia watersheds unless a firm, lasting peace was established not only between the Americans and the Indians but also among the Indian tribes themselves. To the Indians, this last was a novel idea, for since time immemorial they had fought one another over game, territory, honor, or combinations thereof.

So long as their weapons had been limited to the bow and arrow, the war club, the spear, the knife and the tomahawk, the continuing conflict among the tribes had inflicted no serious damage upon any of them. But now that firearms were available, what had been minor skirmishes could become major battles—as witness the serious casualties Chief Broken Arm's war party had wreaked on the Shoshones last fall.

Called *Tin-nach-e-moo-toolt* in the Nez Perce tongue, Chief Broken Arm proved to be a shrewd diplomat as well as a generous host. His longhouse was the largest Matt had seen, measuring one hundred and fifty feet in length, containing cooking fires for twenty-four families, and housing two hundred people. The din of dozens of women pounding kouse roots was so ear-piercing, Captain Lewis said, that it reminded him of a nail factory.

For the comfort of the party's leaders, Chief Broken Arm had ordered a large skin tepee pitched near his longhouse, in which the two captains could live and hold council with him and the other tribal leaders while in the Kamiah area. An ample supply of firewood was piled outside. Two large baskets of camas and kouse roots were sent over as a food gift for the party, but, with last fall's experience still fresh in his mind, Captain Clark was cautious.

"Tell him our men aren't used to an exclusive diet of roots and might get sick," Clark instructed George Drewyer. "Ask him if he'll sell us a horse we can butcher for food."

After Chief Broken Arm had listened to the request, he smiled, shook his head, and made his reply.

"No, he won't *sell* us a horse," Drewyer translated. "But he'll *give* us two fat young horses, which we can butcher and eat whenever we like. And there'll be more for us, whenever we want them."

Warm though the days had become in this sheltered valley, the nights were still cool; both white and Indian hunters roaming the higher meadows and mountain slopes in search of game brought back reports that snowdrifts still lay deep on the Lolo Trail. Bear Claw, Red Elk, and Cut Nose, who had often traveled to the buffalo country, all agreed that crossing the mountains would not be possible before the twentieth of June. But the two captains, who were well aware of how long the return trip to St. Louis was going to be, regarded the prospect of four weeks of waiting and idleness intolerable.

"We'll leave on the tenth," Captain Lewis said.

"Come hell or high water," Captain Clark agreed.

Though he did not verbally express his feelings to the two captains, George Drewyer shook his head and grumbled to Matt, "If that snow is as deep as they say it is, we'll have hell aplenty crossing the mountains, I'm thinking, with high water aplenty in the streams. The Nez Perces know their country a sight better than we do."

Before leaving the Kamiah village, the two captains held a formal council with Chief Broken Arm and the other tribal leaders, during which an attempt was made to explain the policy of the United States as it related to future trade and friendship with the Indians of the Pacific Northwest. Though Matt, Red Elk, and George Drewyer were present and probably had a better comprehension of what was being said by both sides, the two captains seemed to feel that protocol demanded they use Sacajawea, Charbonneau, and the Shoshone boy as official interpreters. Since this meant that the Shoshone boy had to translate what was said in Nez Perce, so that Sacajawea could understand it, with her putting it into the Minataree dialect, with which she communicated with Charbonneau, who then put it into bowdlerized French, which Captain Lewis understood, and who explained it to Captain Clark in English, it was not surprising that the council took up most of the day. Captain Clark called the process "tegious."

Earlier, Chief Broken Arm had pulled the buckskin shirt off his back and given it to Captain Clark, with Clark taking off his own shirt and giving it to the Nez Perce leader. At the end of the council, Chief Broken Arm spoke solemnly.

"We have listened to your advice and are determined to follow it. We have one heart and one tongue on this subject. We wish to be at peace with all nations."

Since making peace with the Shoshones, Blackfeet, Sioux, and Crows was such a radical change in policy, the subject would have to be discussed at length by the elders, Chief Broken Arm said. In due time, a council would be held and a decision reached, following which a vote would be taken. The result, Clark learned, was favorable. He was particularly impressed with the ingenious way Chief Broken Arm set up the voting procedure.

"He took the flour of kouse roots and thickened soup in the kettles and baskets of his people," Clark wrote in his diary, "inviting all such men as had resolved to abide by the decree of the council to come and eat, and requested such as would not be so bound to show themselves by not partaking of the feast. I was told by one of our men who was present in the house, that there was not a dissenting vote on this great national question, but all swallowed their objections, if any they had, very cheerfully with their mush."

After telling Captain Clark what he had witnessed of Nez Perce democracy in action, Matt added, "The queer thing was that all the time Chief Broken Arm was telling the Indians in the longhouse about making peace with the other tribes, the women were crying, wringing their hands, tearing their hair, and making a great fuss. Why do you suppose they did that?"

"As a ritual protest, I imagine. In time past, they've probably lost sons, brothers, or husbands to hostile tribes. Maybe they're more afraid of an untested state of peace than of a known state of war. But at least Broken Arm has promised to give peace a try."

Shortly after the vote was taken, a group of Nez Perce leaders paid the two captains a call, bringing each of them a fine horse as a token of their esteem. Chief Broken Arm said:

"Since we have not seen the Blackfeet and the Sioux, we do not think it safe to venture over to the plains of the Missouri at this time, but we would go there if we knew that these people would not try to kill us.

"When the Americans have established a trading post on the Missouri, as you have promised to do, we will go there and trade for arms and ammunition. It will give us much pleasure to live at peace with these other tribes, although they have shed much of our blood in time past. We are poor but our hearts are good. We must be assured of their sincerity.

"On the subject of one of our chiefs accompanying you to the land of the white men, we have not yet decided. We will let you know before you leave us. Snow still lies so deep in the mountains that if you attempt to cross them now you will surely perish. We advise you not to start out until after the next full moon, by which time the snow will have disappeared on the south hillsides and there will be new grass available for your horses."

Though Matt knew that he was not the only member of the party to have established a relationship with a Nez

Perce woman, Moon Wind's obvious pregnancy and the well-known fact that he had lived with her for two weeks the previous fall could have inspired crude jokes to the effect that the "preacher's boy" had been the first white man to sow Christian seed in heathen soil. But curiously enough none of the men hoorawed him—as they did Captain Clark's big Negro slave, York, who, as the first black man ever seen by the Indians, had attracted female bedmates all along the way.

Perhaps this restraint stemmed from his youth, his innocence, or the sure knowledge that neither George Drewyer nor William Clark would tolerate bawdy jokes aimed at an idealistic young man who had been raised in a religious background. With each passing day, Matt's feeling of guilt increased as he became deeply concerned over the welfare of the Indian girl with whom he had lived, and the child she soon would bear.

As the son of a Presbyterian minister, he knew that neither the Protestants nor the Catholics recognized Indian spiritual life. Indians were heathen, religious white people felt, with no God, no Saviour, and no Holy Ghost; doomed by Catholic tenets to burn eternally as infidels in hell if they died unbaptized, sentenced by Presbyterian belief to the less painful fate of remaining outside the white man's heaven in some vague, unblessed region that would be neither hot nor cold, just uncomfortable.

Since a number of semicivilized tribes were to be found in and around St. Louis, he was familiar with church attitudes toward them there. All the Catholics demanded for Indian membership in their church was a profession of faith, followed by immediate baptism, with the rituals of worship to be learned over an indefinite period of time. But the Presbyterians were stricter, requiring that the Indian reject his heathen gods, take instruction in the tenets of his new faith, then be examined by a board of elders that must be satisfied that he had reached a certain level of grace, before being admitted into membership in the church.

Not surprisingly, the Catholics made converts much more easily among the Indians than the Presbyterians did.

Until now, it had never occurred to Matt to question the doctrine of his father's church. But living intimately with the Nez Perces as he had done, he had come to realize that they had a rich spiritual life. They loved their children and respected their old people. They did not lie or steal. In times of plenty, they shared their food generously with those who had less; in lean times, they went hungry without complaint. They believed that the world had been created by a power far greater than any now existing on earth. In ceremonies that he was just beginning to understand, they paid homage to that power in a manner closely akin to the white man's worship of God. They believed in life after death.

So far as his relationship with Moon Wind was concerned, she made no demands on him, remained cheerful and good-humored, and seemed in no way physically limited in her activity because of her condition. Though he was sure she realized he would be leaving her soon, she gave no sign of concern or regret. But evenings when he sat in the lodge talking to Red Elk about his plans for the future, her dark brown eyes never left his face.

"Once we've crossed Lolo Pass, we'll split the party into two sections," he explained to Red Elk, drawing a crude map on a piece of buckskin with a bit of charcoal. "Captain Lewis will go northeast toward the Marias River country, where he'll try to make peace with the Blackfeet—"

"These are bad Indians," Red Elk muttered. "Captain Lewis should be careful."

"He will be. With the rest of the party, Captain Clark will go south up the Bitter Root Valley, then east through the Big Hole country to the headwaters of the Yellowstone—"

"I know that trail very well," Red Elk said, nodding. "That is the safe route to the buffalo plains, for it goes through the land of our cousins, the Flatheads, and our allies, the Crows. Will you be with this party?"

"I imagine so."

"This large village where you live—how many moons will it take you to travel to it?"

"Three—if we have good luck. Going down the Missouri River by boat, we'll make better time than we did coming upriver against the current."

"You say you will return someday. Can you tell me when?"

"Within a year, our plans should begin to develop," Matt said. "If I haven't returned by then, I'll send you a message telling you when I will be coming."

On the tenth day of June, the Lewis and Clark party broke camp and left the Kamiah Valley, despite Nez Perce warnings that snow still lay deep along Lolo Trail. When Red Elk, his family, Moon Wind, and two other Nez Perce families said that they would accompany the whites as far as Weippe Prairie, where they intended to hunt and dig roots, Captain Clark reacted with unaccustomed testiness.

"What do they expect us to do, Matt, feed them along the way? We've barely enough meat to see us across the mountains to the buffalo country. Kind as they've been to us, we have no food to spare. Tell them that."

"They understand," Matt said, after relaying Clark's ultimatum to the Nez Perce family heads. "They say they'll make out on roots—if they find no game to kill."

"Well, I'm sorry. Truly I am. But if they won't keep their word, we certainly can't feed them."

"What word, sir?"

"Cut Nose promised to supply us with two young chiefs, who would act as guides, go with us to the Great Falls of the Missouri as Nez Perce representatives to the Blackfeet, and perhaps even downriver to St. Louis. But they haven't showed up. Where are they?"

Conferring with Red Elk, who had been present when Cut Nose made the promise, Matt told Captain Clark, "He says they'll be here ten days from now, as Cut Nose told you. He says we should camp and wait."

"We've waited long enough. With or without guides, we'll tackle the pass as soon as we've crossed Weippe Prairie."

Reaching the spot where the party had met the Nez Perces early last fall, Matt was surprised to find the prairie shimmering with blue, waving blossoms of camas in such an extensive field that he first mistook it for the surface of a lake. Small and tender now, the bulbs were gathered, cooked, and eaten eagerly by the three Nez Perce families, whose women waded into the marshy flats and dug till their baskets were full, despite swarms of mosquitoes rising in clouds all around them. To escape the pests, both whites and Indians made camp on higher ground in pine-surrounded clearings at the foot of the Lolo Trail.

It was here, close by the mountain stream where he had first encountered her nine months ago, that Matt said goodbye to Moon Wind.

"You understand I must go?"

"Yes. Men always go."

"The baby will be born soon?"

"I cannot be sure. But I feel that the time is near."

"I want it to know I am its father, Moon Wind. I do not want you shamed."

"It will know, for I will tell it. And I am not shamed, *Moki Hih-hih*. There was no other man but you."

"Red Elk says he will take my place as its father—until I come back."

"He is my brother, so that is his duty. But will you come back?"

"Someday. As God is my witness, Moon Wind, I will come back."

His goodbye was awkward and clumsy. Hugging her briefly, feeling her swollen abdomen against his, remembering when it had been gently rounded and soft, kissing her, blending his tears with hers, wordlessly squeezing her hands, he turned away and stumbled out of the tepee and across the clearing to the white section of camp in the cold night rain. Close as they had been for a while, they were worlds apart now—and would remain so for a long time to come.

But not forever, he vowed. Not forever . . .

8

Though an early start had been planned for Sunday, June 15, hard, driving, cold rainshowers made rounding up and loading the horses a slow, miserable chore. Once they were under way in late morning, the rocky trail was slick and treacherous, causing the horses to slip and fall, with down trees and swollen streams adding to the hazards of travel. By midafternoon the rain ceased, but the going had been so difficult that by the time camp was made the ascent of Lolo Pass was barely begun.

Next morning's start was much earlier. With the terrain steepening and the timber thickening, snow soon covered the trail to a depth of four feet, sufficiently compact to support the weight of the horses but offering dangerous footing on sidehill slopes that must be traversed in order to bypass streambeds raging with high water. At the noon halt, enough grass was found in a south-slope meadow to give the horses a few mouthfuls of grass. As the trail rose and the snowdrifts deepened to eight and then ten feet, all signs of grass disappeared. With slippery rocks and fallen timber buried under the packed snow, traveling became easier for the horses, but the blanket of snow brought on two serious problems.

First, as the Nez Perces had pointed out, the strength of the horses could not be sustained more than two days without grass. Second, with all signs of the trail buried now and with no guides to lead the party, keeping on the safe mountain pass became a matter of by guess and by God. Under such conditions, a mistakenly taken direction or a miscalculation in distance could be fatal to the survival of the entire party.

After camping Monday night, June 16, in a small glade that Captain Clark recognized as the spot where he had killed a horse and left its butchered remains for the main party the previous fall, he took the lead and attempted to act as a guide. Within a mile's travel, the snowdrifts deepened from ten to fifteen feet. Experienced woodsman though he was, the only directional signs he could distinguish were occasional scars on Ponderosa pine trees where hungry Nez Perces seeking food in starving times had slashed the reddish brown bark in order to get at the fibrous, stringy inner bark, which was edible. But these were so scattered that he had no way of knowing how close or how far removed they were from the trail.

"Let's face it, we're in trouble." he said, conferring with Lewis, Drewyer, and Matt Crane. "We can cross Lolo Pass in two or three days—if we don't stray off the trail—"

"Stray off the trail?" Lewis said glumly, waving a despairing hand at the tumbled mass of ridges, valleys, and mountain peaks looming ahead. "Which of half a dozen ridges do we climb? Odds are we'll pick the wrong one."

"Agreed." Clark said. "We can't afford to guess. Under these circumstances, I conceive it madness to go on."

"Damn Cut Nose!" Lewis exclaimed. "Where are those guides he promised us?"

Exchanging glances with George Drewyer, who shrugged and remained silent, Matt Crane blurted, "We may have misunderstood, sir."

"How's that?" Captain Clark demanded.

"Cut Nose said he would send guides in ten days, which

was as soon as he felt the trail would be passable. They're not due until the twentieth."

"We didn't agree to that. We told him we were leaving Kamiah on the tenth."

"Which *he* didn't agree to," Drewyer said bluntly. "When you're dealing with the Nez Perces, Captain, it ain't what *you* say that counts. It's what *they* say. My feeling is, Cut Nose will keep his word—but on his schedule, not yours."

"Well, misunderstanding or not, we've got to have help," Clark said. "Much as it goes against the grain to make a retrograde march, I suggest that's what we do. Your opinion, Captain?"

"We've no other choice. We'll cache our instruments, extra supplies, and papers here, where they'll run less risk of getting damaged or lost. George, I want you, Private Shannon, and Private Crane to go back to Weippe Prairie, Kamiah, or wherever you have to go to find guides. Offer any Nez Perce that is willing to take us to Traveler's Rest Creek a rifle for his services."

"Offer two rifles, if that's what it takes," Captain Clark said. "As an added inducement, offer them ten horses if they'll stay with us to the Great Falls of the Missouri."

"Meanwhile, we'll backtrack until we find grass," Lewis said. "When you've hired guides, send Shannon back to tell us, while you and Crane stick with the rascals and make sure they keep their word."

Traveling downhill over a known, broken trail, unencumbered by laden packhorses, the three men reached Weippe Prairie in midmorning, next day. There they were met by the three Nez Perce guides Cut Nose had promised to send—exactly on schedule by Indian reckoning, as both Matt Crane and George Drewyer felt they would be. Sending Private Shannon to report the good news to the two captains, Drewyer had no difficulty striking a deal with the three Nez Perces.

Yes, for three rifles they would guide the whites across Lolo Pass as far as Traveler's Rest. But staying with the party to the Great Falls of the Missouri in exchange for ten horses struck them as a poor bargain. For one thing, they had plenty of horses. For another, the Great Falls country was in the land of their enemies, with whom peace had been proposed but not yet made. Much as they loved the whites, they cherished their scalps even more.

All three Nez Perces belonged to the Kamiah band and had made many trips across Lolo Pass to the buffalo country, they said. Their names were Bear Claw, Three Crows, and Wolf Ear. It had been Bear Claw, Matt recalled, who had met the party at The Dalles, returned the bag of powder and lead, and then acted as guide upriver. Since he was closely enough related to Red Elk to call him "brother," he good-humoredly called Matt "brother," too.

As a brother, he took pleasure in being the first to tell Matt that he had just become a father.

"What!" Matt exclaimed.

"Moon Wind had a baby," Bear Claw said with a smile. "A healthy man-child."

"When?"

"Yesterday morning."

"Is she still camped in Weippe Prairie?"

"She was there when the baby was born early yesterday morning."

"Are Red Elk and his wife looking after her?"

"She brought the baby to their lodge soon after it was born. In the afternoon, Red Elk and his family packed up and left for the Wallowa country."

"Leaving her alone?"

"No. She rode with them."

"Oh, my God!" Turning in consternation to Drewyer, Matt said, "Did you hear that, George? She had a baby in the morning and they made her get on a horse and travel in the afternoon! What kind of people would be so callous?"

"Injun people," Drewyer said laconically. "Many's the time on the trail when I've seen a squaw drop out of the band, stop in the bushes for an hour or two, then catch up with her people nursing a red-faced papoose she'd just borne. With Injuns, giving birth is no big thing."

"It is to me! That baby is my son!"

"I know, Matt," Drewyer said sympathetically. "Probably just the first of a goodly batch we're leaving behind. Shame you won't get a chance to see it."

Suddenly, to see the child he had fathered, acknowledge it to Moon Wind, to her family, and to the God he believed in so devoutly, seemed a thing he must do. In some measure, the act of acknowledgment would atone for the sin he had committed. It would show Moon Wind that he loved her and the child and that he meant to keep his promise to return to the Nez Perce country someday.

"I've got to see it, George! I've just got to!"

"Well, from what Bear Claw says, they've only got a day's head start on you," Drewyer muttered, eyeing him thoughtfully. "Traveling with his family, it ain't likely Red Elk will be in a hurry. If you ride lively, you'd ought to be able to catch up with 'em, see your woman and the button, then rejoin us before we cross the mountains." Drewyer grinned. "I'll tell Captain Clark I sent you back to Kamiah to thank Cut Nose for the guides—"

"No, George. I'll take full responsibility. But I've got to go!"

"Get started, then. You're burning daylight."

Toughened by the weeks of riding he had done with Red Elk, traveling an easy trail across open, high prairie country, pushing the strong, well-conditioned horse at a steady lope hour after hour through the balmy, long June day, Matt covered in a single afternoon the distance that Red Elk and his family had taken two days to travel. Dusk was falling when he approached the tepee pitched near a scattering of pine trees just off the trail that, a short distance beyond, began its twisting descent to the Middle Fork of the *Koos-koos-kee*. As he dropped to the ground, Red Elk came out of the lodge, saw him, and gave a laughing whoop of greeting.

"Moki Hih-hih! We have a son!"

"I know!" Matt exclaimed as he returned Red Elk's hearty embrace. "I've come to see him."

"Hattia Isemtuks!" Red Elk called into the tepee. "Bring out the great warrior! His father wants to look at him!"

Stooping low to exit the tepee, Moon Wind cradled a small burden in the crook of her left arm. As Matt sank down on his knees before her, she uncovered the baby's face, looked at Matt, and smiled shyly. Wordlessly he held out his arms. She placed the baby in them.

"He is ours, *Moki Hih-hih,"* Moon Wind said softly. "With our love, we made him."

A blinding mist filled Matt's eyes. When he had become a member of the Lewis and Clark party two years ago, he had felt that he was embarking upon the greatest adventure of his life. That it would culminate in his fathering a child by a woman of an alien race, and leaving a son behind in a land far distant from the home in which he had been born and raised, had never entered his mind. But it had happened— and he had no regrets.

"I want him to know he is my son. I want him to bear my name."

"He will," Moon Wind promised.

"We will call him *Moki-Moki Ilp-ilp,"* Red Elk said with a laugh, "after both his father and his uncle."

In the Nez Perce tongue, *Moki Hih-hih* meant "White Crane," Matt knew, while the literal translation of *Moki-Moki Ilp-ilp* would be "Little Red Crane." He nodded.

"That will do fine as his Indian name. But I want him to have a white name, too."

"Tell me the name you would call him by," Moon Wind said. "I will remember."

"I'll do better than that," Matt murmured, gazing at the face of the baby he was holding, in which he imagined he could see a resemblance to his own. "I'll write it down for you."

Before the party left St. Louis, Matt's father had given

him a small New Testament, which fitted inside a waterproof case carried on Matt's person wherever he went. It would have pleased the Reverend Peter Crane if his son had chosen the Presbyterian ministry as his life's work, Matt knew; and indeed until the call of adventure had impelled him to join the expedition he had seriously considered following in his father's footsteps. Now he knew that the ministry was not for him. But he still held strong religious convictions.

Giving the baby back to Moon Wind, he took the case out of his pocket, opened it, and removed the well-thumbed New Testament. During the weeks he had spent with Red Elk and Moon Wind, he had showed it to them and tried to explain its meaning. That it was related to the spiritual world of the white man, just as a feather, a pebble, or a small bone carried in a secret pouch by Red Elk related to the Indian spirit world, was readily understood by the Nez Perces. But with no knowledge of the written word, the tiny black marks of print on the thin pages held no more meaning for them than the symbols painted on their tepees held for a white man unfamiliar with their culture.

Since his father bore the name of the disciple upon whom the church had been founded, it had been natural that Matt be named after the disciple who had written the first book of the New Testament. Because the next three children had been girls, who had been named Mary, Judith, and Ruth, the use of disciples' names had gone no further in Matt's family. But now it would.

"We will call him Mark," Matt said, opening the Bible, taking out a pencil, and printing the letters on the flyleaf. "Here I will write his name, the date of his birth, and the names of his mother, father and godfather. Do you understand?"

"Yes," Moon Wind whispered. "I am very proud."

"Ahh taats!" Red Elk murmured, staring down at the writing. "This is big medicine."

Putting the New Testament back in its case, Matt handed it to Red Elk. "I want you to keep this Bible for him until he is old enough to take care of it himself. For all his life, it will bear witness that he is my son."

"He will never shame you, brother. I will care for him as my own."

"Kneel with me, please, while I give him his name," Matt said in the Nez Perce tongue. When Red Elk had done so, Matt bowed his head, touched the baby gently, and switched to English. "In the name of the Father, the Son, and the Holy Ghost, I christen you Mark Crane. Amen . . ."

Catching up with the party in its camp near the crest of Lolo Pass two evenings later, Matt told Captain Clark he was prepared to accept whatever punishment he deserved for being absent without leave. Clark shook his head.

"Wanting to see your firstborn child is not a flogging offense, Matt. No harm's been done. Truth is, a lot of us likely have left our seed behind, with you the only one to see it. The baby's a boy, you say?"

"Yes. I christened him Mark."

"A good Gospel name. But a word of advice, Matt, from a man who's crossed a hill or two. When we get back to St. Louis, don't tell your father."

"That troubles me, sir."

"Better you than him. He'd never understand . . ."

9

Until the Louisiana Purchase in 1803, the village on the west bank of the Mississippi River had contained less than a thousand souls, most of them Spanish or French, indifferently governed by edicts from New Orleans, Madrid, or Paris. The chief aim of these edicts was annually to drain the adjacent wilderness of two hundred thousand dollars worth of furs obtained from the Osage and other regional Indians, while letting the traders who were given exclusive licenses to deal with the savages pay the least amount of powder, lead, beads, trinkets, and goods that would bring in the pelts. Catholic to a man, the proud Spaniards and the easygoing French had lived in close proximity to the Indians for fifty years without giving a thought to improving their spiritual welfare.

When the Purchase was announced, a horde of rowdy, lawless Americans swarmed into the village and, during the two and a half years Matt Crane had been absent with the Lewis and Clark party, swelled its population to fifteen hundred or so. The freebooters' boast that "God would not cross the Mississippi" soon proved to be wrong. Unlike the Spanish and French priests, who had little missionary zeal, American ministers of the Presbyterian, Congregational, Methodist, and related faiths accepted the challenge offered by the heathen lands and peoples with surprising alacrity.

In fact, it was just that challenge that had compelled the Reverend Peter Crane to move his family and a dozen others from their comfortable homes in Boston to the village of St. Louis just in time to see the flag of Spain lowered, the French flag flown for one day as a token of respect to the citizens of that nation, then the flag of the United States raised on March 20, 1804, as a symbol of American sovereignty.

Admittedly, the move had a mundane as well as a spiritual basis, for it had been underwritten by a prosperous Boston merchant who loved money almost as much as he revered God. Migrating to North America from Holland as a young man thirty years ago, Johann Von Beerbohm had wasted little time Americanizing his name to John Bower and transferring his religious affiliation from the Dutch Reformed to the Presbyterian Church. Trading in furs, tea, rum, and spices on a world-wide basis, he strongly supported President Jefferson's view that true independence and real prosperity for the United States could best be obtained by three aggressive measures: restricting the British southern boundary to the Great Lakes region; establishing a firm American claim to the Pacific Northwest; and making the Mississippi River from source to mouth a totally American artery of commerce destined to control the trade of a nation reaching from sea to sea.

"Let my fat Dutch friend, Jacob Astor, haf New York and the trade of the North Atlantic states," John Bower told Peter Crane, after setting forth his proposal to leave Boston. "Gif me ten years in St. Louis, I'll be as well off as he is."

With typical Dutch energy and single-mindedness of purpose, John Bower, after making the move, had devoted every waking hour, all his skills as a merchant, and a great deal of his financial resources to ending the monopoly of the Spanish and French on the lucrative regional trade, while at the same time encouraging his pastor and the members of his church to make clear to the Catholics that competition to their heretical beliefs had come to St. Louis to stay.

During the brief time he had lived in the village before heading up the Missouri River with the Lewis and Clark party on May 14, 1804, Matt Crane had thought it to be a miserable, muddy, stench-filled, ugly scattering of log huts built in the French manner—standing on end—with slops tossed into what passed for streets in total disregard for sanitation. Though the streets had been given such grand names as Rue Royale, Rue de l'Église, Rue des Granges, and Rue de la Tour, the growing colony of Americans now called them First Street, Church Street, Barn Street, Farmer Street, and Tower Street.

By any name, they had improved little in appearance or smell, Matt noted with disgust. But back away from the river above the bluff, where the Presbyterian church and the houses of its members had been built, the usual cleanliness and orderliness of the Dutch had made a marked contrast to the slovenliness of the waterfront district.

Soon after the return of the Lewis and Clark party, President Jefferson persuaded Congress to recognize the significance of what the expedition had accomplished, by giving tangible rewards to its members. Each enlisted man was awarded a cash bonus equal to his pay and was given a grant of 320 acres of land. Sergeant Nathaniel Pryor was promoted to Ensign and put in charge of returning the Mandan chief, Shahaka, to his people with appropriate presents, a military escort, and a party of traders. Captain Meriwether Lewis was appointed Governor of Upper Louisiana Territory, with headquarters in St. Louis. Captain William Clark was designated Superintendent of Indian Affairs for the Northwest, also to be headquartered in St. Louis. For the next six months, at least, Matt Crane would be employed as a special clerk in Clark's office, helping him transcribe fair copies of the party's journals and correlate maps drawn by Lewis, Clark, Drewyer, and Matt himself.

When the time came to select the 320 acres granted him as a bonus, Matt favored a piece of rolling prairie land

several miles southwest of the village, dotted with good
stands of hardwood trees, well above the boggy, humid,
mosquito-infested lowlands under the bluff along the river.
Though he had no intention of becoming a farmer or a
stock-raiser, he judged this sort of land to be what such a
person would want; thus it would be salable when the time
came for him to leave St. Louis and move to the Pacific
Northwest, as he fully intended to do.

"It's a good piece of land," his father agreed, after hearing
him describe its location. "But before you make a final
decision, Matthew, don't you think you should talk it over
with Lydia and her father?"

One of the reasons John Bower had left Boston was that
an epidemic of diphtheria had taken his nine-, seven-, and
four-year-old sons with stunning suddenness, leaving him
and his wife, Bertha—who was past childbearing age—with
only their sixteen-year-old daughter, Lydia, to carry on the
family name. A deeply religious man, John Bower felt that
God did not want him to stay in Boston and enrich himself in
trade with the morally corrupt European world from which he
had emigrated. Instead, he must lead a colony of Protestant
settlers to the Western frontier as a vanguard of American
expansion.

"He'll never be happy in Boston, with its sad memo-
ries," Peter Crane had said compassionately. "He needs
new country and new challenges to help him forget his
lost sons. God knows, I shall do all I can to ease his
burdens."

Now nineteen, Lydia was fair-haired, blue-eyed, pretty,
slightly plump, and warm-natured. Since her family and
Matt's had been close for many years, the assumption long
ago had been made by both sets of parents that a bond
of affection existed between the two young people, which
someday might mature into a deeper relationship. Truth was,
Matt himself had taken for granted the possibility that he and
Lydia would marry at some time in the future. But that had
been before he had joined the Lewis and Clark party and

made the two-and-a-half-year journey across the continent and back.

While Matt knew how greatly the experience had changed him, his and Lydia's families did not. Busy with getting settled in St. Louis, they had not really missed him. They had only a vague idea of the distance he had traveled. They had only a casual interest in the places and peoples he had seen. Most frustrating of all, so far as he was concerned, they could not even begin to grasp his vision of the nation's size and the excitement he felt in having an opportunity to participate in its development.

Following his father's advice, he had supper with Lydia and her family in their new, comfortable home one evening, during the course of which he told them about the piece of land he had tentatively selected.

"Yah, dot is good land for a farmer," John Bower said with an approving nod. "But do you intend to be a farmer, Matthew?"

"No, sir. For the next six months, I'll be working as a clerk for Captain Clark. After that, he's promised me a position in the fur company he plans to form, as an assistant trader at a post upriver."

"Captain Clark's plans haf not yet matured," John Bower said, shaking his head as he filled his pipe for an after-supper smoke. "Believe me, for I haf discussed dem with him. His company vill need capital, which I vill help supply vhen I'm sure his organization is solid. Right now, it is not. Right now, Captain Clark, Manuel Lisa, Captain Lewis, Pierre and Auguste Chouteau are fighting like cats and dogs over who vill control the Missouri River fur trade, vhich used to be a monopoly of the Spanish and French. Meanwhile, it is good that you vork for Captain Clark. But if it is a clerk or a trader you are going to be, you don't vant dot piece of land."

"Why not?"

"Because unless you build a house on it and farm it, it vill haf little value to you. No, Matthew, vot you should take is land along the river."

"Land under the bluff? Bottomland? But, sir, that sort of land floods every year. It raises nothing but bushes, scrub trees, and mosquitoes."

"True, my boy. But it lies next to the river. Dot is vot is important." Lighting his big, curved meerschaum pipe, Bower inhaled deeply, blew out a mouthful of smoke, then extinguished the sulfur match by waving it admonishingly in Matt's face. "Keelboats and rafts need docks, warehouses, and storage facilities. Vhen St. Louis grows—as it surely vill—land lying along the river vill increase greatly, for vhen it is gone none vill be left. Tomorrow, I vill show you the piece of land you should claim . . ."

10

By early April 1807, some sixty men, at least half of them veterans of the Lewis and Clark Expedition, had signed contracts with Manuel Lisa. While plans for this first commercial venture up the Missouri still were tentative, it was assumed that somewhere upriver at least one permanent post would be built this summer, with more to be established in years to come. George Drewyer told Matt that he felt the best location for the first post would be in Crow country, near the juncture of the Yellowstone with the Missouri.

"Sure, the Crows are tricky," Drewyer admitted. "But they're smart enough to know they need American trader friends if they're going to hold their own against the Blackfeet and the Sioux. They'll steal from us, whenever they think they can get away with it, but they won't do us any physical harm. They need us too much as friends."

"The relationship between the Nez Perces and the Crows is good," Matt said. "Red Elk told me they often meet and hunt together in the buffalo country. Do you suppose we'll be able to persuade any Nez Perces to come to the post to trade?"

"The Yellowstone country is about as far east as the Nez Perces travel, but we may see a few now and then. Particularly bucks like Red Elk, when he hears his white blood brother is in that neck of the woods." Drewyer looked at him shrewdly. "Has Captain Clark agreed to turn you loose from clerking for him?"

"Yes. He says I can leave anytime."

"Do you plan to come back to St. Louis in the fall or stay upriver?"

"That depends upon what you and Manuel Lisa want me to do. If the post is to be a permanent one, I'd be glad to stay upriver through the winter and make it my headquarters for a year or two. After that, if Captain Clark's plans develop, I might move on west to the Nez Perce country."

"What does your pa think of that?"

"To tell the truth, I haven't discussed it with him except in general terms. As I'm sure you know, my family and John Bower's family have been lifelong friends. Mr. Bower thinks there's a great deal of money to be made in the fur trade of the Missouri River country. He expects most of that trade to pass through St. Louis. He thinks it would be good experience for me to go upriver and spend a year or two working as a trader in the field. My father agrees with him."

"But neither of them knows how far upriver you plan to go or how long you intend to stay?" Drewyer said gently. "Is that the way of it, Matt?"

Being half-Indian and half-French, George Drewyer understood what had happened to Matt in the Nez Perce country better than any other person, Matt knew. Between him, Matt, Captain Clark, and other members of the expedition, an unspoken agreement existed that any relationships established with Indian women during their travels were not to be mentioned in journals or in conversations with people who had stayed at home, for the men instinctively knew that those relationships would be misunderstood and condemned.

"The way of it is, I don't want to hurt my family or my friends," Matt said earnestly. "But now that spring's come, I have trouble breathing in St. Louis. I get this feeling of being stifled, closed in. A couple of days ago, when I was down in the bottom threshing my way through the bushes and swamps measuring the piece of riverfront land I'm filing a claim on, I felt like I was choking to death on the steamy, humid air. The mosquitoes and gnats were terrible. If offered the trade, George, I'd gladly swap that whole 320 acres of bottomland for a tepee site in the Nez Perce country, a view of Wallowa Lake, and a lungful of pure mountain air."

"Try to hang on for another month," Drewyer said with a friendly grin. "We'll be heading upriver, then toward the country you're aching for. You'll see plenty of it, I'm thinking, before you're ready to come back to St. Louis and settle down. And likely so will I . . ."

Two mornings after talking to George Drewyer, Matt woke up sick. From the feverish feel of his face, the throbbing ache in his head, and the rapid pounding of his pulse, he guessed he'd gotten a touch of ague from the miasmatic air of the bottomland through which he had chopped and threshed his way while lining out his claim. Supposedly generated by rotting vegetation and animal carcasses, the disease called "malaria" by doctors and "ague" by laymen was endemic among people forced to breathe the pestilential lowland air for any length of time, which was why Matt's first choice for a claim had been the less humid, better-ventilated high ground back away from the river.

Though there seemed to be no way of avoiding catching the disease once a person exposed himself to it by breathing the infected air, the remedy devised by Dr. Benjamin Rush, taught to Captain Lewis, and passed on to Captain Clark, was simple enough: Bilious Pills, containing ten grains of calomel and ten grains of jalap, reinforced with Glauber's salts; stiff doses of quinine pulverized out of Peruvian bark; judicious bleeding to drain the poisons out of the system. If combined with complete bed rest and a light diet containing no red meat, a cure usually was effected within a week to ten days. During the course of the disease, violent chills alternated with high fever, so constant care was required to make sure that the patient did not get too cold or too hot.

Hoping to make as speedy a recovery as possible, Matt stayed in bed, dutifully downing the pills and powders given to him by his mother as directed by Captain Clark. But he stubbornly refused to be bled, even though Captain Clark recommended bleeding, for he feared it would weaken him far more than it would benefit him, and slow his recovery.

"Give me five days and I'll be back on my feet," he told Clark. "Just five days . . ."

"Well, your fever isn't too high and you've had no chills," Captain Clark said, "so you may not have a bad case. I'll stop by tomorrow morning and see how you're coming along."

Strangely enough, Matt still had suffered no chills twenty-four hours later, though the fever, headache, and rapid pulse rate continued. But instead of feeling relieved at this indication that his illness was not ague, Matt began to worry. He was very weak. Reaching out with his right hand for a glass of water on the stand beside his bed, he could not make his fingers and thumb close tightly enough around the glass to pick it up. His breathing was becoming increasingly labored, as if restricted by tight, circular bands around his chest. Rolling over on his side, he removed his right foot from under the covers, placed it on the floor, and started to get out of bed, thinking that lying still for so long had perhaps inhibited the motility of the hand, which would be restored if he moved around a bit.

He felt his bare foot touch the floor. Swinging his left leg out of bed, he started to stand up. Without warning, his right leg buckled at the knee. Pitching headlong to the floor, he pulled the bedside stand down with a loud thump. Shocked by the fact that he had lost all control of the muscles on the right side of his body, he screamed.

"Mother! Help me!"

Hurrying into the bedroom, she knelt beside him, turned him over, and assisted him to sit up. "For goodness sake, Matthew! What happened?"

"The fingers of my right hand—I can't use them. My right leg—it won't work."

"Oh, it's just a temporary effect of the fever, Matthew. Here's your father. Come, we'll help you get back into bed."

With his father aiding on one side and his mother on the other, Matt managed to get back into bed. His mother fluffed up the two fat feather pillows, placed them under his head, and pulled up the blanket. His father's face was puzzled.

"What's this about your hand, Matthew?"

"It won't work, Father! I tried to pick up the glass but my fingers wouldn't close around it. There's something wrong with my right leg. When I got out of bed, it collapsed. I fell. And there's a tightness in my chest, Father. My breath comes so hard—"

As a minister familiar with illness in its many forms, Peter Crane was not a person who panicked easily. But his face showed concern.

"Stay with him, Martha," he told his wife, "while I fetch Captain Clark. Whatever ails Matthew, it's not malaria. Perhaps Captain Clark will know what it is and how it should be treated."

But Clark did not know. After coming to the house and examining Matt carefully, he agreed that the ailment was not malaria. Instead, it was some sort of virulent fever that infected children and young people who were strong, vigorous, and in perfect health one day, then the next either fatally stricken or crippled for life by the loss of control of one or more limbs. The mysterious disease was most prevalent in hot weather, probably nurtured by the same sort of moist, fetid air that generated malaria. All they could do was continue the treatment they were giving Matt, he said, and wait, hope, and pray.

As the day passed, Matt's pulse rate slowed, his headache abated, and his temperature came down. Aided by a dose of laudanum, he got a good night's sleep. When he woke up the next morning, forty-eight hours from the time of the onset of the sickness, he felt fairly normal, save for the

weakness brought on by the purgatives he had ingested
and the sparseness of his nourishment. He still was having
trouble breathing, though the invisible bands around his chest
now seemed to have loosened somewhat, settling down to a
heaviness in his right rib cage. But muscular control of his
right hand and right leg still had not returned.

Blessed with good health all his life, he always had
taken his body for granted. He was strong, he was supple,
he was well coordinated. His eyesight and hearing were
perfect. He was quick afoot, a good horseman, a competent
boatman, an excellent hunter, and confident that physically
he could do whatever needed to be done. That his body
might ever fail to serve his needs had never entered his
mind.

Staring down at his right hand where it lay on the blanket
over his chest, he thought, *It's mine. When I will it to move,
it will move. First I shall extend my arm toward the glass
of water on the wooden stand beside my bed. Like so. Then
I shall will my thumb and four fingers to close around the
glass, pick it up, and move it to my lips. Now! Close now!
Oh, God, close now!*

But the fingers would not close. Refusing to accept the
failure of his muscles to obey his mind's command, he forced
the shaking, useless hand to keep its position around the glass
by clamping the fingers of his left hand tightly down on his
right forearm, concentrating with an intensity that brought
beads of sweat popping out on his forehead and made his
chest muscles go so rigid that his spasmodic breathing came
to a complete halt.

He blacked out. For how long, he did not know, but when
he opened his eyes the glass of water had fallen to the floor,
his mother and father were kneeling beside the bed trying
to quiet him, and he was crying hysterically.

"*Mother! Father!* Am I going to be a cripple the rest of
my life?"

11

By the time the Manuel Lisa party was ready to leave St. Louis two weeks later, Matt had learned to clump around with the aid of the iron and leather brace that a blacksmith and a harness maker had fashioned for him to firm up his right leg. Bitter, he refused to call what he did "walking." Though control of the muscles of his right hand was so completely gone that he could not even pick up a pencil, he could use the upper arm to some degree. His breathing had returned to normal and his general health was good. Aware that he had survived a disease that often proved to be fatal, he knew that he should be grateful just to be alive. His father, his mother, his sisters, and John Bower all told him that.

"God in His infinite wisdom orders our lives in patterns beyond our understanding," Peter Crane said gently. "All we can do, my son, is accept what He gives us."

"This may be a blessing in disguise," his mother told him tenderly. "All the time you were gone with the expedition, I worried about you. If you had gone into the wilderness upriver as a trader, I would have worried even more. Now I know you will be home—and safe."

"We'll help you, however we can," his sisters said eagerly. "If you want papers or books to read, we'll get them for you. You're smarter than all of us put together. If you set your mind to it and practice, you can learn to write left-handed in no time. Captain Clark says he still can use you as a clerk."

Of them all, it was the blunt, plainspoken John Bower who came closest to understanding Matt's deep sense of loss, and who showed him how he could participate in the great venture now unfolding, without leaving St. Louis.

"In the fur trade, Matthew, dere vill be hundreds of trappers risking their lives in the field, vhile the dozen or so men who organize and control the trade stay home and reap the profits. You vill not go back to work as a clerk for Captain Clark. Vith me you vill go to work—as a partner."

"But Mr. Bower, I have nothing to offer—"

"On the contrary, you haf a great deal to offer, my boy. Who knows the upriver country, the Indians, and the trappers who vill be vorking with Manuel Lisa better than you, tell me dot? You come from a goot family whose name is respected in religious and business circles. You own valuable property along the river, vhich is vhere our docks and varehouses vill be built. Also, ve vill need a bank, vhich you vill help me organize and run. Oh, I vill keep you so busy, my boy, you soon vill forget vot you are missing by not going up the river with your goot friend George Drewyer."

Maybe in time he would forget, Matt mused unhappily as he rode in a buggy driven by Lydia Bower down to the river bank, where the heavily laden keelboats of the Lisa party were astir with activity as they prepared to depart this cool, rainy, mid-April day. But as George Drewyer first gave him an awkward, left-handed handshake, then impulsively threw his arms around him and embraced him, he knew that the time would be measured in years, not in weeks.

"Goddam it, Matt, I'll miss you! Don't give up, you hear me? You're getting better every day. Maybe next year you can go upriver with us."

"No, George, my traveling days are over. I'm reconciled to that." Respecting Matt's desire for a private farewell to old comrades and friends, Lydia had parked the buggy well away from the landing, where she now sat out of earshot waiting for him to say his goodbyes. Now he said, "Do me one favor, George. If you should see Red Elk or any of his people, tell them what's happened to me. Ask them to pass the word along to Moon Wind."

"You bet I will!"

"Goodbye, George. God willing, I'll see you in the fall."

Turning away from the river, moving clumsily with the aid of a hickory cane held in his left hand and angled across his body to support his right side, Matt limped back to the buggy, where Lydia sat with her gaze deliberately focused away from him so as not to embarrass him with the pity he knew she felt for him. Awkwardly he pulled himself up into the buggy seat beside her. She looked at him then, smiling tremulously, her eyes brimming with moisture.

"I know how much you wanted to go, Matthew. I'm so sorry you can't."

During the restless, tortured days and nights of the past two weeks, Matt had done a great deal of soul-searching as he tried to understand why he had been stricken. In imagination, he had traveled every mile of the Missouri, the Jefferson, the Beaverhead, the *Koos-koos-kee,* the *Ki-moo-e-nim,* and the Columbia to the Pacific and back again. In his dreams, night after night he had seen Moon Wind's smiling face, heard her cheerful voice, felt her soft, warm body against his. She had been his first love, and he knew such a love would never come to him again. But pure as it had been in his eyes, it was in the eyes of God sin. And for that sin, he had been punished.

Now he must atone.

"It was God's will, Lydia. I accept it."

"Why should God punish you in such a terrible way? What have you done wrong?"

"Let's not question His wisdom, Lydia. Let's look ahead. Let's face the fact that while my body may be crippled for the rest of my life, there is nothing wrong with my mind."

He reached out with his left hand to cover hers as she gripped the reins. "Your father has asked me to go into business with him as a partner. Would you like that?"

"Oh, Matthew! It would be wonderful! Father thinks so highly of you. To him, you're like a son."

"Do you suppose he would accept me as a son-in-law?"

"Is that a proposal?"

"Yes. I want to marry you, Lydia—if you'll have me."

"Of course I'll have you!" Lydia cried, burying her face in his chest. "Oh, Matthew, I've loved you such a long, long time! We'll be happy, I know!"

Stroking her hair, he gazed over her head, watching the lead keelboat swing out from the landing and thrust its bow into the swollen current of the muddy river. For the rest of his life, he would do his best to care for this good white woman whom he respected above all other white women; he would never let her know that his first love, a red woman, and the son she had borne him half a continent away, always would hold first place in a secret recess of his heart.

"I'm sure we will, Lydia," he said softly. "I'm sure we will . . ."

12

Married on Friday, May 1, 1807, Lydia became pregnant within a month's time, bearing her husband a healthy son at four o'clock in the morning on Monday, February 22, 1808. Recalling that his and Moon Wind's son, whom he had christened Mark Crane, had been born on Thursday, June 19, 1806, Matt secretly calculated his Indian son to be just a year and eight months older than his white son. Secretly, too, he wondered if they ever would meet. And secretly, for this would be too hurtful to share now with Lydia, her family, and his family, he resolved that some-day after both sons had become grown men he would let each of them know that he had a half brother, and give them the choice of meeting or not meeting, as they might wish to do.

Selecting a name for the new son caused Matt and Lydia a brief, mild argument. As a dutiful daughter-in-law to a Presbyterian minister, Lydia thought Peter Crane's scheme of naming male children in the family after the Disciples, according to the order of their writings in the New Testament, was an excellent one.

"We'll name him 'Mark,' won't we, dear?"

"No, no!" Matt said hastily. "We can't call him 'Mark.' That would cause too much confusion."

"Why would it?"

"Because Mark is already—I mean, because the names

93

Matt and Mark are too much alike. People would get them confused."

"I certainly wouldn't," Lydia said with a gentle laugh. "But if you don't like Mark as a name, we'll choose another. What would you suggest?"

"How about 'Luke'?"

"If we're skipping one Disciple, why can't we skip two? Let's call him 'John.' That would please Father."

So the child was christened John Crane. By the fur trade grapevine, whose white and Indian couriers carried news, with remarkable rapidity and accuracy, up and down the Missouri River between St. Louis and the Northwest, Matt received word that George Drewyer had met Red Elk in the buffalo country of the upper Yellowstone last fall; Drewyer had told him about Matt's crippling illness, and had been assured that Red Elk would relay the sad tidings to his sister.

"He says *Moki-Moki Ilp-ilp* is bright as a button and growing like a weed," Drewyer wrote cryptically. "But *Hattia Isemtuks* will grieve for *Moki Hih-hih.*"

Smiling wryly, Matt doubted that any person in St. Louis—other than Captain Clark—could make out the meaning of that sentence. So his secret was safe.

Because moving the clumsy keelboats upriver was such slow work, it was early November by the time the Lisa party reached the juncture of the Bighorn River with the Yellowstone and began building the first trading post, Fort Raymond.

"We'll winter upriver," Drewyer wrote, "bringing our fur packs down to St. Louis late next summer. No matter what you hear, Matt, I'm not staying upriver to duck the murder charge against me. I'm staying here for furs. When I get back to St. Louis, I'll surrender and go on trial, if that's what I have to do. Lisa says he'll stand by me."

That a man of George Drewyer's character should shoot and kill a fellow trapper had shocked everyone when word of the violent act reached St. Louis a month after the Lisa party headed upriver. Details had been sketchy. The known facts were that, like all the other *engagés* employed by the company, Antoine Bissonette had signed a contract to hunt and trap for three years, agreeing in writing to accept military discipline. On May 14, 1807, at the mouth of the Osage River, 120 miles upstream, it was discovered that he was missing. Suspecting desertion and anxious to prevent any further such acts, Lisa had ordered Drewyer to track the man down and bring him back "dead or alive."

This Drewyer had done. Catching up with Bissonette, Drewyer told him he must return to the party, the man resisted, and Drewyer shot him. When Drewyer brought the badly wounded man into camp, Lisa said grimly, "Well done. The rascal got just what he deserved."

Because the seriousness of his wound made him useless to the party, Lisa ordered Bissonette put into a canoe and taken downriver to the village of St. Charles, where he could receive medical attention. But before reaching that outpost of civilization, the man had died. Now George Drewyer was charged with murder.

Carrying a season's gather of furs, Manuel Lisa and George Drewyer returned to St. Louis in early August 1808. Drewyer was arrested by the town constable, with Lisa posting $5,000 bail to assure his appearance at next month's trial. Talking to Drewyer, Matt found him a badly shaken man.

"I never meant to shoot him, Matt. Sure, Manuel Lisa said bring him back dead or alive, so in a sense Lisa is as guilty as I am. What he feared was that if one man could desert and get away with it, so could all the rest. Unless it can enforce military discipline, a trapping company can't be held together in the wilderness. We all know that. I had to go after him and bring him back. But, God help me, I didn't mean to kill him."

The trial began September 23, 1808, being held before a jury of townspeople in the court of the Honorable J. C. B. Lucas, presiding judge, with the Honorable Auguste

Chouteau as associate judge. Defending George Drewyer were the ablest attorneys Manuel Lisa could hire—Edward Hempstead, William Carr, and Rufus Easton. Present in the crowded courtroom were all three partners in the fur company, plus William Clark, Matt Crane, John Bower, the Reverend Peter Crane, and a host of St. Louis businessmen with vital interests in the Northwest trade.

That Antoine Bissonette had signed a contract binding him to the company for a period of three years and that he had agreed to accept military discipline were facts easily proved by the contract itself. That he had planned from the beginning to desert also was proved beyond any shadow of doubt, for on the way upriver he had deposited two caches of blankets and supplies which he intended to use during his escape.

"Under the agreed-upon policy of military discipline, which I point out was the same common-sense policy so faithfully adhered to by the Lewis and Clark party, George Drewyer was acting in the best interests of his employer," William Carr told the court. "In fact, it may be said that if anyone is to blame for the death of the deserter, blame should fall on Manuel Lisa, for it was he who gave the order to bring the man back dead or alive.' "

After laying the groundwork for the case, the three attorneys brought witness after witness to the stand, all gave favorable testimony regarding George Drewyer's fine qualities as a man, with lengthy mention of the outstanding services he had performed for the Lewis and Clark party. At the close of the case, the jurymen retired, debated for fifteen minutes, then returned to the courtroom with their verdict.

"Not guilty!"

With the trial over, Manuel Lisa and his two partners, Pierre Menard and William Morrison, split the proceeds from the sale of the furs, each taking $2,667.50, with Lisa allowed an extra $985.00 for leading the party. The three men then gave further evidence of their support for George

Drewyer by agreeing to take him in as a full partner in their proposed expansion of the company. Now that it had been proven that there was money to be made trapping and trading upriver, and that much of that money would come back to St. Louis, a number of merchants formerly hostile to the idea of investing in a far-ranging company realized that they must do so or be frozen out of a lucrative business.

Prominent among them were Pierre Chouteau and Auguste Chouteau, Jr., whose family had long held a monopoly on acquiring furs from the Osage Indians of the region. Reuben Lewis, the younger brother of Governor Meriwether Lewis, became a partner, as did John Bower, Matt Crane, and William Clark. To be known as the "St. Louis Missouri Fur Company," the association of a dozen men was from the outset an uncomfortable one, bound together more by necessity and mutual distrust than by optimism and confidence. Discussed all through the fall and winter before agreement could be reached and the covenant signed March 3, 1809, the object of the company was stated to be "Trading and hunting up the river Missouri and to the headwaters thereof or at such a place or places as a majority of the subscribing co-partners may elect."

One of the provisions in the agreement was that each of the co-partners, or his appointed representative, must accompany the party upriver in the spring of 1809 and stay with it for three years. As his representative, Matt chose George Drewyer, while John Bower selected Reuben Lewis.

"It is not dot I haf anything against George Drewyer," he told Matt. "It is just dot I think it better to spread the votes around."

"Making decisions by majority vote bothers me," Matt said, shaking his head. "If Manuel Lisa is to be the leader of the party, his word should be law. Sure, he should listen to men like George Drewyer and John Colter, which I'm sure he will do. But the final decision should be his."

"He is not liked, Matthew. He made Drewyer kill dot

deserter, Bissonette. Governor Lewis has called him a scoundrel. And some of de men who haf worked for him haf
threatened to shoot him if dey ever catch him two hundred
yards outside of camp."

"Being liked and being a good leader don't necessarily go
together. In our party a few years ago, the captains ordered
several men flogged. Nobody liked them for that, but we
realized it had to be done. In my view, Bissonette got exactly
what he deserved—and the jury agreed. Sure, Lewis called
Lisa a scoundrel, but we all know how quick-tempered he
is. If he really believed that, he never would have offered
Lisa seven thousand dollars to escort Chief Shahaka back
to the Mandan country. So far as threats against him are
concerned, they're mostly wind, made by men who were
tired, mad, or drunk."

"Probably you are right, Matthew. Still, it vexes me dot
de partners should bicker so much. Aren't ve all Americans
now? Shouldn't ve work together to make money instead of
trouble for one another? Vot I'm afraid of is dot de partners
vill be so busy watching one another upriver, dey'll forget
to watch for Indians—and lose dere scalps."

"Well, all we can do is wait and hope. A few profitable
seasons upriver will do wonders for everybody."

News coming downriver for the next twelve months was
a mixed bag of small and large triumphs, of minor and major
tragedies. A year earlier Ensign Pryor and his too-small sol-
dier escort had failed to convey Chief Shahaka safely back to
the Mandan country because of the hostility of the Arickara
Indians farther downriver. Manuel Lisa and Pierre Chouteau
had a much larger, better-armed force, and a much shrewder,
more subtle appraisal of Indian character that enabled them
to buy the friendship of influential chiefs with gifts or to
induce them to keep the peace with an overwhelming display
of rifles, pistols, and swivel-mounted cannons trained from
the keelboats. They managed to return Shahaka to his people
as the federal government had promised to do. The purpose

of bringing the Mandan chief downriver to St. Louis and then east to Washington, D.C., had been to impress him with the wonders and might of the white man's world. He had been impressed. So impressed, in fact, that for days on end following his return to his people he could talk of nothing else but the marvels he had seen—with the sad result that nobody believed him, laughing him off as the tribe's greatest liar.

Despite the fact that the legality of maintaining military discipline by the use of deadly force had been sanctioned by a St. Louis court, desertions by men under contract still plagued the Lisa-Chouteau party. Of the 160 men in the military section of the party, and the 190 men in the trading section, 32 men had deserted by the time the expedition reached the Mandan villages. Though the money advanced them in wages, and the value of the weapons and gear with which they absconded were dead losses to the company, Lisa sent no one after them this time with orders to bring them back "dead or alive," for he had been as badly shaken by the Bissonette affair as George Drewyer.

Bands of trappers left upriver were doing well in the upper Yellowstone country, Matt learned. The Crows were becoming almost as adept in the art of trapping as they formerly had been in the art of stealing horses. Beaver was proving to be plentiful in the Three Forks region along the Gallatin, Madison, and Jefferson rivers, though only whites and imported Indians such as the Iroquois and Shawnees did the trapping there, for the Blackfeet, whose country teemed with buffalo, disdained trapping and were so bitterly hostile to Americans that one of the partners, Pierre Menard, feared that the entire upper Missouri River area would have to be abandoned by the company. Already the Blackfeet had killed eight American trappers. In a desperate effort to abate the Blackfoot menace, Menard told Pierre Chouteau that he planned to ask the Shoshone, Flathead, and Nez Perce Indians, who annually crossed the mountains to hunt buffalo in the region, to join forces and make war on the Blackfeet, compelling them either to cease opposing Americans or run the risk of being exterminated.

William Clark, who for years had been trying to establish peace among the Northwest tribes, did not think much of the idea. Neither did Reuben Lewis. Leading a party in the Jefferson-Beaverhead region, he wrote his brother that he favored giving up entirely on the Blackfoot country, crossing the Continental Divide to the headwaters of the Columbia, and setting up a trading post in the land of the Nez Perces. Discussing the suggestion with Governor Lewis, Matt said, "It's a fine idea, sir. If a post were established where the *Koos-koos-kee* joins the *Ki-moo-e-nim,* it would be on a navigable river, close to good trapping grounds, and among friendly Indians eager to trade with us."

"When we were out there, Matt, I got the impression the Nez Perces weren't interested in any kind of hunting that can't be done on horseback. Where would we get the pelts?"

"We could hire our own trappers to begin with, just as Lisa has done. But instead of taking all our trade goods and traps up the Missouri by keelboat and then across the mountains by packhorse, we could ship them around the Horn to the mouth of the Columbia, transport them upriver by canoe to the mouth of the Walla Walla, then pack them overland on horses bought from the Nez Perces."

"John Astor has that sort of scheme in mind, I'm told. Can the Missouri Fur Company compete with him?"

"If I had my way, sir, John Astor wouldn't be a competitor. We'd invite him to be a partner in our company."

"His capital certainly would strengthen the company," Lewis said with an approving nod. "What do the partners think of asking him in?"

"Your brother favors the idea. So does Captain Clark. But the Chouteaus won't take him in on any terms. Mr. Bower has mixed feelings, he says. He admits we need the kind of capital Astor can supply. But he's afraid two Dutchmen in the company would be one too many."

"I like the idea of establishing a sea link to the mouth of the Columbia River. Of course, if the British push us into another war—as they seem determined to do—supplying a far western post by the Horn route would be a risky gamble." Governor Lewis eyed Matt shrewdly. "If a post were established in the Nez Perce country, would you want to go out and manage it?"

Leaning on his cane, Matt gazed down at the iron and leather brace he must wear for the rest of his life. Though slow afoot, he could get around well enough. He could ride a horse. With someone like George Drewyer to lead trapping parties in the field, he would be perfectly capable of managing a post, for dealing with company trappers and trading with Indians were relatively sedentary tasks. *Do I want to go?* he mused bitterly. *Lord, yes! But I know I cannot go.*

He shook his head. "My family and future are here, sir. I'll never go west again."

"Well, I wish the trip I'm about to make took me west instead of east," Lewis grumbled. "Grizzly bears, Blackfeet, nearsighted hunters, fleas, flu, famine, flux— I'd rather endure them all a dozen times over than deal with the bureaucrats I've got to face in Washington. God help me, Matt, if the government doesn't change its mind and honor those vouchers, I'll be forced to do something desperate . . ."

At the time, Matt had assumed that the "something desperate" Governor Lewis would be forced to do would be to sell or borrow against some of the considerable parcels of land he owned in and around St. Louis in order to cover the vouchers, which totaled five hundred dollars. Used to buy tobacco, powder, lead, knives, hatchets, beads, and blankets given as peace bribes to sullen Arickara and Sioux tribal leaders by the Lisa-Chouteau party as it returned Chief Shahaka to his Mandan village, this relatively small sum no doubt would have been approved without question if it had been incorporated with the seven thousand dollars

the federal government had agreed to pay the escort party.
But as an afterthought—which it admittedly was—it was a
crippled bird that made a perfect target for a bureaucratic
marksman.

The way Matt heard the story, Lisa and Chouteau had
told Governor Lewis how many men, boats, weapons, and
supplies their combined parties would need, and the amount
of wages they would have to pay their people. With the
total cost coming to seven thousand dollars, this was the
sum requested be authorized by Secretary of War William
Eustis. Because communications between St. Louis and
Washington, D.C., were slow, it had taken several months
for his request and bureaucratic approval to make the round
trip. But the seven thousand dollars had been approved.

Just before starting upriver, Lisa and Chouteau had made
a final inventory of the party's supplies—and discovered a
glaring oversight.

"My God! Presents for the chiefs! We forgot them!"

Certainly Meriwether Lewis, of all men, knew that the
price of peace in Indian country was an ample supply of
presents for tribal leaders. By now, the season was too far
advanced for a supplementary request and approval to go
to Washington and back. So Governor Lewis, assuming
that he was dealing with a reasonable man, had issued the
vouchers on his own responsibility, sure that they would
be honored by the federal government. Instead, Secretary
Eustis—whom both Henry Clay and Albert Gallatin earlier had pronounced "utterly incompetent in any field"—
had refused to honor the vouchers, had acidly criticized
Governor Lewis's Indian Policy, about which he knew next
to nothing, and had sarcastically accused him of misusing
federal funds for private commercial ventures.

Even though President Jefferson had been deeply concerned by the failure of Ensign Pryor and his party to escort
Chief Shahaka back to the Mandan country, and had declared
that the honor of the United States demanded that the federal
government keep its promise, Secretary Eustis denied that

the Lisa-Chouteau mission had any official purpose.

"As the object and destination of this force is unknown," he wrote, "and more especially as it combines commercial purposes, it cannot be considered as having the sanction of the Government of the United States."

At the conclusion of his astounding letter rejecting the five hundred dollars' worth of vouchers, he bluntly told Governor Lewis that since his patron, President Jefferson, was no longer in office, taking his protest to the Executive Mansion would do him no good.

"President Madison has been consulted," he wrote, "and the observations herein contained have his approval."

Understandably, Meriwether Lewis was furious. Accustomed to the support of wide-visioned men such as Jefferson and Gallatin, who knew how important retaining the friendship of Northwest Indians was in preventing wholesale blood-letting over a large portion of the Missouri and Columbia river watersheds, he simply could not understand this narrowminded regime. It disturbed him so deeply that he brought out the letter President Jefferson had written him earlier regarding the importance of returning Chief Shahaka to his home, and read it to Matt:

" 'I am uneasy hearing nothing from you about the Mandan chief nor the measures for restoring him to his country,' President Jefferson wrote me a year ago. 'That is an object which presses on our justice and our honour . . . ' "

Angrily waving the letter at Matt, Lewis demanded, "Faced with this expression of the urgency and importance of returning Chief Shahaka to his country, how can Secretary Eustis possibly say that the mission did not have the sanction of the United States Government? How can he make such a stupid statement?"

"It is incredible, sir."

"I've got to bring him to his senses—assuming he has any."

"When are you leaving for Washington?"

"Just as soon as I can arrange some personal business

matters here. Late summer is an ungodly hot time to be traveling, I know. But I've simply got to go."

As Matt understood Governor Lewis's plans, his first intention had been to go down the Mississippi by boat to New Orleans, then by ship to the Atlantic coast. In the city of Washington, he hoped to straighten out the matter of the disallowed vouchers and impress upon Secretary Eustis and President Madison the importance of maintaining friendly relations with Northwest Indians, who were being wooed by the British to side with them in case of war with the United States. While in the East, he also hoped to arrange for publication of the six volumes of his *Journals,* royalty from which would ease his financial problems. After a visit to his mother and to Thomas Jefferson in Virginia, he planned to start back to St. Louis late in December.

But shortly after the boat reached Chickasaw Bluffs, three hundred miles downriver, September 15, Lewis changed his itinerary. After being taken down by a severe, sudden illness, he wrote President Madison from Fort Pickering, detailing his ailment and the reason for his change in plans.

"I arrived here yesterday about 2 o'clock, P.M., very much exhausted from the heat of the climate. But, having taken medicine, I feel much better this morning. My apprehension from the heat of the lower country and my fear of the original papers relative to my voyage to the Pacific Ocean falling into the hands of the British has induced me to change my route and proceed by land through the state of Tennessee to the city of Washington.

"I bring with me duplicates of my vouchers for public expenditures, etc., which, when fully explained, I flatter myself they will receive your approbation and sanction. Provided my health permits, no time shall be lost in reaching Washington . . ."

William Clark, who had been retained by the new administration as Superintendent of Indian Affairs for the Northwest, was not surprised by Governor Lewis's illness or his change in traveling plans. Few people escaped bouts with malaria in the hot, fetid, pestilential country along the river. And the British certainly would regard the detailed, still-unpublished *Journals* being carried by Lewis as a prize acquisition, if given the opportunity to capture them and him on the high seas—as they certainly would be able to do in the event of war.

"The Natchez Trace is a mean, nasty trail," Clark told Matt, "plagued by mean, nasty people of all colors. But Governor Lewis will be traveling with Major James Neely, the Chickasaw Indian agent, and Captain Gilbert Russell, commandant of Fort Pickering. He's got his servant, Pernia, along, too. They're all well armed and should be able to take care of themselves."

Late in October, Matt dropped into Superintendent Clark's office to inquire about a business matter affecting the Missouri Fur Company. He found Clark sitting gray-faced and frozen, staring blankly off into space. After calling him twice by name and receiving no reply, Matt said urgently, "What is it, sir? What's wrong?"

Numbly Superintendent Clark shook his head, as if his mind was refusing to accept the information it had just received.

"I just got word," he said hoarsely. "Governor Lewis is dead."

"Oh, no!"

"Dead by his own hand. A suicide." Bowing his head as if the cares of the whole world lay on his shoulders, William Clark exclaimed in a thick, choked voice, "I fear, Matt, oh, I fear, the weight of his mind has overcome him!"

PART TWO

MOKI-MOKI
ILP-ILP
AND JOHN CRANE

1810-1819

1

Much as she wanted to go to the buffalo country with her brother, Red Elk, in hopes of hastening the day when she would see her man again, Moon Wind obeyed her father and stayed home. No longer was going to the buffalo country the leisurely, enjoyable outing such a trip used to be, for the Blackfeet were getting a steady supply of arms from the King George men now, making them so arrogant and hostile that the Nez Perces dared not venture across the mountains unless their hunting party contained a large number of seasoned warriors.

Each brave going on these meat-making expeditions took his wife and children along, of course, for the trips never took less than three months and sometimes lasted as long as two years. But because of the risk of Blackfoot attack, old people, women without men, or any persons unable to work, fight, or move fast were left behind.

Little Crane, as she called the child, was fourteen moons old and beginning to babble and toddle when Red Elk decided to go to the buffalo land. It would be a slow-paced trip, for Doe Eyes, who belonged to the Kamiah band, wanted to stop off there for a visit with her relatives. Though a few members of the Wallowa band were going along, most of the family heads were from villages east of the *Ki-moo-e-nim* or along the three branches of the *Koos-koos-kee*. By the time two hundred men of warri-

or age joined the party with their wives, children, skin
tepees, belongings, and horses, summer was almost gone.
But once the party began to move, Lolo Pass was crossed
in a week's time, giving the hunters two months of early
autumn weather in which to kill buffalo, elk, antelope, and
deer—good fat meat which the women dried, smoked, or
made into pemmican.

Camping east of the Bitter Root Mountains near their
"cousins," the Flatheads, the sojourning Nez Perces were
gone from their homeland a year and a half. Past three summers old now, black-eyed like his mother but light-skinned
like his father, chubby, strong, and a bright, happy child,
Little Crane thought the world and everything in it had been
created just for his special joy. He petted or pounded dogs,
as the notion struck him. Horses he climbed on and fell off,
accepting either result with stoic calm. When he was cold,
he sought shelter in the nearest lodge; when he was hot, he
went for a swim in the nearest creek or river; when he was
hungry, he ate food offered to him by the nearest mother;
when he was sleepy, he crawled under the nearest
blanket.

Gradually he was beginning to realize that in this big,
friendly family called the Wallowa band, there were a
few people who were particularly devoted to him. First,
his mother, Moon Wind, who was beautiful, warm, and
fun to be around. Second, the plump, heavy woman
with lines in her face and streaks of gray in her hair
who was usually kind but now and then scolded him
when he failed to mind his manners. She was called a
grandmother. Third, a tall, gaunt, stooped man with white
hair, a hawk nose, and a pronounced limp. He was called
grandfather; his sole purpose in life seemed to be to sit
by the fire in the winter longhouse, telling Little Crane
tales of olden times, when *Speelyi,* the Coyote Spirit,
ruled the world.

It was *Speelyi,* Grandfather said, who taught the Nez
Perces not to eat dogs, no matter how hungry they got.

Sheltered by Grandfather's arm, holding a black and white short-haired puppy in his lap, Little Crane listened raptly to the story.

"Long ago, in the moon of *Ah-pah-ahl,* which is the season of making baked loaf from ground kouse roots, a terrible famine lay over the land of the *Nimipu,*" Grandfather said, the tone of his voice and his pronunciation of words quite different from normal usage, for grandfather tales must be related in a special way. "A great forest fire in late summer had burned up the trees, killed many elk and deer, and driven what few animals were left across the mountains toward the buffalo country. When winter came, snow fell so deep and blocked the trails so late the next spring that the hunters could not travel to the buffalo plains, kill wild game there, and bring meat back to their starving families. Because of the fire, the streams running down out of the high country carried bitter-tasting ash into the rivers, which the salmon did not like, so these fish who mean life to the *Nimipu* stayed below the mouth of the *Ki-moo-e-nim* waiting for the water to turn sweet again.

"This was many years before *Speelyi* sent us the horse, of course, for in olden times he did not believe we needed big dogs—which was what we first called horses—in our country. In olden times, when we traveled afoot to the buffalo country, each man, woman, and child carried a pack according to their strength, size, and age. Even the dogs carried packs or dragged loads tied to two sticks—just as your dogs do today in the games you play."

In the buffalo country east of the mountains lived tribes that were different from the *Nimipu,* Grandfather said, for when *Speelyi* slew the monster, cut it up, and threw its parts to the four winds, each piece became a distinct tribe. The monster's feet, which had been dark, calloused, and sharp-clawed, became the tribe called Blackfeet. Since the Sioux sprang from the flesh of the underside of the monster's neck, they were called Cut-Throats by the *Nimipu.* The Crows, who were made of the monster's tongue, were called Big-Talkers; the Pend Oreilles, who were fashioned from its ears, the Big-Ears; the Shoshones, who grew out of its tail, the Wigglers or Snakes; and so on.

"But since *Speelyi* created the *Nimipu* out of the heart's blood of the monster," Grandfather said, "we were his favorite people. And since dogs were made in his image, we always have respected them and never have killed and eaten them, though we know other tribes of Indians and the *Suyapo* do."

"My father is a *Suyapo*," Little Crane said, stroking the puppy in his lap. "His name is *Moki Hih-hih*."

"This I know, *Moki-Moki Ilp-ilp*. You should be proud to have such a man as your father."

"Go on with the story, Grandfather. Tell me about the time of the terrible famine, when *Speelyi* taught the *Nimipu* not to eat dogs."

"Ah, yes, the story!" Grandfather was silent for a time, whether to refresh his memory in recalling a tale handed down from olden times through many generations or to put together the pieces of a new story he was making up as he went along—as the boy knew he sometimes did—Little Crane could not tell. But at last he continued.

"In this time of great hunger, a young brave named Runs Far led a party of hunters into a mountain meadow high above the deep canyon through which the *Ki-moo-e-nim* flows. There they found and killed an elk, which had survived the fire and stayed in the country. Eating only its liver and drinking only a little of its blood to keep up their strength, they cut up the carcass of the elk into loads they could carry on their backs and brought it down the steep, dangerous trails to the village where their starving people waited. Dividing it into equal portions, they built fires in the longhouse and began preparing a feast—the first they had had for a long, long time. But just as they were sitting down to eat, a small black and white, smooth-haired dog—"

"Like mine."

"Yes, just like yours—grabbed the piece of meat Runs Far was about to eat, and ran away with it."

"Was it a big piece of meat?"

"Almost as big as the dog. But the dog was very hungry. By the time Runs Far caught up with it, the greedy dog had eaten it all."

"What did Runs Far do?"

"He was very angry, of course. But he was a just man. He tied a thong around the dog's neck, dragged it back to the longhouse, and insisted that the council of elders put it on trial. Since many people had seen it steal the meat, it was found guilty and was sentenced to die."

"Who did the dog belong to?"

"A boy about your age. His name was Grasshopper."

"What did he do?"

"He offered to give Runs Far his own portion of meat, in place of that the dog had stolen. But Runs Far would not take it. Instead, Runs Far said, since the dog was sentenced to die anyway, he would kill it and eat it. This way justice would be served in two ways: The thieving dog would die, as it deserved to do, and Runs Far would get the piece of meat he had earned. What could be fairer than that?"

Always in the grandfather tales there was a problem—an unexpected complication—and a lesson, Little Crane knew. Always when the problem appeared to be insoluble, *Speelyi* showed up and suggested an ingenious solution.

"It would be fairer," Little Crane said thoughtfully, "if Runs Far took Grasshopper's piece of meat and let Grasshopper keep the dog, which he could eat or not eat as he wished."

"*Ahh taats!*" Grandfather exclaimed, stroking Little Crane's shoulder affectionately. "You grow in wisdom, *Moki-Moki Ilp-ilp*. But that was not what happened. Instead, *Speelyi* appeared and suggested a compromise. At the upper end of the long sandbar on which the longhouse of the village sat, the river swirled around in a slow, deep eddy, forming a pool on whose bottom monstrous sturgeon sometimes groped for food. The size of a full-grown horse, these giant fish were not easy to catch, for the hook made of a peeled, sharpened, hardened tree root must be large and strong, the braided rawhide line to which it was fastened must be sturdy, the bait impaled on the hook must be juicy and tempting, and the stone sinkers pulling the hook down to the bottom had to be placed just right. Even when hooked solidly, the huge fish often moved out of the eddy and got into the main current of the swift-flowing river, from which it could be pulled only with great effort."

"So they fished for a giant sturgeon," Little Crane said, "using Grasshopper's piece of elk meat for bait."

"*Ahh taats!* You grow clever, too!" Grandfather exclaimed. "Yes, that is exactly what they did. Baiting the big wooden hook, fastening stone sinkers to the line, casting the hook into the upstream end of the eddy, then tying the end of the line to a sturdy tree growing near the water's edge—just as *Speelyi* told them to do—they made a pact, which both Runs Far and Grasshopper pledged themselves to honor. For what was left of that day and for all the hours of that night, they would let the baited hook lie on the bottom of the pool. At dawn, the next morning, they would check the line and see if they had hooked a sturgeon. If they had, the black and white dog would live. If they had not, it would be killed and Runs Far would eat it."

"What happened?" Little Crane asked breathlessly.

"The night passed. Dawn came. Runs Far, Grasshopper, and everybody able to run, walk, or crawl hurried to the head of the eddy. The line tied to the tree there was pulled as tight as a bowstring. It was quivering up and down and from side to side, as if, far below the surface of the water, a sturgeon the weight of two horses was trying to tear himself free."

"They had caught one!"

"Not quite, *Moki-Moki Ilp-ilp*. Even as ten strong men ran to seize the line and pull in the big fish, the line broke. Apparently the sturgeon had been hooked for some time and, in pulling this way and that, had chafed the line where it was tied around the tree until it had parted. Now, they all could see, the great fish they had hooked was moving downriver as fast as it could swim. Already the line had floated halfway across the eddy and nothing could be done to retrieve it."

"Couldn't somebody swim out and get it?"

"Runs Far tried. But he missed. Then, just as the end of the line neared the head of a swift rapid downstream from the eddy, a remarkable thing happened. A black and white dog took a running leap off a rock ledge rising above the river, hit the water, swam out to the line, and seized it in his teeth."

"Grasshopper's dog!"

"Indeed it was. But what could a small dog do in the swift rapids of the river to stop a fish the size of a sturgeon? What could it possibly do?"

"I know!" Little Crane cried, excitedly squeezing the black and white puppy so tightly that it yipped in protest. "I know what it could do!"

"What could it do, *Moki-Moki Ilp-ilp?*"

"It could hang on to the line and follow the sturgeon down the river until it came to a quiet pool and stopped. Then it could carry the slack line out onto the bank to a stout tree, run around it three times to snub it off, then lie down and wait for Runs Far and the people of the village to come and pull the big fish in."

"What if there were no tree on the bank?"

"A boulder would do as well. There are lots of them along the banks of the river."

Grandfather smiled and nodded. "As a matter of fact, it was a boulder the dog used to snub off the sturgeon. And he did run around it three times. This was a trick all dogs knew, *Speelyi* said, for he himself had taught it to them."

"How big was the sturgeon?"

"It was as long as a tepee pole and as big around as a horse. Runs Far, Grasshopper, and the people of the village feasted upon its flesh for a week. By then, summer had come, the water in the *Ki-moo-e-nim* had turned sweet again, salmon had come back into the river, the trails to the buffalo country were clear, and no one in the village ever went hungry again. So what is the lesson in that story?"

"Don't eat your dog," Little Crane answered, affectionately stroking the sleeping puppy in his lap. "You may need him the next time you go fishing."

2

Toward the end of the last month of summer each year, the crystal-clear mountain water flowing into Wallowa Lake turned a brilliant reddish-orange as immense numbers of a unique species of salmon made their spawning run to the streams in whose gravel bottoms they had been born. Called redfish, sockeye, kokanee, yanks, or bluebacks, they were not large compared to other varieties of salmon, weighing only three to eight pounds, but were highly prized by the Indians because of the richness of their flesh. Using nets, weirs, gaffs, forks, and spears, the Wallowa band of Nez Perces caught and cured the fish by the thousand. Sharing the food bounty with them were visiting relatives and friends from Lapwai, Kamiah, the Flathead country east of the Bitter Root Mountains, and, from the country of their "cousins" to the west, the Cayuses, Walla Wallas, and Umatillas.

For two consecutive summers now, a handsome, well-mannered young Cayuse brave named Many Horses had favored Moon Wind with polite attention, coming often to sit and smoke with her father, telling bits of news from his part of the country, which her father could not visit as he used to do because age and infirmity denied him long horse-back journeys. Now and then he brought presents for Little Crane—a small bow and a quiver of arrows to match, the tips of the arrows blunted to prevent injury to other children or dogs. As a consequence, Moon Wind's

117

father, her mother, and her son liked Many Horses, and let him know that he was welcome in their lodge.

Because the Nez Perces and other tribes in this part of the country were great travelers, it had become a common practice for young men to seek mates from outside their own band. While the taboos against marrying within the clan were not as strict as in some tribes, they did exist. Furthermore, meeting a man you had not known as a girl or meeting a woman you had not known as a boy was intriguing of itself. And somewhere deep in racial subconsciousness was recognized the value of forming alliances with distant neighbors; such marriages would turn these potential hostiles into relatives and friends.

Twenty-five years old now, Many Horses had been married, Moon Wind knew, but two summers ago both his wife and first child had died. Now, in his patient way, he was courting her. She liked him. She respected him. But until Red Elk returned with news of *Moki Hih-hih,* she could accept no other man.

As the redfish run ended, her brother came back to the Land of the Winding Waters. He was now truly *We-wu-kye Ilp-ilp,* the "Red Bull Elk," for, while sojourning in the buffalo country, he had in several fights with Blackfeet distinguished himself in battle and become a leader of the fighting men. Twice wounded himself, he had killed three Blackfoot warriors and counted coup on as many more by striking their bodies with his war club at close range and then getting safely away.

These kills and coups had been witnessed and sworn to by Nez Perce comrades with whom he shared personal death-songs. By custom, each man memorized death-songs composed by several fellow warriors, so that the final chant could be made by a friend in the event the warrior had had no opportunity to voice the death-song himself before being killed. But Red Elk refused to take the scalps of his victims, as some of the Nez Perce braves were beginning to do in imitation of the Plains and Eastern tribes, who had been taught the practice by the British and French some years ago.

"When we sat in council with the Americans, we agreed to meet the Shoshones, the Blackfeet, the Crow, and the Sioux on the buffalo plains in peace," Red Elk told his father and other elders of the Wallowa band. "We were careful to stay on the south side of the Big Muddy, leaving all the wide land north of that river to the Blackfeet. But as always, they were greedy. They crossed the river and attacked our hunting parties as we were making meat. So we fought and defended ourselves, as we always have done and always will do. But I brought home no Blackfoot scalps to defile my lodge."

In one of the fights, a bullet had broken a rib and still was lodged in his chest, causing him discomfort from time to time. In another, an upward-slashing knife had barely missed his throat, its point catching his left cheekbone and opening up a six-inch wound across his eyebrow and forehead. Though it had bled copiously, Doe Eyes had managed to pull it together and do a fine stitching job on it with the kit of needles and thread she had had the foresight to select as a present from *Moki Hih-hih* when he had offered her a choice between that, some bright blue beads, and a piece of red calico cloth. Long healed now, the wound had given a permanent quizzical frown to the left side of Red Elk's face, however much the right side of his face tried to exude cheerfulness.

After paying his respects to his father and the elders, Red Elk sought out Moon Wind, finding her on a knoll at the north end of Wallowa Lake a short distance away from the level prairie on which the lodges of the village were pitched. In the late afternoon stillness, the dark blue surface of the lake was as smooth as glass, disturbed here and there by a fish rising to take an insect. Above the upper end of the lake, mountains rose steeply, the evergreen forest of their lower slopes splotched with gold here and there, for already frosts had come to the high country, turning aspen and tamarack a rich yellow. Above timberline, the jutting brown peaks

were white-dusted with snow now. Soon the prime hunting
season would be here for deer and elk; then the Wallowa
band would begin its seasonal migration northward toward
the low-lying winter village along the Grande Ronde.

"It is good to have you back, my brother," Moon Wind
said softly.

"It is good to be back, my sister. I am pleased to see that
Moki-Moki Ilp-ilp grows strong and stays healthy."

"He is a fine boy."

"He has good blood." Moving to her, Red Elk put his
hands on her shoulders, looked at her with great affection,
and said gently, "I have news of his father, Moon Wind."

"I would hear it."

"His friend, George Drewyer, the hunter, says he has
been stricken with a crippling illness. That is why he has
not returned, as he promised to do."

"Will he ever return?"

"No. He will spend the rest of his life in the white man's
big village called St. Louis, George Drewyer says, working
as a partner in a fur company. He has taken a white woman as
a wife. Already she has borne him a son. But he wants you to
know that he will never forget you or *Moki-Moki Ilp-ilp.*"

Among the Nez Perce women who had had relations with
members of the Lewis and Clark party, several had given
birth to half-blood babies after the white men had left the
country. Since no stigma was attached to such births, all the
mothers except Moon Wind soon had taken Indian husbands,
who accepted the children as their own. In some cases—such
as that of the boy-child conceived by a young maiden niece of
Chief Broken Arm, who claimed that its father was Captain
Clark himself—the women took great pride in the *Suyapo*
blood running in their children's veins.

As she gazed out over the darkening surface of the lake, a
heaviness filled Moon Wind's breast; a stinging mist glazed
her eyes. But she gave no outward sign of the pain she
was feeling. A crippling illness such as *Moki Hih-hih* had
suffered was part of life. Since he must remain in St. Louis,

he would need a wife. It was natural that she should bear him children. And since she knew now that he would not be returning to the Nez Perce country, Moon Wind would need a husband, too.

"Many Horses is welcome in our lodge, I hear," Red Elk said quietly. "Our father and mother think he is a good man."

"Yes," Moon Wind murmured. "Little Crane likes him, too."

"And you? How do you feel about him?"

"When *Moki Hih-hih* came, I gave him my heart, as he gave his to me. I can never get it all back, just as he cannot. But I know life must go on, dear brother. Speak to Many Horses for me. Tell him I am willing to be his wife."

3

George Drewyer was dead. He had been killed by Blackfeet in prime beaver country on the headwaters of the Missouri in late May 1810. Matt was informed a couple of months later. That Drewyer and the two Shawnee Indians trapping with him had put up a tremendous fight before they died was starkly proven by the savage way their bodies had been mutilated by the Blackfeet—heads chopped off, hands and feet amputated, intestines ripped out and strewn over the surrounding ground. To Matt, the loss of this man who had been a respected mentor and a close friend brought an inner desolation as bleak and grim as that felt by William Clark at the death of Meriwether Lewis.

Now that more details of the tragedy at Grinder's Stand on the Natchez Trace had reached him, William Clark no longer accepted the snap judgment made by Thomas Jefferson that Lewis, in a fit of despondency, had taken his own life.

"A man as skilled in the use of firearms as Governor Lewis does not shoot himself in the head with one pistol, in the breast with another, slash his throat, then his wrists, plead for water, and live from midnight till dawn before he dies," Clark declared firmly. "Why Mr. Jefferson made the statement he did—without a shred of evidence to back it up—will always remain a mystery to me. I'll never believe Governor Lewis killed himself. He was murdered most foully—by someone he knew and trusted. Who that someone was we may never know. But I intend to do my best to find out."

Deeply disturbed in a personal sense by George Drewyer's death, Matt was further concerned by the effect the implacable hostility of the Blackfeet was having on the partners in the company. Trapping beaver and fighting Indians could not be done simultaneously, they agreed. With the death toll now at eleven among the Lisa-Chouteau parties, the eighty American trappers upriver had completely abandoned the Blackfoot country, moving south two hundred miles into the more friendly domain of the Crows and Shoshones. With partner Pierre Menard's approval, Andrew Henry planned to build a fort there, behind whose solid log walls the men would be protected from attack by hostiles.

"They'll trap precious little beaver with that sort of setup," Matt predicted bleakly. "If they can't move out and about the country in small parties, they might as well give up and come back to St. Louis. Either that or move on west to the Columbia River headwaters."

But the bickering partners possessed neither the daring nor the capital that such a move required. Instead they ordered the men to trap in the vicinity of Henry's Fort in large, well-guarded parties, traded on a small scale with Crow Indians, and watched suspiciously as John Jacob Astor developed his grandiose scheme of establishing a monopoly on the fur trade of the Pacific Northwest.

Rebuffed in Montreal by both the Hudson's Bay and the North West Company when he tried to put together an international cartel, frozen out by the partners of the Missouri Fur Company when he attempted to do business with them, he made plans to leapfrog the existing British and American trapping enterprises in one bold, well-capitalized, two-pronged venture aimed at controlling all the fur riches between the Russian posts in the far north and the Spanish settlements in southern California.

By sea, he dispatched the *Tonquin*—captained by an experienced naval man, Jonathan Thorn—from New York, around the Horn, to the mouth of the Columbia River. By land, he ordered a band of men under the leadership of Wilson Price Hunt and Donald MacKenzie to ascend the Missouri by the route Lewis and Clark had blazed, cross to the Pacific slope as the explorers had done, and join the water-borne party near the mouth of the Great River of the West. There they would build a post that would become the commercial heart of a far-flung enterprise called the Pacific Fur Company.

Arriving in St. Louis early in the summer of 1810, William Price Hunt and Donald MacKenzie began hiring men to flesh out the skeleton crew of French-Canadians, Scotchmen, Irishmen, Britishers, and Americans they had previously hired in Montreal and New York. Warned by John Bower, William Morrison, and Auguste Chouteau not to cooperate with the Astor people in any way, lest they derive some commercial advantage from the information given them, Matt Crane did not find it difficult to be coldly formal and closemouthed with Wilson Price Hunt, who impressed him as an arrogant, opinionated, city-oriented man with little knowledge of the wilderness. But big, jovial, outgoing Donald MacKenzie was a man he liked on sight, and one with whom he felt he should talk freely, for in his view a success by the Astor company in the Pacific Northwest would help rather than hurt the efforts of the Missouri Fur Company in the interior.

If ever a person were capable of "going bear-hunting with a switch," Donald MacKenzie was that man. Red-headed and full-bearded, the girth of his chest, arms, and legs was so huge that he weighed a massive 312 pounds, not an ounce of which was fat. Full of far-ranging plans, with a limitless amount of energy, constantly on the move, he was such an elemental force that his associates long ago had dubbed him "Perpetual Motion." Since both Hunt and MacKenzie were full partners in the company, they were supposed to share in leadership decisions; but as summer waned into fall and the party's organization was completed, Matt realized with concern that it was Hunt rather than MacKenzie who was making all the important decisions.

Matt learned that the party of sixty-four men planned to load its trade goods and supplies aboard keelboats and proceed upriver two hundred miles to the village of Nodowa, where it would go into camp for the winter under MacKenzie's leadership, while Hunt stayed in St. Louis and kept in touch with Astor. He was puzzled.

"Won't that be a waste of wages and time?"

"Aye, laddie, that it will. Gi'en my way, I'd head west next week. We'd be at the foot of the Rocky Mountains by Christmas and reach the mouth of the Columbia early next summer. But Jacob Astor listens to Hunt, not to me, for I'm nae good at writing letters, whilst Hunt writes wi' a silver pen."

"That won't do him any good in Blackfoot country."

"Tell me about the rascals, Matt. Is there nae some way we can avoid trouble wi' them?"

"Ordinarily, a party as large as yours would be safe from attack by the Blackfeet," Matt said. "But you've got one bad weakness. The majority of your people are French-Canadians—experts at traveling on water but poor hands at fighting Indians or traveling on land."

"Aye, that's God's truth. On water, one French-Canadian is worth three Americans, I've learned, while on land one American is worth three French-Canadians. But we're stuck wi' the men we've got, Matt, for they're the only ones we could hire. So what's the best thing to do?"

"Don't stay on the Missouri River with keelboats to the Great Falls, as we did. Leave the river in Arickara or Sioux country, well to the south and east of Blackfoot land. Trade with the Rees or Sioux for horses. You'll need at least two for each man. Then head west across Crow country to the land of the Shoshones, Flatheads, and Nez Perces, who will all be friendly. Once you're across Lolo Pass on the upper Clearwater, you can make dugout canoes, as we did, leave your horses with the Nez Perces, and go on down the Columbia by boat."

"D'ye have a map of the country?"

"One you can look at, yes, though I can't let you make a copy," Matt said, spreading out on a table a composite map he had helped William Clark put together. "For some strange reason, the government wants the knowledge our party gained kept secret until they're ready to have it published."

"A look is all I'll need, laddie. I prefer to carry maps in my head—where they won't get wet or soiled."

Matt traced the route he felt the party should take after leaving the river, then suggested that it stop at Andrew Henry's Fort, just west of the Yellowstone country, where it might find guides to lead it on west. Putting his finger on the spot west of the Bitter Root Mountains where the forks of the *Koos-koos-kee* came together, he said that the key to inaugurating a successful fur enterprise in the Pacific Northwest would be in establishing good relationships with the Nez Perces.

"They're the finest tribe of Indians the Lewis and Clark party had dealings with during our two years of traveling. They're honest, good-humored, and generous. They're the cleanest, handsomest, most fearless Indians we met, with by far the best horses. If you're planning to establish a post upriver, their country should be your first choice as a location."

"You know their headmen, I take it?"

"Chief Broken Arm is the most important leader. Twisted Hair and *Tetoharsky* are influential chiefs, too." Matt hesitated a moment, then said, "If you should see a Nez Perce named Red Elk of the Wallowa band, give him my best regards. He's a very special friend of mine."

"I'll make a point of looking him up."

"He has a sister named Moon Wind. During the two weeks we camped with them on our way west, she and I became quite fond of one another. In fact, we . . ."

Choking with emotion, Matt turned away, limped over to the window of the warehouse office, and stared bleakly out at the fallen leaves lying along the muddy street. Over his shoulder, he said, "You've lived among Indians in the wilderness, Mr. MacKenzie—"

"Aye, that I have—for many long, lonely months."

"Then you can understand my feelings for her. She bore me a son. I saw it just before we left Nez Perce country. Through George Drewyer and Red Elk, I have been informed that the boy has thrived. I christened him Mark. He would be four years old by now. If you should see him and his mother, Mr. MacKenzie, give them both my love."

"That I'll do, Matt. Depend on it."

Turning back into the room, Matt crossed to his desk, opened a drawer, and took out a multi-bladed knife encased in a shiny black leather sheath. Made of good British steel, the knife contained a long blade, a short blade, an awl, a corkscrew, a screwdriver, a file, a saw blade, and a small pair of scissors. Though multi-bladed knives had been in existence since first invented in Roman days, this newest import from England was the most compact, useful, and ingenious tool that Matt had yet seen. The moment he viewed it, he knew he must send one to his firstborn son.

"Give him this present from his father. When he uses it, perhaps he will think of me—just as I so often think of him."

"Consider it done," MacKenzie said softly. "And I'll send word back to you meant for your ears alone."

4

It was ironic, Matt Crane brooded after talking to Donald MacKenzie in St. Louis some months later, that the post established by the man he regarded to be the most capable trader in the business, at the most favorable location in the Pacific Northwest, among the region's most friendly Indians, should have produced such meager results. Of course, the entire Astor enterprise had been dogged by failure from beginning to end. Because of his current involvement in the fur business and his earlier experiences with the Lewis and Clark party, Matt had followed the fortunes of the by-sea and by-land segments of the venture with a great deal of interest as news came back to St. Louis between 1811 and 1814. As disaster piled on disaster, he found the end results appalling.

Where the Lewis and Clark party had lost only one man to a fatal illness during its two-and-a-half-year trek to the Pacific and back, the Astor expedition had suffered a stunning total of sixty-three deaths in the same length of time. Most of these, in Matt's opinion, had been caused by the sheer stupidity of the men in command.

Certainly Captain Jonathan Thorn, master of the supply ship *Tonquin*, had been grossly culpable when, in seeking passage over the tumultuous bar at the mouth of the Columbia, he had doomed eight men to death by forcing them to attempt to find a safe channel in small boats during a raging storm; all eight drowned. Later, at Nootka Sound, he showed even poorer judgment when he let so many greedy, hostile Indians aboard the ship that they almost successfully attempted to kill all the whites and take it over, being foiled only by the ultimate desperation of a crew member who dropped a lighted match into the powder magazine, thus blowing himself, Captain Thorn, twenty-five other whites, an unknown number of Indians, and the ship itself to Kingdom Come.

By land on the trip west, five men in the Hunt party had been lost. At Astoria, three more had been killed. When the replacement supply ship, *Lark*, went down off the coast of South America, eight more men were drowned. Later, while gathering furs and fighting Indians in the Shoshone country, nine men died violently. In the final closure of American efforts at Astoria, three more deaths were caused by accidental drowning.

With its sea route of supply cut off by British naval superiority; with the land route difficult and threatened by hostile Indians; and with the Montreal-based North West Company sending a continual stream of men and supplies across Canada and down the Columbia, the partners of the Pacific Fur Company had agreed that their prospects were bleak. Since the senior partner, Wilson Price Hunt, long had been absent on a trading mission to the Russian posts of Sitka and Kamchatka—his return probably to be further delayed by a voyage to the Sandwich Islands—partners Duncan MacDougal, John Clarke, and Donald MacKenzie were forced to assume the responsibility of choosing between a poor bargain or none.

After a great deal of haggling, the North West Company had offered to buy all the assets of the Pacific Fur Company for $80,500. Though John Jacob Astor later complained that the partners in the field had sold him out for ten cents on the dollar, the men who had made the decision were acutely aware of the fact that war between Great Britain and the United States had completely isolated them, and that no military aid would come to their relief. Indeed, the most recent communications from Montreal had brought the news that several privateers and at least three naval vessels were heading for Astoria, intending to take the post with all its supplies and furs as a prize of war. To the partners in the field, selling seemed far better than surrendering, so the transaction had been consummated.

Bringing word of the sale and the $80,500 draft to John Jacob Astor in New York, Donald MacKenzie had been stunned by the vituperative bitterness of Astor's reaction. In St. Louis to confer with Wilson Price Hunt, who now was making that city his headquarters as he tried to reorganize the shattered company, MacKenzie told Matt Crane how surprised he had been at the reception he received in New York.

"Would ye believe he would call me a traitor? That he would accuse me, MacDougal, and Clarke of selling out to the North West Company in hopes of personal gain? That he would curse me and say that, gi'en his way, he would rather have surrendered all the holdings of the Pacific Fur Company to the British at gunpoint, without being paid a dollar, than to make a sale under duress? D'ye ken such thinking, Matt?"

"Certainly I do," Matt said with a wry smile. "If title to the assets of the Pacific Fur Company had been taken from him by the British as an act of war, he could have put in a claim for compensation when the war is over. But a sale, even under duress, is a commercial transaction, which probably will stand up in court."

"Weel, all I can say is we struck the best bargain we could. I offered to work wi' him and Hunt, opening up an overland route to the Shoshone and Nez Perce country, but he nae would listen to me. So now I weel go to Montreal and seek a job wi' the North West Company."

"Will you go back to the Columbia?"

"Aye—but not to the lower river. As I tried to tell Astor and Hunt, the best beaver country is inland. The key to unlocking it, as ye told me, is in establishing good relations wi' the Nez Perces. It took me a while to reach an understanding wi' them, but I finally did."

"You say Red Elk was helpful—"

"Aye, that he was. And your son is a handsome lad, Matt. Ye'd be proud of him, I know."

"Moon Wind has a husband—?"

"A Cayuse named Many Horses. A fine man, so far as I could tell, who treats her and the lad well, and is liked by all her people."

When he learned that Moon Wind had accepted a husband, Matt's feeling had been mixed—jealousy that she now lived with another man; relief that she had found someone to take care of her. He was pleased to hear that his son knew he had a white father and was proud of it. But when MacKenzie told him about Red Elk's fights with the Blackfeet in the buffalo country, and his growing reputation as a warrior, it disturbed Matt that the boy should be given violence, bloodshed, and the killing of fellow human beings as examples of manhood to be emulated.

"I had hoped that the Nez Perces would persuade their neighbors to live at peace with them and one another," he said thoughtfully. "Do you see any chance of that?"

"While the war between England and the United States lasts, no. After it ends, peace of a sort could be imposed on all the far-western tribes, I would say, if both nations insist that a truce be made before any trading is done."

"For all practical purposes, the war is over now. At least the fighting was stopped and they're discussing a treaty in Ghent."

"Aye, the war is over in the East, the South, and on the high seas. But as I hear the news, neither England nor the United States will give up their claim to the Pacific Northwest. All they'll do is agree to leave the country open to settlement and trade by citizens of both nations for a term of ten years. To civilized white people like you and me, laddie, that may be peace. But to the Blackfeet, Sioux, Nez Perces, Shoshones, and all the far-western tribes, it means nothing's been settled yet. Which to them means war."

"No doubt you're right. But knowing that my own flesh and blood is growing up in those conditions troubles me."

"The lad lives in an Indian world, Matt. A heathen world of force and violence."

"Must it always be so?" Matt demanded passionately. "In the time I spent with the Nez Perces, I learned that they're a kind, compassionate, intelligent people, with a well-developed spiritual life—"

"But different from ours, lad—far different indeed. For instance, Red Elk told me that in a couple of years your son will go on his *Wy-a-kin* quest—"

"What kind of quest?"

"*Wy-a-kin*. Among the Nez Perces, when a boy gets to be twelve or thirteen years old, he goes alone to some isolated spot where he fasts until he sees a vision. An animal, a bird, lightning, thunder, an avalanche, a landslide, a fire, a falling tree. He goes without food and shelter until he falls into a kind of trance, with the wild elements of nature putting on a show for him that will change his way of life forever."

"That's paganism!"

"Aye, so it is. But it's the Indian world, Matt. The world your son was born into and must grow up in."

"It can be changed. It must be changed. Enlightenment must be taken to these poor, heathen people. They must learn the ways of God and how to live at peace with one another."

Shaking his head sympathetically, MacKenzie said, "Weel, lad, playing the role of a priest or preacher is nae for me. But when I build my post in Nez Perce country, as I intend to do, a man of the cloth would be most welcome in it and would be gi'en my strong support in his efforts to Christianize the Indians."

"If I were younger and stronger, I would like nothing better than to go as a missionary to the Nez Perces myself,"

Matt said fervently. "But since I cannot, I will do the next best thing."

"Aye? And what is that?"

"Raise my son, John, to do so for me. With proper guidance, he'll become a minister in the Presbyterian church and will go into heathen lands as a missionary."

"Does he know he has an Indian brother?"

"Not yet. But at the proper time, I will tell him. I want my two sons to know and love one another."

5

For months now, *Moki-Moki Ilp-ilp* had been thinking about where he would go on his *Wy-a-kin* quest. He mused that high in the massive, snowcapped mountains looming above Wallowa Lake, there must be an alpine meadow far above timberline that few human eyes had ever seen; a place of mystery and danger, as close to the sky spirits as a person could get, where after a long period of fasting and solitary meditation the rules he must live by and his adult name would be revealed to him. Even as the deep snowdrifts of winter melted under the warm spring sun to form the little rivulets that became streams, lakes, and rivers, so there must also be a source of magical power in the pure air of that high land next to the sky.

When he told his second father, Red Elk, and his third father, Many Horses, the general area where he wanted to go, they both said he had chosen a good place. In olden times, Red Elk said, it was through this mountain wilderness that their enemies, the Shoshones, had come to attack the *Nimipu* as they made their bountiful harvest of redfish from the Wallowa River in late summer.

"This was when the Shoshones had horses and we did not," Red Elk said. "They could move so much more swiftly than we could that a small party of warriors could ride through the mountain passes, swoop down on our fish-gathering families, and do great damage before we knew they were there. But we soon learned how to stop their raids."

"What did you do?" Little Crane asked curiously.

"We posted guards in strategic places overlooking the mountain passes through which the Shoshones had to come. In some places, the trails were so steep and narrow that men fighting afoot had a great advantage over warriors on horseback. After two such battles, in which they lost many men and horses, the Shoshones came no more."

"But we were glad they had come," Many Horses said with a smile. "If they had not, we would have to go to their country to steal the horses. As it was, they brought the horses to us."

Because the second moon of spring, *Ke-khee-tahl*—the season of harvesting wild potatoes—was only half done, with the lakes of the alpine country still frozen and snowdrifts still deep in shaded places along the trail from the Grande Ronde village to their summer camp, the Wallowa band had not yet begun its annual migration from low to high country. But with Little Crane eager to go on his *Wy-a-kin* quest while the rivers, lakes, and mountains of the Land of the Winding Waters still were untenanted by their usual summer visitors, Red Elk agreed that now would be a good time to travel.

In keeping with the dignity of the occasion, Moon Wind pretended not to regard the departure of her son and her brother as an event of any special importance. But catching her eye in unguarded moments the day before he was to leave, Little Crane noted the sadness in them. A tight, hard lump formed in his throat. Though his mother had borne Many Horses a girl-child two years ago, and was six months pregnant now with what she firmly believed would be a boy-child, he was her first-born and best-loved son. She was about to lose him, she knew, for when he returned from his *Wy-a-kin* quest he would be a boy no longer; he would be a man.

During the past year, his chubby body had changed remarkably, his growth becoming vertical rather than horizontal; instead of being broad-chested, muscular, and medium-statured like his second father, Red Elk, it now appeared that when he got his full growth he would be tall, slim, and rangy, like his first father, *Moki Hih-hih*. Though his hair, which he wore Nez Perce fashion—combed straight up and back over his head—was gleaming black, like his mother's, his skin was a shade lighter than hers, his face thinner than Red Elk's, and his cheekbones not as broad. Sobered by the instructions given him by Red Elk on the duties and responsibilities of becoming a warrior and a man, he showed no outward evidence of being frightened—though he inwardly was—nor of doubting that he could endure the ordeal ahead—which he secretly did.

While his mother dared not show, by fussing over him unduly, that she still regarded him to be a child, every stitch she put into the elkskin moccasins she had made for him, every bead threaded as decoration on the soft deerskin leggins and fringed jacket; every bone, quill, and piece of dentalium worked into the beautifully fashioned neck choker she created for him; and, most especially, the waterproof bag in which he would keep his secret, personal medicine pieces, was done with utmost loving care.

The New Testament carried by his first father from St. Louis to the Great Stinking Water and then back to Nez Perce country, where it had been inscribed with his white name, the date of his birth, and the name of his mother and father, was his to care for and keep now. Also placed in his medicine bag, which was tied around his neck and suspended down his chest inside his jacket, was the many-bladed knife sent to him by his first father as a gift carried by the giant white trader, Bearded Red Grizzly Bear. Though an excellent tool, he used it only on special occasions for special purposes, when an everyday tool would not serve, for to him it must last a lifetime as tangible proof of the white father he would probably never see.

Leaving the winter village at the mouth of the Grande Ronde on a cool, misty morning with three horses apiece, a

small skin hunter's tepee, and enough dried jerky, pemmican, and camas cakes to last them for a week, Little Crane
and Red Elk rode up the winding, steep, muddy trail from
the low-lying valley to the high, rolling, grassy plains of the
Wallowa country. In no hurry, they took three days for
the journey. Beside the fire each night, Red Elk told him
about the trip he had made with *Moki Hih-hih* thirteen years
ago, just before *Moki-Moki Ilp-ilp* was born.

Saying that it was important to his *Wy-a-kin* quest that
Little Crane know exactly what kind of man his *Suyapo*
father had been, Red Elk described his appearance, his
bearing, and his manner of speaking in such careful detail
that the image of the man was imprinted indelibly in Little
Crane's mind. For the first time, Red Elk told him the story of
his name: How *Moki Hih-hih*'s father back in St. Louis was a
highly respected *Shaman* with close ties to the *Suyapo* Great
Spirit called God; how when God's son, Jesus, came down
from the sky to live on Earth many years ago, twelve men
had become special chiefs who would spread His message
to the world; how the *Shaman*'s name, Peter, meant the
rock upon which the church would be built; how Matthew
was the first special chief to write a chapter in the Book
given Little Crane, Mark the second, Luke the third, John
the fourth, and so on.

"These stories are all written in the New Testament which
you now possess," Red Elk said. "Someday you must learn
how to read it."

"Who will teach me?"

"I have spoken of this to Bearded Red Grizzly Bear. He
says there are two possibilities. One is that a *Tam-tai-nat*—
a white *Shaman* who preaches—may come to live and teach
at his trading post on the great river. If this happens, you
could go there to learn."

"I would like that," Little Crane said thoughtfully. "What
is the other possibility?"

"That several Indian boys your age be sent east to live
and study in the land of the crowned ones. When he spoke

of this possibility, I at first thought it a fine idea, for if you went to St. Louis, you could meet your father. But when Bearded Red Grizzly Bear said he could not send the Indian boys to the land of the Americans, but must send them to the land of the King George men, I told him I would not let you go there."

"So we must wait for a *Tam-tai-nat* to come to us before we can learn what the Book says?"

"It would seem so, yes."

"Did my father ever talk to you about what was in the Book?"

"Many times. As I understood him, the teachings of the Jesus-God do not differ greatly from those rules by which the *Nimipu* live—except in one important matter, which I find difficult to accept. Instead of being wary of our enemies and killing them before they kill us, the Jesus-God Book says that we should open our hearts to them in peace."

"This is a strange way to treat enemies."

"It is, indeed. But to *Moki Hih-hih* and the two leaders of his party, this was the most important message they brought us. They wanted us to live at peace with all our neighbors, no matter how untrustworthy they have proved themselves to be. We have tried. To the Shoshones, to the Blackfeet— time and again we have offered the pipe of peace. They have refused it."

Touching the disfiguring scar on his face, Red Elk said bitterly, "This mark shows what it costs to trust a Blackfoot. Yet now that the war between the Americans and the King George men is over, Bearded Red Grizzly Bear says we must try again to make peace in the buffalo country. As a warrior, I never will. But you are young and unscarred. In your *Wy-a-kin* quest, you must ask for a sign as to how peace might come."

Pitching the small skin tepee on a knoll overlooking the lower end of Wallowa Lake, Red Elk and Little Crane dug a circular pit, cut limbs off a willow tree, shaped and bound them into an oval framework for a small sweat bath, covered it, then filled it with stones heated in the campfire. After pouring water on the stones and raising the temperature to an almost unbearable height, man and boy stripped, entered the sweat lodge, closed off the narrow entrance, and squatted inside, moisture pouring off their bodies until their senses reeled and every vestige of impurity had been boiled out of their systems. Then, trembling with weakness, they threw back the hide cover over the entrance, staggered down to the shore of the lake, on whose surface floes of ice still lay, and plunged into the paralyzingly frigid water.

Purified now, and following the strict ritual prescribed by Red Elk, Little Crane dried himself, dressed, then sat in silence in the hunter's tepee, staring meditatively into the small fire. From this moment on, he would ingest nothing but water, would not speak, would not sleep, would not even close his eyes until the nights and days of his *Wy-a-kin* quest ordeal had passed, however long it might be.

Though under no compulsion to fast or stay awake with him, Red Elk kept Little Crane silent company through the long night, eating no food, seeking no sleep. He kept the fire going to provide a bit of light and warmth. When the darkness began to fade, he touched the boy gently on his shoulder and made a sign: "It is time."

"Yes, I know," Little Crane signed in return. "And now I go."

Outside the entrance to the tepee, which faced east, the sky was paling. The air was bitter cold, damp with the fog and mist rising off the surface of the lake. Because deep winter still would prevail in the high country into which he was going, Little Crane was permitted to wear a tightly woven, gray and white, two-point North West Company blanket over his jacket and leggins, but a shelter of any kind was not permitted, nor could he build a fire. He carried no weapon. Since Little Crane himself did not know where he was going or how long he would be gone, he would have no hope of being rescued if he fell and injured himself.

If attacked and wounded by a wild animal, if caught in an avalanche, if incapacitated by illness—no help could be expected to reach him in time. For the first time in a life so far spent sheltered, cared for, and protected by a loving family and community, he was completely on his own.

By the time he reached the south end of the lake where the trees began and the mountains sloped steeply upward, the sun had climbed above the high ridge of gravel and boulders carelessly cast aside by *Speelyi*, the Coyote Spirit, when he had gouged out the lake bed in olden times. According to the grandfather tales, he had quarreled with a big sturgeon—for whom he had agreed to create the lake as a summer cooling-off pool—over what shape it should be and what kind of food should be placed in it.

After arguing until exhausted, *Speelyi* had reluctantly promised to send a migration of redfish into the lake in late summer each year. But these tasty fish were primarily for the benefit of the *Nimipu*, he said, with the sturgeon forbidden to eat any of them until after the Wallowa band had taken its allotted yearly supply.

Growing very hungry one evening, the big sturgeon rose out of the depths of the lake during a violent storm, when he thought no one would notice, and seized and ate a young Nez Perce maiden, who had fallen out of an overturned canoe. When *Speelyi*, who noticed everything, learned what the big sturgeon had done, he became very angry.

"Since you have behaved like a monster, I will turn you into one!" he declared. "For the next thousand winters, I will block the lower outlet to the lake so that you cannot get out. For a thousand winters, you will live without the company of your kind in this deep, cold lake. Never again will you be permitted to come to the surface in daylight, to be seen by the people who once regarded you as the finest fish in their country. You will be feared, hated, and reviled as the monster you have become—the devil-fish of Wallowa Lake!"

"There are worse places to live," the big sturgeon replied smugly. "So long as I can devour a young maiden now and then . . ."

How much truth was in this particular grandfather tale, Little Crane could not say. He did know that from time to time sightings of a water monster twenty, thirty, perhaps even fifty feet long had been reported just before dawn or just after dusk. And when sudden storms whipped the surface of the lake into foam-topped waves, all *Nimipu* canoe paddlers headed hastily for shore—with young maidens leading the way.

As the terrain above the lake steepened, the rapids-filled stream flowing down from the mountains divided into two forks, one from the southeast, the other from the southwest. Without making a conscious choice, he crossed the southeasterly fork on a fallen tree, found a game trail leading along the bank of the southwesterly fork, and followed it upward. By mid-morning, he had reached a twenty-foot-high waterfall over which the stream tumbled. He remembered that two summers ago he had come this far hunting with Red Elk. He remembered Red Elk telling him that half a day's climb up the stream lay timberline, where a small alpine lake fed by snowmelt nestled just below the high, jagged crests of the Wallowa Mountains.

The tallest of the peaks was conelike and pointed. Jutting proudly upward, it was called *Ha-yat Kaas*—"woman's breast." Now he knew where he must go. If he followed the stream to its source, with the sun crossing the sky above and before him, he would reach the lake and the glacier lying just below the base of the peak in late afternoon. There, with an unimpeded view of this highest, most beautiful of mountains, with nothing beyond it but cold, clear air through which messages from the sky spirits could be sent to him without earthly interference, he would sit down and begin his vigil, enduring whatever might come for however long it might take . . .

• • •

Directly below the white granite boulder against which he had placed his back—this was the warmest, most sheltered position he could find—lay the frozen surface of the small, circular lake. Heat from the spring sun had melted the snowdrifts covering a narrow stretch of pure, light-colored sand at the near edge of the lake, though on the lake's surface the ice still was intact. Beyond the far side of the lake, the cone-shaped mountain rose steeply, for the most part covered with snow and glacial ice, though here and there its slopes were so steep that snow could not cling to them, and the dark brown rock of which the mountain was formed showed in stark contrast to its pristine white covering.

At first, *Ha-yat Kaas*, as might be expected of a beautiful woman being courted by a would-be lover, ignored Little Crane's presence and refused to speak to him. He did not press her. For hour after hour, while the westering sun bathed her slopes, passed over her peak, then sank beyond her into the darkening sky, he sat in immobility and silence, letting her recognize the fact that he was there, giving her his reverence, waiting patiently for the time to come when she would speak to him.

When night came, she did speak—not in words but in sounds. A boulder loosened by the day's snowmelt thumped downward to the lake's far edge, booming the message "Beware!" A small snowslide hissed into a cirque, whispering, "What are you doing here?" An immense snow cornice overhanging the northern face of the peak collapsed with such force that the avalanche it created sent a wave of wind roaring into the dark, commanding, "Know and respect my power!"

He lost track of time. Day blurred into night; night faded into day. At times he was comfortably warm; at times uncomfortably cold. Warned by Red Elk that he must supply his body with moisture or he would die, he had positioned himself within arm's reach of a small rivulet from which he dipped a few swallows of water every hour or so with a hollowed-out gourd. Though he had never before gone through a day without eating, the gnawing pangs of hunger, which he had felt after a night and a day without food, dwindled and bothered him not at all.

He was getting light-headed. He was falling into a languorous state in which he was not sure whether he was awake or asleep, whether the sounds he heard and the sensations he felt were real or imagined, whether words were spoken to him by materialized spirits or were phrased in his own mind. At times, rain fell; at times, snow drifted down. In the darkness of the third night, a brilliant light suddenly appeared high on the slope of the mountain, moved downward steeply, then shot across the lake as a shimmering, silvery bridge, across which human figures that he recognized to be his mother, his grandfather, Red Elk, and Many Horses walked, danced, and sang seemingly to exhort him to live by the rules they gave him. But their voices were so jumbled and run together he could make no sense of what they were trying to tell him.

Making a fist and shaking it at them in exasperation, he cried, "One at a time! Speak one at a time! Speak more clearly so that I can understand you!"

But before they could do so, the monster rose out of the depths of Wallowa Lake, huge mouth agape, and devoured them all.

Devastated by the knowledge that he was now completely alone in the world, he broke down and sobbed piteously. Then he heard a firm voice say, "Peace, my son. Peace."

He opened his eyes. His first father stood facing him. Yes, there was no doubt of it; the man standing in the circular pool of brilliant light in the middle of the lake just below him was *Moki Hih-hih*, his *Suyapo* father, looking exactly as Red Elk had described him. Joyously, Little Crane called out, "What must I do, Father? How must I live to honor you and my people?"

"Learn to read the Book, my son."

"Yes! I will learn!"

"Do not kill."

"Not even enemies?"

"If you follow the ways of peace taught by the Book, you will have no enemies."

"Will I ever meet you, Father?"

"The future is not completely clear to me, my son. I see you preparing to make a long journey. I see you beginning it. I see you traveling far in company with other members of your tribe. You are making a journey eastward in search of wisdom."

"Then I will see you!"

"Some of your people will see me, my son. But my vision of the future is not complete. I see something bad happening near a big river. There is difficulty crossing it. There is sickness. There is death. The vision fades . . ."

Now the pool of light and the figure illuminated by it vanished, leaving only darkness, cold, and silence. Overcome by sadness and bewilderment, Little Crane cried out in anguish, tried to rise to his feet and rush down to the spot where the vision of his father had appeared, but his weakened legs would not support him. Fainting, he fell back into the hollow of snow against the face of the granite boulder. By the time he regained his senses, the first faint light of what he judged to be the fourth day of his *Wy-a-kin* quest was spreading over the scene before him. A voice deep inside him whispered that the climactic moment of his vigil had come.

Through the translucent mist which hung between the base of the mountain and the frozen surface of the lake, a large creature was striding, gliding, floating, moving toward him in some mysterious way. It was taller than a full-grown man; it had wings, which rose and fell in a slow rhythm used more as a matter of balance than an effort at flight; it had two long legs, like those of a wading bird, but much thicker; its shiny coat of feathers was a resplendent mixture of red, yellow, and white. In its beak, it carried a walnut-sized stone that glittered with the brilliance of a star plucked down from the sky.

Knowing that he must observe and remember every detail of what this name-vision-creature did, Little Crane watched hypnotically as it crossed the lake, moved across the sandy beach and the untrodden snowdrift just below him, then paused and loomed over him. He felt no fear. Even when the creature lowered its beak and let the glittering stone fall downward and strike his chest, he somehow was sure that the gesture was that of bestowing a gift rather than that of casting a weapon. Then suddenly the vision-creature vanished, disintegrating like smoke into the cold morning air.

Meticulously, he put the words together that described in detail what he had seen and experienced in his *Wy-a-kin* vision, out of which his name as a man must be constructed. *Peo-peo*—"large bird." *Te-ne-ik-se*—"to cross a lake on the ice." *Maig*—"sand." *Meke*—"snow." *Te-mug*—"track." *Ue-tu*—"no." *Ips-kel-i-nik-se*—"walks."

Strung together in their proper order, the words gave both a visual image of what he had seen and a verbal meaning to his new name. It would be: *Peo-peo Te-ne-ik-se Maig Meke Te-mug Ue-tu Ips-kel-i-nik-se*: "Tall Bird Crossing a Lake on the Ice, Leaving No Tracks on Sand or Snow."

Only he himself and a few of his closest relatives and friends would ever know or use the entire name or understand its significance. Probably he would be known simply as *Peo-peo Te-ne-ik-se*—"Tall Bird Crossing a Lake on the Ice." On most occasions the name would be shortened to "Tall Bird." But his boy's name, *Moki-Moki Ilp-ilp*, "Little Red Crane," would be used no more.

The light was growing. Getting to his feet, he felt an object fall off his chest; groping over the ground where he had sat, he found the walnut-sized stone that had been given to him by the creature in his vision. Slightly opaque as he held it up toward the rising sun, it contained the vague outline of a mountain, a lake, a feather, and a bird. It was what the *Nimipu* called a "picture-story-rock," he knew, and was considered great medicine, for such rocks—whose imprisoned pictures became much clearer when the rock was polished—were made by *Speelyi* himself and were given only to individuals who were high in his favor.

Knowing that he must treasure the picture-story-rock for the rest of his life, Tall Bird—as he now thought of himself—took off his blanket and shirt, placed the rock in his medicine bag, and donned his shirt and blanket. After a final inclination of his head in a gesture of respect to *Ha-yat Kaas*, he left this sacred spot and set out on the triumphant journey back to the camp where his second father, Red Elk, awaited him . . .

6

At the age of eleven, John Crane was blond, blue-eyed, and tall, like his father. In temperament, he was outwardly placid and good-humored, like his mother, but concealed under the surface amiability lay a streak of dogged stubbornness that could only have come from his Dutch grandfather, John Bower. When it suited his purpose, he would go to great lengths to tailor his behavior so that it pleased his elders; but only because life was less troublesome that way.

Strong, full of energy, and no shirker where physical effort was required, he breezed through such chores as cutting wood, cleaning the stable, and sweeping out the church with so much apparent zest, neither his father nor grandfather seemed to notice that as soon as these tasks were done he would head for the woods or the waterfront. There, with gun, horse, boat, traps, and the most disreputable of white or Indian companions, he reveled in outdoor life with the same enthusiasm his father had felt toward it before his crippling illness. That he cared little for books or pursuits requiring intellectual effort did not greatly trouble his father, for Matt felt that his son was still a child and not yet ready to put away childish things.

But as John Crane neared his twelfth birthday, his father agreed with the Reverend Peter Crane that the time had come to make a serious commitment of the boy's future to religious service. Since there were no schools for the

Presbyterian faith in the area, and the boy was far too young to become a minister, his elders decided that the commitment should take the form of a "Consecration," a ceremony to be held in the church on a Sunday afternoon between morning and evening services. During this time he would be surrounded by his relatives and friends, and in their presence he would make a few solemn promises regarding the direction his life would take in the years to come.

"There will be no formal vows," the Reverend Peter Crane declared firmly, "such as those forced on novitiates by the Catholics. Whatever promises he makes will be made of his own free will, in the full knowledge that if he has a change of heart in time to come, he need not keep them. Compulsory vows are not a part of the Presbyterian faith."

When talked to on the subject, John Crane had no particular objection to taking part in the Consecration ceremony. Secretly, he had no particular desire for it, either, but since his parents, grandparents, and the members of the church seemed to regard it as such an important event, he saw no harm in going along with it and making them happy. After all, the only things he was agreeing to do were becoming an apprentice lay worker in the church, studying the Bible, and planning to go into the ministry five or six years from now—which at his age was so far in the future that he could not even imagine what his life would be like then.

The ceremony took place one day before his twelfth birthday, Sunday, February 21, 1820. The church was full, for in prosperous, growing St. Louis, a great number of American merchants, craftsmen, farmers, and fur traders belonging to the Protestant faith had come here during the past fifteen years; they had begun to alter the nature of the city from that of a Catholic, Spanish-French, provincial community to one that was Americanized, business-oriented and expansion-minded.

Though his new suit, stiff collar, and polished black boots were uncomfortable, as he walked down the center aisle of the church with his mother on his arm, he could hear the approving whispers of his mother's women friends, could see the approving nods of the older men in the congregation, and could sense without hearing or seeing the quickening of breath and the subdued gasps of admiration from young girls; until now these girls had regarded him as just another rowdy, ill-dressed boy who was fun to tease and be teased by and whose hands must be watched when sharing church cleanup chores in shadowed quarters.

To them all, he was a somebody now. Seating his mother in the first row pew, he bowed to her with what he judged to be great dignity and affection, turned, and mounted the raised platform on which the Reverend Peter Crane, his father, John Bower, and the elders of the church stood waiting.

Though solemn, the Consecration ceremony was neither tedious nor long. Interested more in what kind of impression he was making on certain special members of the congregation, John did not listen too closely to the prayers made in his behalf, in behalf of the church, and in behalf of the benighted heathen Indians who eventually would receive light from the torch of salvation being ignited here. But since he had been given detailed instructions on what the questions asked him would be, he was prompt, humble, and sincere in his replies.

Yes, he was prepared to devote the next five years of his life to doing lay work for the church, he said solemnly. But even as he spoke the words aloud with irreproachable dignity, a devilish voice inside him snickered, *Like Audrey Burchardt, Ruth Allen, Esther Madden, and that sweet little redhead, Susan Swan—I'll do a lay in the hay with them anytime!*

"And your highest aim in life?"

"To carry God's word to the heathen."

"Bless you, my son, in your great endeavor."

You're purely welcome, Grandfather. And I'll endeavor to lay a few heathen maidens, too. We good Christians must spread our lay works around.

"And now, let us pray . . ."

PART THREE

JOURNEY IN SEARCH OF THE BOOK OF HEAVEN

1820-1832

1

Though proud of the fact that he long ago had proved himself to be a warrior, Red Elk accepted without question the *Wy-a-kin* order given his young nephew Tall Bird that he must not kill a fellow human being. Personal rules of life acquired during the sacred manhood ordeal were to be respected and never violated, no matter how greatly they caused an individual to deviate from what was considered to be normal behavior.

For instance, if a young man revealed that his *Wy-a-kin* had decreed that during any battle fought in daylight his body would cast no shadow and become so thin that no arrow, spear, or bullet could hit him, he would be permitted to place himself in the position of greatest risk, confident that he would not be wounded or killed. But if a battle were begun in daylight and continued after sunset, thus nullifying his protection, he would be permitted to withdraw to a less exposed position without his courage being questioned.

If his *Wy-a-kin* told him that spiritually he was brother to a fish, a horse, a buffalo, or a bear, he would be selected to lead any party going in search of these creatures as the man most in tune with their ways. If his *Wy-a-kin* told him that he possessed the secret powers of a *tewat*—a medicine man—no one would challenge his right to start practicing that mysterious art, though if he were so inept as to kill a paying client's ill father, wife, or son, the *Wy-a-kin* that had persuaded him to take up that career could be pronounced evil, with both it and him being put to death by the aggrieved party.

Even if his *Wy-a-kin* told him, as it now and then did, that he should have been born a female instead of a male, and that from now on he must wear a skirt and become a *Neke Hayat Hama*—a half-man-woman—the *Nimipu* would accept his status without question. This was the Nez Perce way.

Bearded Red Grizzly Bear had won his wager with Red Elk that he could take a bateau through the Big Canyon of the Snake. Using a towline much of the way, scrambling over endless slides of volcanic rock, wading in icy water far more than they rode in the bateau, he and his band of men had required two months of superhuman effort to make the round trip; thus, when he came to the summer camp of the Wallowa band to lay claim to the blue stallion with the white-spotted rump, he told Red Elk that he would not attempt such a feat again. With typical good-humored generosity, he gave Red Elk the new rifle he had offered as part of the wager.

"Gi' to the lad, if ye like," he said. "It'll outshoot any guns he'll come up against in Blackfoot country."

"He will be grateful to have a good rifle to use hunting game," Red Elk said. "But he never will kill a Blackfoot. His *Wy-a-kin* forbids it."

"Weel, I'm pleased to hear that. The Nez Perces need men of peace."

"He wishes to learn English so that he can read the Book given him by his father. In a vision, his father's spirit told him that he might be going on a long journey to the east in search of wisdom. Can this be done?"

Donald MacKenzie nodded. "Aye—if peace lasts. Ye ken that Great Britain and the United States signed a Joint Occupancy Treaty giving citizens of both countries the right of access to the Pacific Northwest for the next ten years?"

"Yes."

"And that the North West Company has been absorbed by the Hudson's Bay Company, wi' the nabob in charge of operations in North America being his lordship Sir George Simpson?"

"I have seen this man at Fort Nez Perces, traveling down the Columbia in the style of a high chief. He appears to be a man of great power."

"Aye, that he is. And he intends to use that power to make sure that this part of the country becomes British rather than American. So far as he's concerned, the only things of value in it are fur-bearing animals and the trade of the Indians. Though I cannae agree with his methods, I must obey his orders. One is to send trapping parties over the inland country every year, stripping it bare of beaver, so there'll be no reason for Americans to come into it. The other is to send several young Spokane Indians to eastern Canada, where they'll be taught English and religion, hoping that when they return home in a few years they'll be tame Indians, like the Iroquois, with trade needs that only the British can supply."

"The Iroquois are a weak, foolish people," Red Elk said contemptuously. "I doubt that my brothers the Spokanes ever will become slaves like them, no matter how civilized the white man makes them."

"Weel, ye're probably right there. But I nae can help Tall Bird learn English and religion unless ye'll let him go to eastern Canada."

"His father is an American," Red Elk said stubbornly. "If he goes east, he must go to St. Louis. Otherwise, we will wait for the Americans to return to *Nimipu* country, as they long ago promised to do."

"Why should they come back, if there's no beaver for them here? In their system, if trappers can't make money from a season in the mountains, they seek more profitable fields."

Remembering the long talks he had had with *Moki Hih-hih* when he had lived with Moon Wind, Red Elk refused to believe that making money was the only thing that motivated the *Suyapo*. Like the *Nimipu*, they were full of curiosity about new country and loved to travel. It had been the Americans, not the British, who first crossed the mountains and laid claim to the country adjoining the mouth of the Great River. In view of that, he doubted they would give up their claim to an empire-size territory simply because it had temporarily been stripped of beaver.

"They will return," he said. "I am sure of that."

Saying that he was more interested in gathering furs than in empire building, Bearded Red Grizzly Bear shrugged and prepared to set out on yet another trapping expedition over the headwaters of the Snake River country. This one was to be his last. Since he had established the pattern of such pelt-gathering ventures, with each of his trips resulting in a larger harvest of plews than the one preceding it, he was being rewarded by a transfer to Montreal and appointment as chief factor there. Succeeding him as field leader of the trapping parties was the astute young clerk who had been his assistant at Fort Nez Perces, Alexander Ross.

Tall Bird soon became his close companion and friend.

In his late teens now, and far more interested in the traveling and trading of the trapping parties than in the doings of the Wallowa band of Nez Perces, Tall Bird spent most of his time living with Ross and his itinerant trappers. Since he was proficient in the regional Indian tongues, knew both the sign language of the Buffalo Plains Indians and the Chinook jargon of the Columbia River tribes, and quickly acquired a working knowledge of English and French, he made himself useful to Ross in communicating with his motley and at times dense employees.

The Hudson's Bay Company now had three principal posts in *Nimipu* country—Fort Nez Perces, Spokane House, and Flathead Post. In early October each fall, Tall Bird would join Alexander Ross at Fort Nez Perces and help him wade through the tangled thicket of language barriers as the coming season's expedition was assembled. Acquiring all the horses, most of the supplies, and some of the employees the party would need at Fort Nez Perces, the expedition would travel first to Spokane House, then to Flathead Post, where the rest of the personnel and the supplies required for the next six months would be obtained. To Ross, who was a stickler for organization, the process was an exercise in frustration and exasperation.

"Just look at this list of personnel," he complained to Tall Bird before heading into the mountain wilderness from Flathead Post in early November 1823. "At Spokane House, I was authorized to hire eighty men. I could muster only forty—with many of them questionable. At Flathead Post, I managed to hire fifteen more, making the party total fifty-five in all. Supplying each man with a rifle, three horses, eight traps, and enough clothing and ammunition to carry him through the season, the company has made an investment in the expedition that will turn the reddest hair of its Scotch accountants white overnight. And the mix of race and language is a veritable Babylon of confusion."

"Babylon?" Tall Bird said with a frown. "This is a place I do not know. Is it in eastern Canada?"

"No, it's in the Bible. When the people got to squabbling over how to build a tower, ages ago, the good Lord punished them by causing them to speak in a confusion of tongues—just as He's punishing me now. Look what we've got in our party: two Americans, seventeen Canadians, five half-breeds from the east side of the mountains, and twelve Iroquois. Also, two Abanakee Indians from Lower Canada, two natives from Lake Nepissing, one Saultman from Lake Huron, and two Crees from Athabaska. Plus one Chinook, two Spokanes, two Kootenays, three Flatheads, two Kalispells, one Palouse, and a Snake slave. Five of the Canadians are above sixty years of age, and two are on the wrong side of seventy. Talk about a mixed bag . . ."

"It is like a band of *Nimipu* when we go to the buffalo country, a village on the move."

"Exactly! According to my count, twenty-five of the men are married and have their wives and sixty-four children along. In the party are 75 rifles, a brass three-pounder, 212 beaver traps, and 392 horses, not to mention a goodly stock of powder and lead and a supply of trading articles. Sir George Simpson may call this a trapping expedition. But I would call it an invasion!"

Large and unwieldy though the party appeared to be, it survived through the fall, winter, and spring with only a few casualties; it lived off the country, consuming every sprig of vegetation available, killing every edible game animal that could be shot, and trapping everything that wore fur, leaving behind a wide wake of devastation that literally obeyed Sir George Simpson's edict to "strip the country bare."

Yet, curiously enough, it was the wanderings of this party that brought a band of Americans into a region that supposedly offered no attractions. Wanting to investigate the fur possibilities of the southeastern part of the Snake River country, Ross sent a dozen Iroquois there to trap and explore. After they did so, they were to rejoin the main body in the high-country basin called Pierre's Hole, just west of the Teton Mountains. Not surprisingly, the band of Iroquois got into trouble, blundering into an encounter with hostile Shoshones from which they salvaged their scalps and a hundred beaver plews, but lost their powder, lead, supplies, and their sense of direction.

After wandering around for a few days, totally disoriented, they met a small party of American trappers led by a remarkable young man named Jedediah Strong Smith. Barely twenty years old, Smith had proved himself to be so bold, shrewd, and capable that his employer, William Henry Ashley, had instructed him to penetrate into the Pacific Northwest territory now being exclusively trapped by the Hudson's Bay Company. He was to scout it carefully, then make a report on why the Britishers were trapping it annually when their usual practice was to visit a fur-producing region only once every four years in order not to deplete its resources.

A New Englander by descent, Jedediah Smith combined the instincts of a Yankee trader with the principles of a

Wesleyan Methodist Church member. Thus, when the lost Iroquois asked if he would lead them back to Pierre's Hole, where they were due to rendezvous with their employer, Alexander Ross, he was happy to oblige.

He would be pleased to guide them, he said. However, since they had managed to save a hundred beaver plews, he would charge a slight fee for his services. Say, a hundred beaver plews? Improvident as always with their employer's assets, the Iroquois accepted the offer. Upon meeting Jedediah Smith and learning of the bargain that had been struck, Alexander Ross was furious.

"He's a damnable American spy!" Ross exclaimed to Tall Bird. "I'd like to boot him out of camp!"

But use of the boot as a means of dealing with American trapper rivals was strictly forbidden by Sir George Simpson. "Joint Occupancy" meant exactly that, he had told his factors, traders, and field leaders in the Pacific Northwest, and they must never use the threat of force to discourage American competition. Of course, if they could lose an inept competitor by laying a false trail into barren desert country where he might starve or die of thirst, or into an area filled with hostile Indians who might rob him or lift his hair, that would be permitted—so long as it were done politely and with no blame to be placed on the Hudson's Bay Company.

Trouble was, Ross discovered during the next few weeks, there was no losing Jed Smith and his men, no matter how many false trails were laid. Wherever detached bands of the Ross party wandered in attempts to lead Smith astray, the shrewd young Yankee always managed to discover the direction in which the main Ross party intended to go, where they planned to make their next camp, and even what kind of meat would be cooked for supper.

Truth was, the Americans supplied more meat for meals than they consumed, for their hunters were far superior to those of the Ross party. In traveling and making camp, they were helpful, efficient, and willing to do more than their share of the work. Smith made no secret of the fact that he was curious about every aspect of the Hudson's Bay Company operation and intended to report on it in detail to his employer in St. Louis, where it quickly would become common knowledge to the American fur trade; but he was so well mannered and polite that Ross could not dislike him. As for Tall Bird, he was fascinated by Smith's behavior as a sincere, practicing Christian.

Before each meal, Jedediah Smith would bow his head and say a brief prayer of grace. After supper each evening, in the long twilight of the late spring days, he would read aloud from the well-thumbed Bible he carried with him, discuss the passage with anyone who cared to talk about it, then open a hymnbook and lead the singing of sacred songs praising the white man's God.

At first, Tall Bird was shy and silent during these periods of evening worship, simply watching and listening as Smith read, talked, and sang. But after the combined parties had returned to Flathead Post, where a resigned Alexander Ross treated Smith like a respected guest, Tall Bird summoned up the courage to ask Smith a few questions about the route he had traveled on his way west.

"You came from St. Louis?"

"Yes."

"By boat or by horse?"

"By horse on this trip, though the trail does follow the river route up the Platte and the Sweetwater to South Pass."

"How many moons did it take you?"

"Two and a half, but I think we can do better than that. Next year we'll be carrying our supplies out and our pelts back in wagons instead of on horses, which should cut down on our traveling time."

Not long ago at Fort Nez Perces, Tall Bird had seen the marvel called a wagon, which was made like a large dugout canoe, with wheels instead of travois pole skids, and was drawn by two or more horses. From what he had observed, such a vehicle could be used only on relatively flat terrain.

This meant that the country between St. Louis and the place Smith called South Pass must be free of mountains and easily traveled.

"Do the Americans plan to build a trading post near South Pass?"

"No, we're going to try something different. What you might call a 'rendezvous.' You see, we'll select a place where there's good water, wood, and grass—like Pierre's Hole, say—and meet all the trappers and Indians there for two or three weeks in early summer. When we get our business done, the trappers and Indians can head back to their home grounds with enough supplies to last them a year, while the fur company brigade takes the plews they've bought back to St. Louis. We think it's a system that'll beat all hollow the one used by the British, allowing us to pay twice what they do for beaver and still make money."

"The Nez Perces have no beaver," Tall Bird said. "But we do have many good horses. Will you trade for them?"

"No. But the white trappers and the Buffalo Plains Indians will, you can be sure of that. From what I've seen, a good Nez Perce horse is worth twice the price of any other breed."

Having observed how indifferently the children with Indian mothers and French-Canadian fathers were treated by Alexander Ross and British employees of the Hudson's Bay Company, Tall Bird was reluctant to admit his white blood to Jedediah Smith, for fear he would be relegated to the status of a half-breed not entitled to the pride and dignity of either race. But he was so full of questions regarding the mysteries hidden in the Bible from which Smith read each evening that he finally was compelled to reveal his secret in an oblique way.

"I, too, have a Book of Heaven," he told Smith shyly. "But it is smaller than yours."

"May I see it?" Smith asked. Tall Bird took the New Testament out of its waterproof case and gave it to him. Before opening it, Smith frowned down at it and said, "Where did you get this?"

"From my second father. It was given to him and my mother the day after I was born."

"By whom?"

"My first father. He told my mother and second father that he wanted me to know who I am. He told them he would always be proud of me and wanted me to be proud of him."

"Who was he?"

"A *Suyapo*. A white man. An American. His name is written in the front of the Book."

Opening the Testament, Jedediah Smith read the inscription written on the flyleaf, then gave an exclamation of surprise.

"Matthew Crane is your father! How remarkable!"

"You know him?"

"Not well. But I've met him. He's become an important man in the St. Louis fur trade. Have you ever seen him?"

"My mother tells me he held me in his arms when he gave me my name. Since I was only two days old at the time, I do not remember this. But later, in a vision, my *Wy-a-kin* brought him to talk to me. He said that someday I might go on a long journey to see him."

"God willing, you shall," Jed Smith said softly. "Let me tell you how such a journey could be made . . ."

2

Ever since the visit of Lewis and Clark, the possibility of sending a delegation to St. Louis had been discussed by the Nez Perces. In the habit of traveling widely and acquiring whatever new things appealed to them from other cultures, the *Nimipu* were far too proud and independent to put their boys in the care of white men and permit them to be transported to a faraway city, there to be taught civilized ways. Instinctively, the chiefs knew there was more danger than value in letting the minds of future Nez Perce leaders be shaped by white men in a strange, distant land.

But as word came down from Spokane country in 1830 that one of the boys sent east to be educated five years ago had returned and now was teaching, preaching, and demonstrating what he had learned to his fellow tribesmen, several Nez Perce headmen decided to journey north and find out what useful knowledge their neighbors had acquired. Because of his skill as a linguist and the breadth of his travels with the Hudson's Bay Company trapping parties, Tall Bird was invited to come along.

Now twenty-four years old and married, with a son three and a daughter one, Tall Bird twice had followed the instructions given him by Jedediah Smith, and journeyed to the American fur rendezvous held annually in high-country basins just west of the Continental Divide. In contrast to the tightly controlled trading sessions of the Hudson's Bay

Company, these early summer meetings proved to be times of riotous drinking and carousing by the white free trappers who came to exchange the pelts they had gathered for next season's supplies. During the two or three weeks the rendezvous lasted, the Indians who came to the gatherings—Utes, Shoshones, Flatheads, Nez Perces, Crows, and Sioux—kept the peace, for trading, not warfare, was the purpose of the meetings.

From the rendezvous grounds, Tall Bird learned, a delegation of Nez Perces could travel in safety through the normally hostile country of the Sioux, Cheyenne, and Pawnee Indians to St. Louis, for it would be under the protection of the returning American fur brigade, which these tribes dared not attack for fear of jeopardizing their supply of trade goods and arms. But the idea of making such a journey was so momentous to the Nez Perces that it must be considered and discussed through many a long council before it would be undertaken.

Because Red Elk was a war leader and this was a mission of peace, he stayed home and let a thirty-year-old cousin, *Tu-eka-kas*, represent the Wallowa Band. A quiet-spoken, handsome man, above average in height and weight, *Tu-eka-kas* was respected for his piety and his deep love for the high mountain valley in which he had been born.

With the Big Horn chief, *We-ark-koomt*, now dead, leadership of the band living in the Alpowa area west of the juncture of the Clearwater with the Snake had been taken over by *Ta-moot-sin*, who was a relative and close friend of *Tu-eka-kas*. A gentle-natured, thoughtful, unassuming man, *Ta-moot-sin* recalled having hidden in the bushes as a child twenty-five years ago, watching the members of the Lewis and Clark party as they camped, talked, and ate, but too shy to show himself.

Certainly there was nothing shy about the third of the three Nez Perce chiefs. The eldest son of Twisted Hair, he was the peace leader of the Weippe Prairie and Kamiah Valley Nez Perces. Widely known among both Indians and whites for the breadth of his vocabulary, his intelligence, and his oratory, he was named *Ish-hol-hoats-toats*—"Bat That Flies in the Daytime." Because he spoke good English and was an eloquent talker, white men called him "The Lawyer," a name which he used with pride.

The visiting Nez Perces were made welcome by the Spokanes, who were pleased with the attention being paid their newly returned prodigy, who had been given the white name "Garry" in honor of the Hudson's Bay Company stockholder who had sponsored him. Though only fourteen years old when he had gone east to Winnipeg and only nineteen now, he had proved to be such an excellent student that Sir George Simpson had designated him head chief and principal spokesman for his tribe.

"That will bring trouble," Lawyer predicted shrewdly. "He is too young to be a head chief."

"The Spokanes are not like the *Nimipu*, among whom becoming a war chief, a peace chief, a hunting chief, or a fishing chief must be earned by proving skill in that particular field," *Tu-eka-kas* said quietly. "They want so badly to please the King George men that they will accept whatever rules are given them. Because it is simpler to deal with one chief than with many, this is what the King George men make them do."

Observing the twenty-by-forty-foot wooden building put up under Chief Garry's supervision by his fellow tribesmen as a school and church, noting the leather-bound Old Testament, New Testament, and hymnbook which he used in services conducted in both English and the Spokane tongue, admiring the vegetable garden he had laid out and planted, *Ta-moot-sin* was lavish in his praise of the useful knowledge that his Spokane brothers had acquired.

"This is great medicine!" he exclaimed. "We must go home and persuade our leaders to seek the same kind of wisdom from the Americans."

"It will not be the same," Tall Bird said, shaking his head. "Among the *Suyapos*, there are many different kinds of religion and many different *Tam-tai-nats*."

"What kind of religion was Garry taught?"

"It is called the Church of England kind."

"Is this the same as that practiced by the Iroquois?"

"No. That is the Black Robe kind."

"What kind do the Americans practice?"

"There are so many, I have been told, that no man can know them all. Jedediah Smith, who has twice visited our cousins, the Flatheads, and has urged them to go to St. Louis and ask that a *Tam-tai-nat* be sent to live in their country, belongs to the Wesleyan Methodist Church. *Moki Hih-hih*'s father—who is my grandfather—is a *Tam-tai-nat* in the Presbyterian Church."

"Perhaps we would be wise to visit the Flatheads," Lawyer said thoughtfully, "and ask if they would join us in sending a delegation to St. Louis. If they could obtain a *Tam-tai-nat* of one kind, while we obtained one of another, we would be twice as well off as the Spokanes, and thus become twice as strong."

"What need have we for more strength?" *Tu-eka-kas* asked. "No enemies have invaded our country with any success since we acquired horses and guns."

"True, my brother. But knowledge is the best kind of strength. That is why I have learned to speak, read, and write English—and why Tall Bird is learning. Though we have not yet discovered all the secrets written in the white man's Book of Heaven, we know they are there. The sooner we learn them, the stronger we will be. Obtaining *Tam-tai-nats* to teach us will make us wise more quickly."

"I agree," *Ta-moot-sin* said. He looked questioningly at Tall Bird. "If a delegation is chosen, would you guide it to the American fur rendezvous?"

"Yes. I would be pleased to guide it."

"I have heard that your father is a man of importance," Lawyer said. "Perhaps in St. Louis you would see him."

"Yes, I would hope to do that."

"It is settled, then. We will go home and spread the word among our people. When the snow melts in the Lolo Pass

next spring, we will send a delegation of Nez Perces and
Flatheads to the American fur rendezvous on the upper Green
River. From there, it will go to St. Louis with the returning
brigade—and ask that *Tam-tai-nats* be sent to teach us the
wisdom of the Book of Heaven . . ."

3

In time to come, the grandfather tales—by means of which *Nimipu* history was recorded and passed on to future generations—would be hazy as to the motivation that inspired the quest. Jealousy of the Spokanes; a yearning to learn the secrets of making such marvels as metal pots and pans, tools of steel, and gunpowder; simple curiosity to see how white men lived—one or all may have been factors. But it is known beyond all doubt that six far-western Indians traveled to the American fur company rendezvous in the upper valley of Green River in early summer 1831. Chief Lawyer later recorded their names. They were:

Le-pit Ga-Gaz, or "Two Bears"; *Peo-peo Te-ne-ik-se*, or "Tall Bird Crossing a Lake on the Ice"; *Hi-youts-tohan*, or "Rabbit-Skin-Leggins"; *Ta-wis-sis-sim-nim*, or "No-Horns-on-His-Head"; *Tip-ya-lah-na-jeh-nim*, or "Black Eagle"; and *Ka-ou-pen*, or "Man-of-the-Morning."

Of the six, Two Bears and Man-of-the-Morning were Flatheads, the first a young brave about Tall Bird's age, the second an important chief in his mid-fifties. Of the remaining four Nez Perces, Tall Bird, Rabbit-Skin-Leggins, and No-Horns-on-His-Head were young men, while Black Eagle was an older chief highly respected by the Lapwai band.

Though Chief Lawyer at first talked of going along, he finally decided to stay behind, using the coming year to assemble a large band of Nez Perces that would cross

171

the mountains next summer, meet the party of American missionaries which he felt sure would respond to the appeal of the far-western Indians, and escort them to their posts in safety.

Warned by Tall Bird of the drinking, carousing, and riotous behavior they would see among the white trappers, mixed-bloods, and some of the Indians during rendezvous, the delegation of Flatheads and Nez Perces observed, abstained, and patiently waited for the breakup of the meeting. Of the two hundred or so free trappers assembled at the rendezvous, and the half-dozen traders there to supply them with their needs, Tall Bird judged that a young French *bourgeois* named Lucien Fontenelle, whom he had met two summers ago, was the man most likely to be receptive to the delegation's request that it be allowed to travel back to St. Louis in his company.

"Why do you want to go to St. Louis?" Fontenelle asked.

"We seek wisdom and teachers. We want the Americans to know that our loyalty is not to the King George men but to them. We want to remind them of the promise made us long ago by Lewis and Clark that they would come to our country to live among us and trade."

"You know that Governor Lewis is dead?"

"Yes. But we have heard that General Clark still lives and is agent for our country. We also have heard that another good friend, Matthew Crane, is an important man in the fur trade and would listen to our requests with sympathy."

"He probably would," Fontenelle said, nodding. "He's been after the church people for years to send missionaries out to your parts of the country. He's even tried to make a missionary out of his son, John, though if I'm any judge he'll have no luck there."

Though deeply curious about his first father and his half brother, Tall Bird refrained from telling Fontenelle of his relationship for the same reason he had been reluctant to reveal it to Jedediah Smith. In the Nez Perce world, his white blood was no cause for shame. But in the white world, he sensed that a similar tolerance for Indian blood did not exist.

"You will let us travel with you?" he asked. "We will not be a burden to you."

"That much I know about you Nez Perces," Fontenelle said. He smiled and held out his hand. "Sure you can travel with us. But once we reach St. Louis, I'll have to leave you on your own."

Following the breakup of rendezvous, the fur brigade led by Lucien Fontenelle wasted no time loading the three wagons in which the baled furs were packed and getting under way. Though in many ways the country across which the party traveled was similar to that Tall Bird was familiar with to the west and north, there were subtle differences which grew greater day by day. There were more stretches of desert here, fewer mountains, wider reaches of plains. Once the Continental Divide had been topped and the streams began flowing east instead of west, the water lost its sweetness and took on a bitter, alkaline taste. The wind was different too, blowing strong, hot, and dry out of the southwest, often filled with dust, and carrying no moisture, as the winds of *Nimipu* country did on occasion even during the heat of summer.

Used to learning landmarks and drawing mental maps of the country traversed, Tall Bird observed and remembered the white man's names for rivers, rock formations, and other distinctive features. Knowing that the experienced traveler looked backward as often as he looked forward, so that he would recognize the terrain when riding in the opposite direction, he noted the fissure cut by the Sweetwater called "Split Rock"; the mass of rounded granite boulders on which many of the white trappers had scratched their names, giving it the name of "Register Rock" or "Independence Rock"; and the tall, spirelike formation near the spot where the two branches of the Platte River came together called "Chimney Rock."

It was strange traveling across a country in which there were no mountains to be seen in the distance. He had not realized such a flat, featureless country existed. Accustomed to bathing every day in a cold, clear stream, or at least cleansing himself by taking a sweat bath, he found the warm, turgid, scum-covered pools along the Platte repulsive, the swarms of mosquitoes and other insects annoying, and the water often so gritty with sand that he could not drink it. Though the party had been traveling two months now, and the last moon of summer was past, the cool currents that at this time of year made the air of his beloved Wallowa country such a delight to breathe were not present; instead, humid heat lay like a stifling blanket over the lowlands flanking the river, cooling little even after nightfall.

"This is a poor country," Two Bears grumbled, "fit only for outhouse Indians."

Where Two Bears had picked up the term "outhouse Indians," Tall Bird did not know, though he suspected what the Flathead meant by it was that the dwellings of those Indians who no longer hunted, rode, fought, or made any effort to exist by their own labors looked like the privies of the white men.

"St. Louis will be better," Tall Bird said with an optimism he did not truly feel. "I am sure of that."

"St. Louis could not be worse, brother. Of that I am sure. How much farther do we have to go?"

"Tomorrow we will come to the Big Muddy, I am told, which we will follow for two weeks to the south and east. Then we will reach St. Louis."

Camp was made next evening on a bluff overlooking the Missouri River, near the village of a band of Omahas. Heeding Fontenelle's warning that this particular band was not to be trusted and was apt to be diseased, the men of the fur brigade and four members of the Indian delegation stayed close to camp on the bluff above the Omaha village. But Two Bears and Tall Bird felt so hot, sticky, and in need of a cleansing bath that they made their way down to the bottoms flanking the river, threshed through the bushes in a roundabout detour of the Omaha village, and a hundred yards downstream from it found what appeared to be a reasonably clean, cool pool in which they went for a long swim. In fact, the water was so refreshing following the sudden rain-shower that fell while they were bathing that they drank copiously from it.

A few mornings later, both Indians woke up violently ill.

Learning their symptoms—sharp intestinal pains, high fever, and vomiting—Lucien Fontenelle was puzzled, for no other members of the party had fallen ill and he knew of nothing different that they had eaten, drunk, or done for the past few days. When told of their bath in the pool downstream from the Omaha village, he groaned.

"God in heaven! They've caught virulent fever!"

Impatient as he and the other members of the fur brigade were to finish their journey, Fontenelle insisted on staying with the two seriously ill Indians until he could arrange for their care by a French-Canadian settler named François Le Roux, who, with his Shawnee Indian wife and their brood of five children, ran a small store and a reasonably clean roadhouse on a Missouri River landing two days' travel downriver from the spot where Two Bears and Tall Bird had been taken sick.

"Do what you can for them," he said. "We can't take them with us."

"With ze fever, *m'sieu*, I think dey soon die. All I can do is bury them."

"So be it. Here's two dollars for your trouble. We've got to be moving along."

If the two older Indians, Black Eagle and Man-of-the-Morning, or the two young braves, Rabbit-Skin-Leggins and No-Horns-on-His-Head, had any desire to stay behind and try to nurse their brothers back to health, they did not express it. To them, disease was a fact of life beyond their power to cure, particularly when it came on so suddenly in a strange land so far from home. All they could do was make signs meant to wish the ill persons well, express a hope that the same sickness would not affect them, and say goodbye so far as life in this world was concerned.

Ten days later, the party reached St. Louis . . .

4

Preoccupied with business affairs, Lucien Fontenelle paid no attention to what the four Indians who had accompanied the brigade did when his party reached St. Louis. With Tall Bird left behind and none of the four able to speak any language understood in this big, teeming city, the three Nez Perces and the Flathead wandered around aimlessly, stunned by the sights that met their eyes, questioning indifferent local Indians in their strange tongue and in sign language that the St. Louis Indians had never bothered to learn, until finally they came upon a large building topped by a symbol they recognized—a cross.

That the church was Catholic, they did not know. But the Jesuit priest in charge kindly took them in. After querying them at length, he sent word to General William Clark that he needed help unraveling a mystery that might be related to his expedition of twenty-five years ago. When the messenger came to Clark, Matt Crane happened to be in his office discussing fur trade business.

"If you can spare a few minutes, Matt, I'd like you to come with me and talk to these Indians."

"I'd be glad to."

The Right Reverend Joseph Rosati, the priest who found the Indians, had given them quarters in an unused stable behind the church. Because the October day was cool, the stable door was closed and the light filtering through the small, dusty window was dim, making it difficult for Matt and William Clark to make out the facial features and the dress of the four Indians sitting cross-legged on the dirt floor.

"The best I can make out, they belong to some tribe from beyond the Rocky Mountains," Father Rosati said. "When one of them saw our church, he became very excited, made the sign of the cross, touched his mouth, then his ears, as if saying: 'Fill me with your holy words.' "

"Are you sure he didn't touch his stomach, too," Matt said caustically, "and ask you to fill it with food?"

William Clark, who was staring intently at one of the older Indians, suddenly seized Matt's arm. "What did the Nez Perces call themselves, Matt? Do you remember?"

"*Nimipu.*"

"And the Flatheads?"

"*Tush-e-paw.*"

"They have a greeting ritual, if I remember correctly, which they use when meeting strangers, asking who you are. Do you remember the signs?"

"Lord knows, I should remember," Matt said wryly. "The man who taught it to me had a knife in his hand which he would have used if I hadn't given him the right answers."

"Try it on the older one now."

Raising his right hand to shoulder level with the palm open, Matt shook it from side to side, inquiring, "What is the name of your tribe?"

Passing the index finger of his right hand just under his nose, as if thrusting a skewer of dentalium through the septum, the Indian signed, "Nez Perce," at the same time saying, "*Nimipu.*"

Nodding vigorously, the two young Indians made the same sign and said the same word, but the other older Indian shook his head, passed his right hand from eye level to the top of his head, signing, "Flathead," at the same time saying, "*Tush-e-paw.*"

Matt tapped the older Nez Perce lightly on the chest, signing, "What is your name?"

First touching the dark dirt floor of the stable, then his feet, the Indian made the sign Matt read as "Black," made the sign for "Bird," then specified it more closely by moving his arms and hands in majestic winglike motions that could only mean "Eagle." At the same time, he said, "*Tip-ya-lah-na-jeh-nim*."

Before Matt could translate these signs and words to William Clark and Father Rosati, the Indian leaned forward, tapped him on the chest, made the signs for "Crane" and "White," and said, "*Moki Hih-hih*."

"Good Lord!" Matt exclaimed. "He knows me—and I know him! So do you, General Clark!"

"From when? The trip out or the trip back?"

"The trip back. He was a young brave with Chief Broken Arm's band, which was gone to make war against the Shoshones when we were on our way out. When we came back, he'd covered himself with glory by killing three Shoshones, so he was honored by being permitted to use the tail feathers of the most respected bird in Nez Perce country, the golden eagle, in his headdress. Red Elk told me that he was likely to become an important chief of the Lapwai band."

"Can you find out why they came and what they want?"

Matt tried. What he learned astonished him. Father Rosati appeared to be right when he said that the delegation had come in search of religious knowledge. Aware that for several years the Catholics had been urging the hierarchy of their church to send missionary workers to the Indians of the Oregon country, just as he and his father had been trying to get the Protestant Church to do, Matt felt a sudden angry resentment that by a stroke of blind luck the delegation of Indians had fallen into Catholic rather than Protestant hands. Hoping to remedy that, and aware that Father Rosati was watching and listening intently, Matt's interpretation of the Indian's words and signs was purposefully vague.

"He says that twenty-five years ago you invited his people to send a delegation of chiefs to St. Louis so that you could show them how white men live. He says they want to stay for six months or so, learn all they can about our ways, then return to their country full of wisdom to be passed on to their people. It would be very helpful, he says, if we would send teachers and missionaries to live with them."

"We will go!" Father Rosati exclaimed. "I will write my superiors at once, requesting funds and workers. Oh, what a dramatic story this will make for the religious Catholic press! To think that these poor, ignorant savages have traveled thousands of miles through a trackless wilderness, seeking truth—"

"The Nez Perces and Flatheads are not as poor and ignorant as you might think, Father Rosati," Clark said testily. "So far as tracks go, American explorers and fur brigades have made trails that are easy to follow all the way to the Northwest Coast."

"I was speaking metaphorically, sir. The point is, they came. And their thirst for religious instruction must be slaked!"

"It was my invitation that brought them to St. Louis, Father. Therefore, it is my duty—"

"An invitation twenty-five years old? That is ridiculous, sir. It was God himself who inspired their quest. And it will be the Catholic Church that instructs them and sends missionaries to their country."

"So far as saving their souls is concerned, I'll let you fight that out with the Protestants," Clark said curtly. "But as Superintendent of Indian Affairs for the Northwest, I must make them welcome as guests of the American Government. As soon as I can find quarters for them, I shall have them moved."

"They have quarters now, General Clark. They are guests of my church. Unless you formally order me to turn them over to you, I shall not give them up."

William Clark scowled. If there was one thing he did not need, it was a public argument with a belligerent Jesuit priest over the saving of Indian souls.

"Well, you may keep them for the time being. If there's anything my office can do for them, please let me know."

Now that he had absorbed the shock of seeing an Indian he had known in the distant past appear in the present, Matt studied Chief Black Eagle more closely. Twenty-five years had elapsed since Matt had attended the meeting in the Kamiah village longhouse during which the Nez Perces had debated adopting the policies recommended to them by Lewis and Clark. During that council, he recalled, a tall, slim, arrow-straight young brave named Black Eagle had gotten to his feet and made an impassioned speech urging acceptance of the policies.

"I am a warrior, as all of you know," he had said. "But if the Americans say make peace with our neighbors, I will make peace. Hear me, *Moki Hih-hih*, blood brother to Red Elk. Since you are his brother, you are my brother, too. I vote for peace."

In the dim gray light of the stable, to which Matt's eyes were becoming accustomed now, he could see that Black Eagle had aged greatly. Every winter since that council on the *Koos-koos-kee* had written its hardships in the deep wrinkles of the Nez Perce's face, in the tiny wisdom lines around the eyes, in the sag of facial muscles no longer young—years that made a ghost of the young warrior who had once called him "brother." Remembering, Matt suddenly had a searing thought. Black Eagle and Red Elk had been close friends and probably still were. So Black Eagle must know about Matt and Moon Wind's son. Leaning forward, he made a question sign.

"Moki-Moki Ilp-ilp?"

For long moments, the elderly Nez Perce stared at him. Then he solemnly shook his head. Slowly his hands moved as he made a series of signs. Softly words formed in his throat and passed over his lips as he spoke with great care

and a sincere desire to be understood. In a kind of frozen
trance, Matt watched and listened. When Black Eagle was
done, the Indian drew his blanket closely about his shoulders,
bowed his head, and began chanting what Matt recognized
as the personal death-song of a friend. Hearing it, the old
Flathead chief, Man-of-the-Morning, started chanting too,
though the death-song he was voicing was slightly different
from that being sung by Black Eagle.

Stunned by what he had heard, Matt got to his feet, lurched
to the stable door, tried to open it, but found himself too weak
to do so. General Clark rose and moved to him.

"What's wrong, Matt? You're white as a sheet!"

"I'm ill, General Clark. I need fresh air."

Opening the door, Clark took his arm and helped him get
outside. As Matt limped along the narrow alleyway leading
to the street, Clark eyed him with concern.

"What did Black Eagle say to you, Matt? Why did he
sing that awful chant?"

"You remember I fathered a son by a Nez Perce woman?"

"Yes, I certainly do."

"His Indian name was *Moki-Moki Ilp-ilp,* which translates
as 'Little Red Crane.' I asked Black Eagle if he knew about
the child. He said that he did. He said that Moon Wind had
married, which I learned years ago, and that she, her Cayuse
husband, and Red Elk had raised the boy to be proud of his
white blood and aware that I was his father."

"That was decent of them."

"When Little Crane went through the manhood ritual, he
changed his name to Tall Bird. He had a vision, Black Eagle
said, decreeing that he must live a life of peace, learn how to
read the New Testament I gave him, and be prepared to travel
to St. Louis to see me, if his people ever should decide to
send a delegation here in search of religious instruction."

"Good Lord! Wouldn't that have been a strange thing!"

"It happened, General Clark. He guided the delegation to
the fur rendezvous on Green River, where he'd been twice

before. From there, the Indians traveled to the Missouri River in the Council Bluffs area with Lucien Fontenelle's fur brigade. Originally, there were six Indians in the group— two Flatheads and four Nez Perces. But when they reached the Missouri, one of the Flatheads and one of the Nez Perces took sick and died."

Halting, Matt leaned on his cane, trembling so uncontrollably he could barely stand.

"The Flathead's name was Two Bears, Black Eagle said. The Nez Perce's name was Tall Bird. It was their personal death-songs the Indians were chanting in there, sir. I have lost my Nez Perce son, who I loved dearly. He died on his way to see me . . ."

5

Because there was no way he could pry the four Indians
loose from the embrace of the Catholic Church, with which
he had no desire to cooperate, Matt did not see the two
elderly chiefs again. Black Eagle, who had a bad cough
the day Matt and General Clark talked to him, developed
pneumonia a week later and died. Given the Christian name
"Narcisse" by a Jesuit priest, he was administered the final
rites of the Catholic Church and was buried in the church
cemetery October 31, 1831.

Two weeks later, Man-of-the-Morning also fell ill and
died. He too was administered the final rites, was given
the Christian name "Paul," and was buried beside his Nez
Perce friend November 17, 1831.

Through William Clark, Matt heard that Father Rosati
was having no luck acquiring funds with which to establish
a Catholic mission among the Nez Perces or Flatheads. But
he was so afire with religious zeal that he had written an
impassioned letter to the editor of a Jesuit publication in
Lyons, France, a copy of which he gave General Clark, who
let Matt read it. Dated December 31, 1831, it contained several errors of fact, but it certainly put the St. Louis Catholic
Church in a good light.

"Some three months ago four Indians, who live at the
other side of the Rocky Mountains, near the Columbia River,
arrived in St. Louis," Father Rosati wrote. "After visiting

185

General Clark, who, in his celebrated travels, had seen the nation to which they belong and had been well received by them, they came to see our church, and appeared to be exceedingly well pleased with it. Unfortunately there was no one who understood their language.

"Sometime afterward two of them fell dangerously ill. I was then absent from St. Louis. Two of our priests visited them, and the poor Indians seemed delighted with their visit. They made signs of the cross and other signs which appeared to have some relation to baptism. This sacrament was administered to them; they gave expression of their satisfaction. A little cross was presented to them; they took it with eagerness, kissed it repeatedly, and it could be taken away from them only after their death. It was truly distressing that they could not be spoken to. Their remains were carried to the church for the funeral, which was conducted with all the Catholic ceremonies. The other two younger Indians attended and acted with great propriety.

"We have since learned from a Canadian, who has crossed the country which they inhabit, that they belong to the nation of Têtes-Plates (Flatheads), which, as is the case with another called Pieds-Noirs (or Blackfeet), has received some notions of the Catholic religion from two Indians who have been to Canada.

"These nations have not yet been corrupted by intercourse with others; their manners and customs are simple and they are very numerous. We have conceived the liveliest desire to not let pass such a good occasion. Mr. Condamine has offered himself to go to them next spring with another. In the meantime, we shall obtain information on what we have been told, and on the means of travel."

Noting the priest's statement that the two young Indians had returned to their country, Matt shook his head.

"He's wrong in saying Rabbit-Skin-Leggins and No-Horns-on-His-Head have left St. Louis. They were in our store this morning looking at beads and trinkets to take home."

"I know," Clark said. "They came to me a week ago and said they were tired of living with the Black Robes and had been filled with all the religious wisdom they could hold. They asked me to find other living quarters for them, which I did."

"If you understood them that well, your knowledge of their language isn't as rusty as you thought it to be."

"I had an interpreter, Matt. Your son, John. He has an amazing gift for Indian tongues."

"I wish he had the same gift for his chosen calling," Matt said bitterly. "He seldom comes near the church anymore."

"He's how old now—twenty-three?"

"He'll be twenty-four next month."

"As I recall, Matt, his 'chosen calling,' as you put it, wasn't chosen by him. It was chosen by you and your father."

"We tried to guide him into it, yes. But he just isn't interested. All he wants to do is hunt, ride, fish, fool around on the river, and go on trips into the wilds with his trapper and Indian friends."

Now sixty-two years old, his shock of thick red hair gone to seed and turned white, fleshier in the face, and not as hale and hearty as he had been in his prime, William Clark moved to the window of his office and stood with his hands clasped behind his back, his head cocked to one side as if his thoughts were far away. He chuckled softly.

"What were you doing, Matt, when you were his age?"

"Times were different then, sir. I took part in the tremendous adventure of exploring an unknown country. But a young man today should be participating in a greater challenge—that of civilizing a heathen race."

"Establishing trade with the Indians is as big a step toward civilizing them as making religious converts of them would be, Matt. The fur trade we've developed in the Oregon country during the past fifteen years has done more to create a peaceful relationship among the natives than the missionary efforts of all the churches."

"That's true, General Clark. But this delegation from the Nez Perces and Flatheads proves how sincerely they want missionaries sent to their country. The churches must respond. Since neither my father nor I can play an active role, we had hoped John would do so as a representative of our family and church."

"From what I've seen of him, he's intelligent, energetic, and gets along well with people. In many ways, he's like you were at his age—restless, romantic, adventurous. Has he told you what he would like to do?"

"Yes—and I don't approve at all. He wants to be a free trapper."

"What's wrong with that?"

"Everything! Free trappers, as they call themselves, are a drunken, lawless, wild class of men. Some of their acts of debauchery at rendezvous are appalling."

"With nothing lost in the retelling," Clark said with a smile. "For that matter, when rivermen and wintering trappers tangle in barroom brawls on the St. Louis waterfront, their acts can be appalling, too. I agree that most of the free trappers are a carefree, improvident lot. On the other hand, there are men like Kit Carson, Tom Fitzpatrick, Bill and Milton Sublette, and, before the Comanches killed him last summer, Jedediah Smith, who are models of propriety. If your son John is the sort of young man that can be led astray by bad examples, he'll find them in St. Louis just as easily as he would find them among the free trappers at rendezvous."

"I suppose that's so. But I don't want him to waste his life as a trapper. There's no future in it."

"May I suggest, Matt, that John might be intelligent enough to see that for himself? Why don't you give him a chance by letting him take a trip west this year? From what I've heard, 1832 is going to be the biggest year the fur trade has ever known. The Sublettes, Fontenelle, Nathaniel Wyeth, and Captain Bonneville all are planning to take companies to rendezvous in Pierre's Hole. The *Yellowstone* is scheduled to make her second trip up the Missouri at least as far as Fort Union. She'll be leaving sometime in April. I'm planning to send the two Nez Perces home on the boat. If you'll let John go along as an escort and interpreter, I'll be glad to give him the job."

"I appreciate your advice, sir. I'll talk with John and let you know."

Because his father's crippling illness had stricken him before his son was born, John Crane had never been able to visualize his father as a strong, mobile, physically powerful man. Tall and gaunt, perpetually stooped over, his right arm hanging useless at his side, his right leg artificially stiffened at the knee joint by the heavy leather and iron brace, Matt seemed always to view the world with a fierce-eyed, humorless intensity, as if he must make up for his physical defects by triumphs in the financial and spiritual world.

Though in awe of his father, John at times felt sorry for him, too, sensing that the paralysis had so drastically changed his way of life that it had distorted his judgment. Respecting his father as he did, John wanted to please him—up to a point. But beyond that point he stubbornly refused to go.

Working as a clerk in the store that outfitted the brigades and in the warehouse that sorted, graded, and resold the furs, John was well aware of the fact that most of the money in the business was made by the men who took the least physical risk. But what the hell did that matter? It was the free trappers, the mountain men, the hard-drinking, horny, piss-and-vinegar, reckless studs who roamed where they chose and obeyed no law but their own desires who had all the fun.

Respectful as he was of his father, fond as he was of his mother, and proud of the success he'd had the past few years doing lay work with hot young ladies like Audrey Burchardt, Ruth Allen, Esther Madden, and the most passionate piece of all, sweet little redheaded Susan Swan, he'd about reached the point where he was ready to tell them all to blow it up their you-know-what, with him heading west for far places. But before he could do so, his father surprised him by suggesting the same thing.

"I've been talking to General Clark," Matt said. "He tells me you were quite helpful in interpreting for the two Nez Perces."

"Aw, that was no great chore. We talked mostly in sign language, which I've picked up hanging around with trappers and Indians who've been west."

"Do you still want to go west, John?"

"So bad I can taste it."

"Well, it might be good experience for you to spend a season in the field, seeing how things are done. General Clark tells me this will be a big year. He says he's sending the two Nez Perces home on the *Yellowstone*. If you'll go along as their escort and interpreter, he'll give you the job."

"That's mighty kind of him," John said. "But spending six months on a stern-wheeler fighting a muddy, snag-filled river doesn't strike me as much fun. If I'm going west, I'd prefer to go to rendezvous with one of the overland brigades."

"You'll have several to choose from. Would you like me to speak to the Sublettes or Fontenelle?"

John shook his head. "Father, don't think I'm ungrateful for the offer, but I'd rather stand on my own two feet. Of all the parties heading west this year, the one that intrigues me most is the one being put together by Captain Bonneville. He's been given a two-year leave from the army, I've been told, and claims that the federal government has nothing to do with sponsoring his party. If that's so, where is he getting his money?"

"I've heard John Astor is secretly backing him."

"With the American Government secretly backing Astor?"

"That's possible, I suppose."

"Well, it sounds mighty interesting to me. If you have no objection, I'm going to try to hire on with Captain Bonneville."

"You'll go west with him to rendezvous, spend the summer in the mountains, then come back to St. Louis in the fall?"

"That's my plan, yes," John lied.

"Then you have my approval."

During their talk, they had strolled several blocks along the teeming, busy waterfront, which this early February day was bathed with the warm sunshine of false spring. Not able to walk far, Matt Crane sat down on a bench near the wharf to which the new stern-wheeler *Yellowstone* was moored, leaned upon his cane, and gazed somberly at the muddy surface of the river.

"John, there is something I must tell you," he said in a thick, choked voice. "Something that has to do with the delegation of Indians that came to St. Louis last fall from the Nez Perce country. Something that I fear will shock you."

"Oh?" John said.

"Two years before you were born, I fathered a son by a Nez Perce woman."

The hell you did! John mused. *Why, you randy old goat! I didn't know you had it in you!* But the tortured, haunted, suffering look on his father's face kept the words unspoken.

"I am surprised, Father. But I know such things happen."

"It was an innocent, pure relationship in my eyes, John. But in the eyes of God, it was a sin for which I had to be punished. And I was."

Oh, you sorry bastard! John thought with a sudden wave of sympathy. *Just because you bedded down an Indian girl and she whelped a child, you think God singled you out as a terrible sinner and struck you down with a special punishment. If that's the way God treats his children, I'm glad I refused to do his dirty work.*

"Did you ever see the child?"

"Yes."

"In Nez Perce country?"

"The child was conceived on our way west in early October 1805. He was born in late June 1806. I saw him, held him in my arms, and gave him the Christian name Mark, the day after he was born. His Nez Perce name as a child was *Moki-Moki Ilp-ilp,* which translates as 'Little Red Crane.' When he went through the manhood ordeal at the age of thirteen, he took the Nez Perce name *Peo-peo Te-ne-ik-se,* which translates into 'Tall Bird Crossing a Lake on the Ice.' I understand he was usually called 'Tall Bird.' "

"Where did you learn all this?"

"From Black Eagle, who I had known years ago in Nez Perce country. Through white and Indian friends in the fur trade, I had kept track of my Nez Perce son over the years, hoping that someday you and he would meet and love each other. That can't happen now because he is dead."

"When and how did he die?"

"He and a Flathead named Two Bears were with the delegation when it reached the Council Bluffs area last September. They contracted virulent fever there and died."

"Does Mother know about him?"

"Not yet. But I intend to tell her."

"Please don't. It will only hurt her." Reaching out, John impulsively took his father's hand and squeezed it. "I understand, Father—truly I do. I wish I had met him. I would have liked having an Indian brother . . ."

6

Although Two Bears died within half a day of being left at the roadhouse, Tall Bird lingered on. In great pain, burning with fever, and completely out of his head, he lay on the pallet of skins upon which he had been placed, holding on to life by the thinnest of threads. Used to caring for her husband and children during their illnesses, the Shawnee woman kept him clean and comfortable, saw to it that he had water and a medicinal sassafras tea to drink when his system would accept moisture, and meat broth when his intestinal lesions began to heal and his stomach would tolerate food.

In addition to the two dollars in cash which Fontenelle had given LeRoux, the fur trader had left the rifles, powder, lead, knives, and other personal belongings of the two Indians with the roadhouse keeper, as well as the six horses which they had brought from home. Because they would fetch better prices here than in St. Louis, LeRoux could sell them, Fontenelle told him, retaining half of what he received for his trouble, holding the other half for Fontenelle on his upriver trip next spring. Eventually Fontenelle would give the net proceeds to a responsible Flathead and Nez Perce at rendezvous as tokens to be returned to the dead Indians' grieving families.

An illiterate, incurious, provincial man, François Le-Roux had no idea of where the two Indians placed in his care had come from or why they were going to St. Louis. A good-hearted, honest man, he sold the rifle, personal effects, and horses belonging to Two Bears within a month of the Flathead's death; but, as Tall Bird continued to survive, he held on to the Nez Perce's possessions. When the fever at last departed and it became apparent Tall Bird would live, LeRoux was troubled for a time, wondering how he would be paid for the Indian's care. Then the answer came to him.

"We will give *M'sieu* Fontenelle a bill," he told his wife, "ze same amount as what he has coming from ze sale of ze dead Indian's things. Then we can keep all ze money."

Truth was, he was not an inhospitable man, and as Tall Bird's strength and vigor slowly returned during the golden autumn, the cold, snowy winter, and the windy, rainy spring, he was pleased to find the Nez Perce an excellent hunter capable of putting more than his share of meat in the pot, and a fine horseman, fluent in English and the sign language of the upriver tribes. In addition, he was a fascinating story-teller whose tales of Coyote, Fox, and the monstrous fish that ate Indian maidens kept the children entertained for many a night.

As for Tall Bird's own feelings, he accepted what had happened with no inner protest, for years ago when his first father had come to him in his *Wy-a-kin* vision, he had predicted a long journey, illness, and death by a great river. All these things had come to pass. Because the sky spirits obviously did not want him to take part in the quest for the Book of Heaven, he would turn his face back to the West when spring came, join the first party of American fur traders headed for this summer's rendezvous in Pierre's Hole, and travel to that place and rejoin his family, which would be coming there with Chief Lawyer and the large band of Nez Perces he was assembling to meet the *Tam-tai-nats* that would be traveling out from St. Louis.

"Ze Sublettes will be first, I t'ink," LeRoux predicted. "Zey always are. Zey will put dere overland party together at Independence, two days' ride south of here. Next week, you should go."

Next week, Tall Bird said farewell to the family that had treated him so well, rode south to Independence, and found a large body of men, animals, and equipment being assembled on the muddy plains above the river landing. As LeRoux had predicted, this brigade was employed by William and Milton Sublette, veteran, hard-bitten brothers who were well aware of the fact that first travelers got the best grass and game en route, and on arrival at rendezvous struck the best bargains with fur-rich, thirsty trappers.

This year, Milton Sublette had stayed west, wintering with a band of trappers in Ogden's Hole in the Salt Lake area. With William Sublette, who had brought the party out from St. Louis, were sixty-two men of the Rocky Mountain Fur Company, the most experienced of the companies now fiercely competing for the highly profitable trade of the West. A week to two weeks behind, and bound for the same destination were parties led by Lucien Fontenelle and the mysterious, enigmatic Captain Benjamin Louis Eulalie de Bonneville, the United States Army officer who insisted he was on leave and engaged in a strictly commercial enterprise but whose every movement and act reeked of deep intrigue.

While Tall Bird did not begin to understand the political issues involved, he did know that the Joint Occupancy Treaty signed between the United States and Great Britain in 1818 had been renewed and now would hold until 1838. Convinced that a good-sized portion of the Oregon country would become an American possession if private enterprise played its cards right, a remarkable man from Boston named Nathaniel J. Wyeth had mounted a wide-ranging scheme almost as ambitious as the Astor venture that had failed so spectacularly twenty years ago.

An energetic, aggressive merchant of thirty, Wyeth had managed a farm and ice-selling business in New England.

Outfitting a ship filled with ice, barrels, salt, and trade goods, and sending it around Cape Horn to the lower Columbia, he had led a party of twenty-three men overland to Independence. Following a few months' stay in the Pacific Northwest, the ship would sail back to Boston with a highly profitable cargo of salmon caught in the Great River of the West and valuable packs of beaver trapped inland. Or so Wyeth planned. Falling in with the Sublette party at Independence, Wyeth asked for permission to travel with it to Pierre's Hole.

"You're perfectly welcome, so long as you keep up," William Sublette said curtly. "But if you straggle, we'll leave you behind."

"My men are well disciplined," Wyeth said. "We'll keep up."

Learning that Tall Bird was a Nez Perce and familiar with the Snake and Columbia river watersheds, William Sublette suggested that he offer his services to the Wyeth party as a guide and interpreter. This Tall Bird did.

"We'll be glad to have you," Wyeth said. "Do you know the beaver country well?"

"I have been over it many times with parties of Hudson's Bay Company trappers."

"I'm hoping to fill a ship with a cargo of salted salmon from the Lower Columbia. Can you help me there?"

"I can take you to where the salmon are caught and introduce you to the Indians who catch them. Whether or not they will work for you, I cannot say."

"Well, if they won't, we'll do the fishing ourselves. It can't be too difficult to learn."

Despite the fact that the discipline of Wyeth's men was not what he claimed it to be, the combined parties made good time on their journey west. Crossing the Continental Divide, Jackson Hole, and Teton Pass, the mixed bag of greenhorns, veterans, half bloods, and Indians reached the rendezvous grounds in Pierre's Hole in midmorning, July 8, 1832.

Visible for miles in all directions across the wide, grass-covered floor of this well-watered, beautiful mountain basin were the tepees, tents, horse herds, and campfires of the largest number of people ever assembled in this part of the West . . .

PART FOUR

THE GREAT COMMAND—"GO YE THEREFORE . . ."

1832-1836

1

One hundred and twenty lodges of Nez Perces and Flat-heads—nearly a thousand people—had come to Pierre's Hole to greet the hoped-for missionaries. But much to Tall Bird's disappointment, his wife, *Ha-ne-sa La-tes*—"Flower Gatherer"—and their five-year-old son and three-year-old daughter were not among them. Red Elk, who had come, explained their absence.

"In the second moon of winter, Flower Gatherer bore you another son. With three small children to care for and the trail across the mountains difficult and tiresome, she thought it best not to make the trip."

"She was wise. Has she given our new son a name?"

"Because he is so lively and keeps flapping his arms as if trying to fly," Red Elk said with a smile, "she calls him '*Peo-peo Kuz-kuz.*' "

"*Ahh taats!* 'Young Bird' is a good name for a third child. It goes well with that of our oldest son, *Teg-Teg*—'Cricket'—and of our little girl, *Pis-Ku*—'Cabbage.' When they are older, we will give them more suitable names."

"You came back alone, I see. Where are the men who went with you?"

Sadly, Tall Bird related what had happened, saying that the same illness that had killed Two Bears had prevented him from reaching St. Louis and seeing his first father, *Moki*

Hih-hih. From William Sublette, he had heard that Black
Eagle and Man-of-the-Morning had talked to William Clark
before they took sick and died. But Sublette did not know
if General Clark had made them any promises regarding
sending missionaries west. Clark had said that he planned
to send Rabbit-Skin-Leggins and No-Horns-on-His-Head
home on the boat that belched smoke and paddled itself
up the river. But where the two Indians would leave the
steamer *Yellowstone*, what route they would take overland
from the Missouri, and when they would return to Nez Perce
country Tall Bird did not know.

"They will have to cross Blackfoot country and that is
dangerous," Red Elk said thoughtfully. "I will tell Chief
Lawyer what you have told me. Perhaps he will send a
party of warriors north to the Big Muddy to meet them
and escort them home."

Daily for the next week or so the white and Indian
camps spread out over the grassy floor of the wide valley,
which teemed with the comings and goings of riders, pack
trains, villages on the move, and the arrival and departure
of trapping parties from or to the adjacent mountains. If
Chief Lawyer was displeased that white missionaries had
not responded to the Indians' appeal, he soon forgot it in
the excitement of visiting half a dozen brigade leaders, all of
whom were vying with one another for beaver and trade.

As the first arrival, William Sublette had skimmed off the
cream, Tall Bird knew. Milton Sublette and his party, which
had wintered in the Salt Lake area, had arrived, turned in
their pelts, and reoutfitted. It planned soon to depart on a
southwesterly trapping venture, going first to the Snake River, then on down to the Humboldt region, which, despite its
desertlike physical features, was said to abound in beaver. In
the Wyeth party, half of his men had threatened to quit unless
their pay and working conditions were improved, so he had
fired them and told them to find their own way home.

"Which is no great loss," John Ball, a firm-minded New
England schoolteacher who remained loyal to Wyeth, told

Tall Bird acidly. "They were all loafers he picked up around Boston, city men with no understanding of what they were going into."

Down to only eleven men now, Wyeth refused to abandon his plans, making arrangements to travel with the Milton Sublette party to the westward bend of Snake River where it entered the desert, then being guided on to the Blue Mountains and the Lower Columbia by Tall Bird, who had agreed to take the party as far as Celilo Falls.

Two days' ride to the southeast, the large body of men with the twenty heavily laden wagons belonging to Captain Bonneville had arrived in the upper valley of Green River, made camp there, and was now engaged in building a log-walled fort. The wagons were to be left there, with the chubby, good-natured, bald-headed captain sending trapping, exploring, or information-gathering parties out in all directions over the intermountain country. To the free trappers and the leaders of the St. Louis–based fur brigades, building such an elaborate post in a spot as high, remote, and unpopulated as the upper valley of the Green appeared ridiculous.

"Don't the damn fool know snow'll be ass-deep by October an' won't melt till April?" Jim Bridger muttered. "What's he up to, anyways?"

"Maybe he's heard the British are comin'," Joe Meek mused. "Maybe he's gittin' ready fer a war."

"Wal, it shore looks like a big piece of nonsense to me. I'd call it that, too—Fort Nonsense. Or Fort Folly."

Somewhere between Bonneville's Fort and Pierre's Hole, the party led by Lucien Fontenelle was traveling, trading, and scheming for the trapping rights to productive fur-gathering grounds. Despite the ever-present danger of Blackfeet, a band of free trappers led by Jim Bridger was planning to head north, following the breakup of rendezvous; they would go toward the Yellowstone country, make a swing northwesterly to the Missouri, then circle back through the Three Forks area—a region still as rich in beaver as it was full of hostiles.

Chief Lawyer, intrigued by what he had heard about Captain Bonneville, sent couriers inviting him to visit Nez Perce country. So did Chief *Kow-so-ter* of the upper Salmon River band, who sweetened his invitation by telling the bald-headed chief that he might find a female companion to keep him warm during the winter.

With hundreds of white trappers and thousands of friendly Indians spread out over the broad, sun-drenched basin, the likelihood of an encounter with hostiles seemed remote. But after leaving rendezvous July 17, 1832, and riding eight miles in a southerly direction, the combined Sublette-Wyeth parties blundered into just such a confrontation, next morning. Actually, it was the northward-traveling Indians that blundered, for only a village on the move, with all its women, children, and old people along, could have been so careless as to ride into such a trap.

"Would you look yonder!" Milton Sublette exclaimed in surprise, halting the party and squinting through the early morning haze at the swarming figures on horseback half a mile away, "Who'd that bunch be, Tall Bird—Fontenelle's or Bonneville's?"

"They are Indians," Tall Bird said after a moment's study. "A village on the move."

"Can you make out what tribe?"

"Gros Ventre, I think. What the Nez Perce call the 'Big Bellies' or 'Beggar' Indians because their stomachs never get filled. For many years, they have lived among the Blackfeet, who dislike them as leeches, as do their cousins to the south, the Arapahoes. Every few years they go south for a long visit with the Arapahoes, then, when their laziness and gluttony become too great for their southerly cousins to bear, they leave, journey north, and live with the Blackfeet for a while. They are bad Indians, not to be trusted."

"Well, we damn sure could make good Indians out of them, if we had a mind to," Sublette muttered. "We've caught them out in the open where they don't stand a chance of getting away." Shading his eyes against the sun, he watched a lone Indian wrapped in a scarlet blanket ride toward them. "What do you suppose he wants?"

"He is waving his right hand, signing that he is unarmed. In his left hand, he carries the greenstone medicine pipe, which his people smoke when they want to make peace."

Moving up beside Milton Sublette, a French-Canadian trapper named Antoine Godin and a Flathead brave named *Kei-Tse Pi-Sa-Kas*—"Bitter Smoke"—suddenly began talking excitedly to each other in a mixture of French and Flathead so garbled that Tall Bird, who knew both languages well, could barely understand what they were saying.

"That is him!" Godin exclaimed. "That is the dung-souled mother-defiler who killed my father two years ago!"

"Yes!" Bitter Smoke grunted. "He is the female-organ-kisser who came to your father bearing the pipe of peace, struck him down with his war club when he turned his back, and took his scalp!"

"He will not live out this day!"

"He does not deserve to, brother. How shall we kill him?"

"By treachery, just as he killed my father. Listen—this is what I want you to do . . ."

With so many Gros Ventre killings of whites and Indians to be avenged, Tall Bird did not think it likely that the scarlet-blanketed chief approaching them could have made peace on any terms under the present circumstances, which offered such a fine opportunity for slaughter. Even so, he was surprised by the brutal act that initiated the hostilities. Handing a short-barreled musketoon to Bitter Smoke, who concealed it under his jacket, Antoine Godin reined his horse over to Sublette's side.

"You wish me to parley wiz him, *m'sieu*?"

"Yeah. See what he's got to say."

Extending his right hand in the sign for peace, Godin moved forward. As they approached each other, the French-Canadian offered his hand to the Indian. For just an instant, the Gros Ventre chief hesitated, as suspicion and pride fought within him. Pride won. Reaching out, he took Godin's hand.

"Now!" Godin cried. "Kill the *cochon!*"

Pulling the musketoon out from under his jacket, Bitter Smoke thrust its barrel into the Gros Ventre's chest and pulled the trigger. Killed instantly, the Indian fell off his horse, which squealed in terror and bolted. Still gripping the Gros Ventre's hand, Godin toppled with him to the ground, pulled his knife out of its sheath, and with expert, savage strokes took the scalp, then leaped to his feet and waved it exultantly at the milling mass of Gros Ventres on whose behalf the chief had tried to make peace. As Godin's wild yell of triumph filled the air, Nathaniel Wyeth stared white-faced and horror-stricken at the bloody trophy and the man who was flaunting it.

"Good God in heaven! What a horrible thing to do!"

Ignoring him, Milton Sublette jerked the protective leather case off his long rifle, raised it high over his head, and shouted, "After them, men! Cut 'em off 'fore they make cover! Joe, hustle your butt over the ridge and tell Bill we've got us a passel of Injuns to kill! Tall Bird, you go with him and fetch the Nez Perces and Flatheads. I reckon they'll want a piece of this fight, too. Haul ass, boys! Haul ass!"

Of the hundred and fifty Gros Ventres in this band, only a fourth were warriors, giving them a force of fighting men roughly equal in number to that of the combined Sublette-Wyeth parties. But once word reached the two hundred or so white trappers and the four hundred Nez Perce and Flathead warriors still in Pierre's Hole that a band of their mortal enemies had been cornered and were ripe for killing, the Gros Ventre band would be doomed.

Skirting the hostiles as he rode with Joe Meek toward the low ridge dividing this basin from Pierre's Hole, Tall Bird saw that the Gros Ventre warriors were forming a sagging arc of defense, behind which the old men, women, and children, with their horses and belongings, were falling back to the cover of the cottonwoods, willows, and bushes growing along the course of a small stream which cut across the northwest part of the basin. Though because of his *Wy-a-kin* order never to kill a human being he had no intention of taking an active part in the battle, Tall Bird was not at all disturbed by the prospect of wholesale slaughter. Nor did he feel inclined to condemn Antoine Godin and Bitter Smoke for the manner in which they had killed the Gros Ventre chief. Treachery called for treachery and blood called for blood, where enmities of such long standing as those between Blackfoot allies and the Nez Perces, Flatheads, and whites were concerned. Chief Lawyer would be pleased with this opportunity to cover himself with glory in battle, Tall Bird knew, for though Lawyer took pride in being a peace leader and respected for his wisdom, he could never be regarded as a truly great chief—such as the late, legendary Broken Arm had been—until he had distinguished himself by leading a band of warriors in a victorious battle.

Before the day was done, Lawyer had indeed made a name for himself as a war leader. With William Sublette directing the tactics of the white and Indian forces, charge after charge was made against the beleaguered Gros Ventres, who dug in behind the thin shield of trees and bushes. During a long day of fighting they put up a surprisingly strong defense. Knowing that Wyeth's men were without experience in fighting Indians, and accepting Tall Bird's noncombatant status, Sublette ordered Tall Bird to take the Wyeth men to a spot away from the conflict, set up a shelter, and tend to the casualties. These soon proved to be far more than anticipated.

William Sublette himself was one. Catching a rifle ball in the fleshy part of his upper right arm, he had it bandaged, then coolly went on directing the attack. In the second charge of the Nez Perces and Flatheads, which Chief Lawyer led against one flank of the entrenched Gros Ventres, Lawyer stopped a bullet with his left side. Striking the hipbone just above the leg joint, the small-caliber, partially spent ball

burrowed so deep that it could not be removed; it would
cause him to walk with a cane for the rest of his life. A chief
of the Lapwai band, *Tack-en-su-a-tis,* also was struck by a
small, low-velocity rifle ball, which penetrated his stomach
and made an ugly, festering wound that would take so long
to heal he would be given the name "Rotten Belly"—a name
he carried with pride as evidence of his support for his white
friends.

Sometime during the night, the Gros Ventre survivors
slipped away in the darkness. Though he had taken an
active part in the fighting, Nathaniel Wyeth was appalled
by the results of what he felt had been a needless conflict.
In describing what would be called "the Battle of Pierre's
Hole," he wrote:

> The Indians, finding they were caught, fortified them-
> selves in a masterly manner in the woods. We attacked
> them and continued the attack all day. They decamped
> during the night, leaving most of their utensils, lodges,
> etc., and many dead. Probably 20 of them were killed,
> and 32 horses were found dead. We had lost three
> whites killed, eight badly wounded, among them
> William Sublette, who was extremely active in the
> battle. About ten of the Nez Perces and Flatheads
> were killed or mortally wounded. In the morning
> we visited their deserted fort; they had dug into the
> ground to reach water and to secure themselves from
> our shot. It was a sickening scene of confusion and
> bloodshed . . .

No longer a greenhorn, Wyeth separated his small party
from Milton Sublette's a few days later. Under Tall Bird's
guidance, the party traveled west across the lava deserts and
parched valleys of the Snake River country, then climbed
steep, rocky trails over the crests of the Blue Mountains.
Pointing north at a range of sharp, rugged peaks piercing
the clear blue sky, Tall Bird told Wyeth of the beautiful

lake, the sparkling streams, and the rich stands of grass that made his homeland a summer paradise.

"We call it '*Wallowa.*' "

"What does it mean?"

" 'Land of the Winding Waters.' According to the grandfather tales, *Speelyi*, the Coyote Spirit who made the world, shaped the Wallowa Valley as his final act of creation ten thousand snows ago, then gave it to the *Nimipu* as a place of eternal beauty to be cherished by us for all time."

"I'd like to see it someday."

After crossing two wide, grass-covered valleys, the trail led downward through gradually thinning timber to the bleak sagebrush plain where the Columbia River turned westward toward the sea. The British trading post built here by Donald MacKenzie and Alexander Ross thirteen years ago was no longer called Fort Nez Perces, which from the beginning had been a geographic misnomer. Because the land on which it stood belonged to the Walla Walla tribe, the post now was called Fort Walla Walla.

" '*Walla*' means 'little stream,' " Tall Bird told Wyeth. "When the word is repeated as in '*Walla Walla,*' the meaning is 'Place of Many Little Streams.' Where the Walla Walla River goes into the Columbia near the fort, it is called '*Wallula,*' meaning 'Mouth of the Waters.' "

By now summer was gone and the chill of autumn was in the air. Low on provisions, out of tobacco, and so raggedly dressed that they looked more like scarecrows than men, the Wyeth party sought to purchase supplies from the Hudson's Bay Company, payment to be made by a draft against the profits Wyeth expected to gain from future fur-gathering and salmon-salting endeavors. The response of Pierre C. Pambrun, the taciturn Scotch-Irishman in charge of the post, was cool. Curtly refusing to sell Wyeth any supplies unless he agreed to abandon his venture and return to the East, he declared that the Hudson's Bay Company had a monopoly on the trade of the Pacific Northwest, which it did not intend to give up.

Angrily, Wyeth responded that under the Joint Occupancy Treaty Americans had the same right to engage in trade in the Oregon country that Britishers did.

"Under the terms of the treaty," Wyeth said sharply, "either nation may cancel it by giving a year's notice. I can assure you, sir, that if the Hudson's Bay Company persists in monopolizing the trade of the Pacific Northwest to the detriment of American businessmen such as myself, I shall urge my government to give such notice."

"This is not my personal policy, Mr. Wyeth," Pambrun said in a more conciliatory tone. "It is the policy of the Hudson's Bay Company as conceived by the director of operations in North America, Sir George Simpson, and passed on to me by the regional factor in Fort Vancouver, Dr. John McLoughlin."

"In that case, when I go downriver and meet the supply ship that will be waiting for me there, I'll tell Dr. McLoughlin what I've just told you. With an American ship anchored on his doorstep, he may be more inclined to be reasonable than you are."

Realizing that this tough New Englander was not to be intimidated, Pambrun grudgingly gave him and his men enough clothes to protect them from the increasingly cold autumn weather, then passed them on to his superior at Fort Vancouver by providing them with bateaux and boatmen to transport them downriver.

With his services no longer needed as a guide, Tall Bird said farewell to Nathaniel Wyeth, whom he had come to like and respect, and rode east to greet his family, which he had not seen for over a year. Because of his interest in Wyeth, he kept track of his doings during the next few months by means of the Indian-trapper-trader grapevine, which passed on news with remarkable speed and accuracy.

Reaching Fort Vancouver October 29, 1832, Nathaniel Wyeth received a piece of bad news. His supply ship, the *Sultana,* had been wrecked on a South American reef and all its supplies had been lost. Though he found Dr.

John McLoughlin "a fine old gentleman, truly philanthropic
in his ideas . . ." he was told politely but firmly that the
Hudson's Bay Company and the Indians under its control
would not trade with him on any terms or supply him with
any necessities beyond food and clothing. However, if he
wished ship passage back to Boston or an escort overland,
that could be arranged . . .

Curtly, he told Dr. McLoughlin he wished neither.

Accompanied by two still-loyal men, he headed east
February 3, 1833, going up the Columbia and the Snake,
then across the Spokane country. Though Tall Bird missed
seeing him, he heard later that Wyeth had made a special
point of looking up Nez Perce and Flathead friends he had
met at last summer's rendezvous, later calling them " . . .
the best of Western Indians . . . devout, honest, brave . . ."

After the reverses he had suffered, a less determined man
would have gone back to farm-managing and ice-selling.
But according to what Tall Bird heard, giving up never
entered Wyeth's mind. Somewhere en route east, he met
Milton Sublette, who mentioned the fact that the Rocky
Mountain Fur Company would be needing trade goods
next year. Saying he knew where to buy quality goods at
bargain prices, Wyeth drew up a contract for three thousand
dollars' worth of supplies, promised delivery at rendezvous
midsummer of 1834, and returned to the East.

He was not beaten yet. In fact, he was just beginning to
fight . . .

2

Lord, it's big country! John Crane mused. Big, beautiful, and wild—with a man able to do whatever in hell he wants to do, whether it's traveling or trapping, fighting or fornicating, drinking himself blind or going bear-hunting with a switch, and no pious old fogeys around to stifle his yen for freedom and fun by telling him he's supposed to behave like a civilized white man.

Sure, as a green hand he'd borne his share of hoorawing from the party's tough old mountain men on the way out from Independence. But after he'd shown them that he could take the worst tenderfoot-baiting crap they could dish out without whining or getting riled, after he'd laughed off some insults and refused some fights, bridled at other insults and accepted other fights, whipped a few of his tormentors and in turn been whipped by a few of them, the greenness had begun to wear off and he'd been accepted for what he was—a willing and eager young stud who admitted he didn't know much yet but one that was, by God, willing and eager to learn.

Among rivals, talk was that Captain Bonneville didn't know his ass from a hole in the ground when it came to the fur trade. Maybe not. But he knew how to lead men in the military style, for of the one hundred and ten trappers, traders, camp tenders, packers, and teamsters in the well-supplied train of twenty wagons and hundreds of horses, oxen, and mules there wasn't a man or beast that

213

had not learned his place and job by the time the caravan was two weeks on the trail. What was more important, the men all liked him, carrying out his quietly given orders with a cheerful alacrity that gave his company the tone of a happy one.

By the time the fort was finished, the main rendezvous in Pierre's Hole had broken up. If Captain Bonneville was disappointed in not getting there in time to trade for a substantial pack of furs, he managed to conceal it by saying all he'd hoped to do this first summer was "find the dens where the foxes hide." Broaching a keg of rum with which all hands toasted the completion of the fort, he got pleasantly mellow, then conferred with his two assistant leaders, Michael Silvestre Cerré and Joseph Reddeford Walker, in regard to future plans.

Leaving the wagons, some of the supplies, and enough men to guard them here at the new post for the time being, he wanted the rest of the men to split up into three parties, which would explore the country and fur possibilities to the south, west, and north. Cerré, who impressed John Crane as pompous, arrogant, and supercilious, would lead the party headed northward toward Crow and Blackfoot country; Walker, who struck John Crane as a down-to-earth, practical man, would lead the party headed southward toward the Salt Lake region; while Captain Bonneville himself would lead the party headed westward to the head-waters of the Snake and the Nez Perce country.

No, Captain Bonneville said when gently chided by Cerré, the promise made by Chief *Kow-so-ter* of the upper Salmon River Nez Perces that he would supply the Bald Head Chief with an Indian maiden to keep him warm during the winter had not influenced his decision. It was simply a matter of strategy toward the British.

"In that quarter, the United States is most vulnerable to the enemy," he said solemnly. "Therefore, as a good commander, I must expose myself in the post of greatest danger."

"C'est la guerre!" Michael Cerré said gallantly, raising his tin cup of rum in a toast. "We drink to the exposure of our brave *capitaine!* Long may he wave!"

Though given no voice in the matter, John Crane guessed that his friendship with Joseph Walker and William Craig, both of whom were from the Virginia hill country, likely had something to do with the fact that he was chosen as a member of the party bound for the Salt Lake area. A stocky, rusty-headed man of medium height, Bill Craig was an old hand in the trapping game, being now in his fourth season as a free trapper, even though he was only a year older than John himself. Campfire talk was he'd killed a man back home, and thus had been forced to flee from civilization. Maybe he had, John mused. But who in hell cared? Well mannered, quiet-spoken, good-humored, and so well thought of by the Crows, Shoshones, and Nez Perces that he need never sleep without a female companion when families of those tribes were around, he was also generous enough to share his knowledge of Indian women with a greenhorn like John Crane.

When the party first made camp on Green River, a band of Crows had been camped nearby. Asked by Captain Bonneville if he thought they would be friendly, William Craig said he'd be happy to take some beads, hawks-bells, and trade foofaraw over to their village that evening and find out.

"Jest in case I need some he'p," he said, giving a wink to John Crane, "meebee John here oughta go 'long. We git in a jam, we kin fight our way out, coverin' each other's rear, so to speak."

"Shore I'll go 'long," John muttered, grinning as he returned the wink and deliberately imitated Craig's exaggerated Virginia hill-country drawl. "An' I declare I'll do my best to cover Bill's rear."

As often happened when dealing with Indians in general and Crows in particular, William Craig solemnly told Captain Bonneville when he and John Crane returned to the white camp two hours after daylight next morning, assaying the mood of the nearby band had taken longer than he'd figured it would.

"You know how it is, Cap'n. Injuns don't like to be rushed. Seein' talks were goin' so well, we couldn't insult 'em when they gave us an invite to stay the night, now could we?"

"Certainly not. What is their mood?"

"Friendly, I'd say." William Craig gave John Crane a quizzical look. "Ain't that the impression you got, John?"

"Shore is," John answered, trying to but not quite succeeding in suppressing a self-satisfied smirk. "Real friendly. The females in particular."

"Well, I'm glad to hear that you kept each other's rear covered," Captain Bonneville said dryly. "With the nights as cold as they are, parleying with Indians bare-assed could frostbite a man's privates."

Because of the wound William Sublette had suffered during the Battle of Pierre's Hole, he had postponed the departure of his brigade for St. Louis a couple of weeks; so it was well into August when he met with Bonneville and picked up whatever messages and men the captain wanted to send east. Hearing about the fight with the Gros Ventres, veteran mountain men Joseph Walker and William Craig were not disappointed in being too far removed from the battle to take part.

"Lord knows, I'd gun down the red bastards, should a bunch of Gros Ventre bucks cross my path," Walker said. "But charging a dug-in band of women, children, and old people, like them trappers, Nez Perces, and Flatheads done, seems plumb foolish to me."

"Likewise to me," Craig grunted. "Makin' war on women ain't my kind of doin's."

Though John Crane did not particularly want to discuss the matter with him, William Sublette sought him out and asked him about his plans for the future.

"Before I left St. Louis last spring, your father asked me if I would make a place for you in the returning brigade. I told him I would. But you seem to be planning on wintering in the mountains. At least, Captain Bonneville tells me you've signed on with him for a full year. Is that true?"

"Yes, sir, it is. He made me an offer too good to turn down."

"What were his terms?"

"Three hundred and fifty dollars in cash guaranteed for the first year. Seven hundred for the second. For the third, if he gets his leave extended and decides to stay west another year, one thousand."

"Promises cost him nothing, John. When the time comes, I have a suspicion that he'll pay off in wind rather than dollars."

"I'll risk that, sir. Truth is, I'm enjoying myself so much I'd work for nothing if I had to. This winter, I'll be with Joe Walker and a party headed down to the Salt Lake country. Next year, we may be going all the way out to California. That's a country I've always wanted to see."

"If the Spanish are as suspicious of Captain Bonneville's motives as I am, the members of the Walker party will see nothing of California but the inside of a jail," Sublette said stiffly. "Well, you're old enough to make your own decisions. I'll pass on the word to your father. After his travels with the Lewis and Clark party, he should be able to understand your feelings."

Sure he should. But he probably won't even bother to try. Because if what I think is going to happen does happen, the arrival of William Sublette's brigade in St. Louis and the little surprise Susan Swan threatened to drop in Pa's lap if I didn't come home and marry her by the first of October will take place at about the same time.

Which will be a great time for me to be two thousand miles away . . .

3

Because of his father-in-law's failing health during the past two years, Matt Crane had taken over direction of the warehouse, store, shipping company, and real estate office operated by the Bower & Crane Mercantile Bank to such a degree that he now held almost total control. Too old and feeble to act as pastor of the Presbyterian Church anymore, the Reverend Peter Crane had retired a year ago. Though Matt and his wife, Lydia, still attended church services regularly and gave the church generous financial support, they were no longer as closely involved in its activities as they had been when John was young and they were hoping that he would become a minister.

Early in marriage as Lydia's first child had been conceived, and easy as its birth was, she had borne no more. Twice she had suffered half-term miscarriages. An eight-month female baby had been born dead. Since then there had been no more conceptions. Though her warm, cheerful nature had not cooled, and her health remained good, Matt knew that she secretly grieved that she could have no more babies, compensating for the lack by lavishing love on him and the one child they did have, giving so much of her time to young mothers, their new babies, and showers thrown for their benefit by the matrons of the church that she was fondly called "Aunt Lydia" by many of the church's children and their mothers.

Aware of this, Matt was not surprised when he came home just before dark one mild October afternoon and found Lydia, a young lady, and a baby in the sitting room. Though he did not at first remember the young lady's name, he recalled having seen her in church a number of times during the past few years, for the sheen and texture of her rich, red hair made her stand out in any crowd. A sprinkling of brown freckles dusted her cheekbones; her eyes were green and large; her skin was milk-white; and she was strikingly beautiful. At the moment, she appeared to be under great emotional stress.

Lydia was cradling the baby in her arms. That his wife's cheeks were streaked with tears as she rocked back and forth, wordlessly crooning to the baby, did not surprise Matt. More than most women, Lydia was inclined to get emotional about babies.

"Well!" he said cheerfully as he took off his hat and coat. "What do we have here?"

Instead of answering proudly, as he expected her to do, the girl dropped her head, raised a handkerchief to her mouth, and sobbed hysterically. Lydia kept her gaze fixed on the baby in her arms.

"Matthew—there's no easy way to tell you this—"

"Tell me what?"

"This is Susan Swan. Her parents died several years ago, remember? Her Aunt Agatha took her in and has cared for her ever since."

"Yes, I remember her now. So what is not easy to tell?"

"Susan and our son, John, have been friends for years. Well, more than friends." Raising her eyes, Lydia gazed at him with tremulous defiance. "Susan says that John is this baby's father. And I believe her, Matthew! Truly I do!"

Matt sat down. Leaning on his cane, he gazed at Susan, who was sobbing softly into her handkerchief, then turned his head and stared at Lydia, who was gently rocking the baby. Because the object of his anger was not present, he tried to keep his voice calm. "How old is the baby?"

"Six weeks," Susan said, at last finding her voice. "He was born September third."

"It's a boy?"

"Yes. I named him Luke."

"Isn't that interesting, Matthew!" Lydia exclaimed. "That was the name you wanted to give our baby, remember? But we settled on 'John.' "

He remembered well enough. With his Nez Perce son already bearing the name "Mark," which was what Lydia first wanted to call the child, he had had no choice but to accept her second suggestion. He looked questioningly at Susan.

"When was the child conceived?"

Crimson with embarrassment, she lowered her head and murmured, "Late last December, I think."

"And you *think* our son, John, is the father?"

"Oh, I *know* he is, Mr. Crane!" the girl said spiritedly. "He has to be, because—well, because there was never anybody else but him! I loved him! I really loved him!"

"When did you know you were pregnant?"

"A couple of months later. In February, I guess it was. At least, I thought I was."

"Did you tell John?"

"I tried several times. But I don't think he really listened. What I mean is, he didn't want to listen because he didn't want to believe it."

"He left for the West in April. Surely he knew by then."

"Well, I kept telling and telling him. But he kept saying, 'Things happen to women who think they're going to have babies. Sometimes they don't have them.' Anyhow, he couldn't do anything about it then, he said, because he'd signed a contract with Captain Bonneville that he couldn't break. He'd be back in St. Louis around the first of October, he said, and if I'd really had a baby by then, he'd marry me, he said."

"The lying rascal!" Matt muttered angrily.

"Oh, Matthew!" Lydia exclaimed. "How can you accuse our son of lying?"

"Because that's exactly what he did. When we talked about his going west, he knew about this. He knew he did not intend to come back. But he told me he would come back."

"He will, Matthew! Surely he will!"

"No he won't, Lydia. I saw William Sublette this afternoon, just arrived with his brigade. He says John has signed on with Bonneville for another two or three years. Did you know that, Susan?"

"Yes. When I heard Mr. Sublette was back, I went to see him. He told me about John. That's why I came to see your wife."

"We've got to help her, Matthew," Lydia said urgently. "If we don't, her aunt will pledge her out."

"She's threatened you with that?" Matt said.

Tight-lipped, Susan nodded. "Yes. When she found out I was pregnant, she threatened to disown me unless I told her who the father was. When I told her, she made me stay out of people's sight until after the baby was born. She would wait and see if John came home and married me, like he'd promised to do, she said. If he didn't, she would send me to you. If you refused to take me and the baby in, then she would find a family as far away from St. Louis as she could—and pledge us out."

In theory, the custom of "pledging out" a young unwed mother and her baby to any good Christian family that would agree to take them in seemed humane enough. In practice, it often was little better than slavery. An unmarried mother had no rights. Neither did her bastard child. With their welfare and their future totally controlled by the head of the household that took them in, mother and child became charity cases who were expected to be grateful for whatever food, shelter, clothing, and care was given them. Often the reason for taking in a young unwed mother was the poor health of the household head's wife; thus, the drudgery of cooking, washing, and caring for a large brood of children was dumped on the frail shoulders of the new woman in the family, who, because of the act of immorality she had committed, was given little honor or respect.

Getting to his feet, Matt limped to his wife's side, put a hand on her shoulder, and said gently, "Do you want to take them in, Lydia?"

"More than anything in the world."

"Then we will."

"John will come home sooner or later," Lydia murmured, her eyes brimming with tears. "I'm sure he will. When he comes home, he'll do the right thing and marry Susan. I truly believe that."

"My belief in the young rascal is not as strong as yours," Matt said. "But we'll hope for the best."

"I'll write him a long letter, telling him what a beautiful son he has, and how we've taken Susan and the baby in, just as if she and John were already married. In the eyes of God, they are, Matthew. Don't you believe that?"

"What I believe is, you're the happiest grandmother in St. Louis," Matt said with a smile. Putting on his coat and hat, he turned to Susan. "Come along, my dear. We'll go see your aunt and pick up your things. You and Luke are part of our family now . . ."

4

Late in March 1833, Matt Crane stopped by William Clark's office to discuss a business matter. He found Clark studying a religious publication, printed in Pittsburgh, called the *Christian Advocate and Journal and Zion's Herald*, which apparently had just arrived. Scowling as he looked up, Clark said testily, "Just the person who can answer my question."

"Regarding what?"

"Why do religious people become such consummate liars when they write letters promoting their faith? For example, in the letter Father Rosati wrote to the Catholic publication in Lyons, France, a year or so ago, he made several misstatements regarding the visit of the Nez Perces and Flatheads in their so-called search for the Book of Heaven. Now it's the Methodists who are telling lies."

"On the same subject?"

"Yes. Do you recall a man named William Walker, a well-educated, part-blood Wyandotte Indian I introduced you to in November, year before last?"

"Vaguely. Wasn't he with a delegation of Ohio Indians that was considering a government offer to relocate them farther west?"

"That's right. He was in St. Louis shortly after the first chief died, a little before the second chief passed away. After getting back to Ohio, he wrote a letter to a Methodist friend—

a gentleman named G. P. Disosway—who passed it on to this religious journal, which has just published it. Read it, please, then tell me what relation it has to the truth."

Donning his spectacles, which had become a necessity nowadays, Matt picked up the journal, moved over to the window in search of stronger light, and began to read aloud.

" 'Immediately after we landed in St. Louis, on our way west, I proceeded to General Clark's, Superintendent of Indian Affairs. He informed me that three chiefs from the Flathead nation were in his house . . . ' " Matt looked at Clark. "That isn't true, sir. At that time, they were guests of the Catholics."

"Correct. But you wouldn't expect a Methodist to say that, would you? Read on. It gets further from the truth as it goes along."

" ' . . . and were quite sick, and that one (the fourth) had died a few days ago. They were from the west of the Rocky Mountains. Curiosity prompted me to step into the adjoining room to see them . . . ' " Matt frowned. "How could he see them if they weren't there?"

"A minor detail, Matt. Read on and find out what he *says* he saw."

" 'I was struck by their appearance . . . small in size, delicately formed, except the heads . . . ' " Matt snorted. "My God, General, he's drawn an atrocious sketch of an Indian with a *pointed* head. He certainly never saw that kind of Indian anywhere!"

"Read on! Read on!"

" 'The head is flattened thus: From the point of the nose to the apex of the head, there is a perfect straight line; the protuberance of the forehead is flattened or leveled. You may form some idea of the shape of their heads from the rough sketch I have made with the pen, though I confess I have drawn it most too long for a flat-head. This is produced by a pressure upon the cranium while in infancy . . . ' "

Matt shook his head in amazement. "He's describing the head-flattening process used by lower Columbia River Indians many years ago, which they seldom practice now, and which the Flatheads, despite their name, never practiced at all. In fact, their tribal identification sign is to indicate that the top of their head is like yours and mine, not slanted, like the head of a lower Columbia River Indian."

"Keep reading, Matt. It gets even better."

" 'General Clark related to me the object of their mission, and, my dear friend, it is impossible for me to describe to you my feelings, while listening to his narrative. It appeared that some white man had penetrated into their country, and happened to be a spectator at one of their religious services. He informed them that their mode of worshiping the Supreme Being was radically wrong . . . that the white people away toward the rising sun had been put in possession of a book containing directions how to conduct themselves . . .

" 'They called a national council to take this subject into consideration. Some said if this be true it is certainly high time we put ourselves in possession of this mode. They accordingly deputed four chiefs to proceed to St. Louis to see their great father, General Clark.' "

Shaking his head, Matt peered over the rim of his spectacles at Clark. "Did you really tell William Walker that, General?"

"As I recall, all I told him was that a group of far-western Indians had come to St. Louis apparently seeking religious teachers. The rest is embroidery. Read the comment G. P. Disosway made on the letter. If that doesn't start church bells ringing all over the Burnt District, nothing will."

The term "Burnt District," which recently had come into use, referred to a section of upper New York State and a portion of New England, whose church pastors and members now burned with zeal to go to far places and convert the heathen. The more colorful the heathen, the hotter this missionary zeal burned. Were there cannibals in Fiji and unclad natives in the Sandwich Islands? If so, the cannibals must be Christianized and put on a vegetarian diet; the unclad must be Christianized and clothed. So far, the Indians of the Pacific Northwest had ranked well down on the list, so far as being colorful was concerned. But Disosway appeared to be about to change that.

" 'How deeply touching is the circumstances of the four natives traveling on foot 3,000 miles through thick forests and extensive prairies, sincere searchers after truth. The story has scarcely a parallel in history. May we not indulge the hope that the day is not far distant when the missionaries will penetrate into these wilds where the Sabbath bell has never tolled since the world began!' "

Accepting the journal as Matt handed it back to him, William Clark chuckled. "The course of empire follows a crooked path, Matt, as westward it makes its way. In spite of all the effort we expended, all the maps we drew, all the flora and fauna we gathered, all the words we wrote and published regarding the nature of the Far West—we reached only a few people. At one time, I've been told, Daniel Webster offered to trade the whole Oregon country to Great Britain for a Newfoundland codfish bank. The deal fell through because England offered a small codfish bank, while Webster wanted a medium-sized one."

"Good heavens, sir, if people only realized the vastness and the resources of the Oregon country!"

"In time, they will—despite Sir George Simpson's sly scheme to exterminate the country's most obvious asset— fur. And if I'm any judge, this sort of story, foolish and untrue though it is, may be the sort of thing that will turn the trick. What could be more precious to the moral leaders of our country than immense numbers of poor, benighted heathens, with flattened heads and souls to be saved, eager to be converted . . . ?"

5

It's been some year, John Crane mused drunkenly, *the likes of which this child won't live again. Traveling west from Salt Lake over the worst desert I ever seen to the Humboldt. Killing them pesky Digger Indians. Crossing the High Sierras into balmy California. Spending a winter and spring there with the padres and easygoing Spaniards. Bullfighting, bear-baiting, wine-swilling, and chasing hot-blooded wenches around the missions. Freezing, starving, nearly dying of thirst on the way east. Christ on a crutch, what a purple-peckered pistol of a year it's been!*

"Digger-Killing Crazies!" That's what Old Bonny was calling the men who'd been in the California expedition. Well, sure we did kill a passel of Diggers, John Crane maudlinly admitted to anybody who would listen at the Bear River rendezvous. But they ain't hardly human, you know. Like Joe Walker kept trying to explain to the captain, the thieving, ignorant, dirty bastards brought it all on themselves.

This summer, the main fur rendezvous was being held on Green River, two days' ride northeast of where Bonneville had met the returning Walker party, As usual, there was a good deal of traveling back and forth between camps, a lot of tall tales told, gossip traded, and changes of employment or allegiance made from one brigade to another. Sobering up after a week of heavy drinking, during which John

229

Crane vaguely recalled having been hailed as a horny,
hairy-chested hero by mountain men envious of the Injun-
killing, bear-and-bull-baiting, and wench-screwing of the
California contingent, he began to do some serious thinking
about his future.

On paper, his yearly salary from Bonneville had risen
from three hundred and fifty, to seven hundred, to one
thousand dollars a year. But on paper, Old Bonny was
broke. A year ago, he had shipped only twenty-three packs
of beaver east. This year, John heard, the total was even
slimmer, coming to no more than fifteen packs. Unless
his mysterious backers in the East were prepared to supply
him with unlimited funds, the prediction made by William
Sublette that he would pay off with wind rather than dollars
was likely to come true.

Still, Bonneville remained optimistic. Sending this year's
harvest of furs back to St. Louis with Michael Cerré, he wrote
a letter to the Secretary of War requesting a two-year exten-
sion on his leave of absence—which he blithely assumed
would be granted—then made plans for a second journey
to the lower Columbia, where this time, he was sure, he
would succeed in competing with the British. Told that he
was to be one of the twenty-three men chosen for the party,
John Crane shrugged laconically.

"Why not, Captain? I got a yen to see that part of the
country. From what Joe Meek tells me, it's right purty—
when it ain't raining."

"By the way, John, I ran into an Indian relative of yours
last winter," Captain Bonneville said. "A Nez Perce named
Tall Bird."

"The hell you did! I thought he died."

"From what he told me, he came close to dying. But he
pulled through and made it home. Did you know about
him?"

"Yeah. Pa told me he'd whelped a half-breed son by a
Nez Perce woman, years ago. Didn't seem ashamed of it,
either. What sort of a buck is he?"

"Handsome, intelligent, honest. He's been quite helpful to me. I told him you'd be at the Bear River rendezvous, in case he wanted to meet you. But he hasn't showed up."

"Well, if he's anything like them Diggers we tangled with on the way out to California, not meeting him will be no great loss. But I am curious to see what he looks like. Maybe later . . ."

6

Maybe later he would ride over to Bear River, Tall Bird was thinking, where he would cautiously check on his white half brother to see what kind of a man he was. But right now, events transpiring at the larger fur rendezvous on Green River—to which he and a sizable contingent of Nez Perces and Flatheads had journeyed because of the great news that white missionaries at last had come out from the East— compelled his attention.

The missionaries were Methodists, he learned. Traveling west from St. Louis with Nathaniel Wyeth and his party were the Reverend Jason Lee, his nephew, Daniel, and three lay brethren. Seeing them, the Nez Perces and Flatheads were first delighted, then disappointed.

"Sorry," Jason Lee said. "We do not plan to establish a mission in your country, which we hear is uncivilized. We're going on west to the Willamette Valley, near Fort Vancouver. Perhaps later . . ."

Though the Indians were baffled, Tall Bird understood what had happened. In addition to the Rocky Mountain Fur Company, American Fur Company, Wyeth, and Bonneville brigades, a Hudson's Bay Company brigade was there. Led by Thomas McKay, it had been sent east from Fort Vancouver by Dr. John McLoughlin with instructions to do everything possible to persuade Americans to settle south of the Columbia in the vicinity of Fort Vancouver, where the Hudson's Bay Company could keep an eye on them, rather than inland among the Nez Perces and Flatheads, who were altogether too friendly toward Americans to suit British aims. Without doubt, it had been Thomas McKay who had convinced the Lee party that establishing a mission in the Willamette Valley would be far easier and more pleasant than building one in the country of the Nez Perces and Flatheads.

This trip, Wyeth's preparations for serious competition with the British were even more extensive than before. He had chartered another ship, the *May Dacre*, which he planned to meet on the lower Columbia. Accompanying him were two scientists, Thomas Nuttall, a Harvard botanist, and John K. Townsend, a Philadelphia physician and ornithologist. Because these two men had so rapturously classified flora, fauna, and birds, filled journals with copious notes, and behaved with such reckless disregard for their scalps while passing through dangerous Indian country, the hostiles, thinking them mad, had left them strictly alone, Tall Bird was told.

Also with the party, observing the stars, shooting the sun, and making accurate recordings of longitude and latitude with his feet set firmly upon the ground rather than on the heaving deck of a ship, was Wyeth's second-in-command, an old sea dog, Captain Joseph Thing.

As he had done two years ago, Wyeth asked Tall Bird to come with the party as a guide and interpreter as far west as Celilo Falls. Again, Tall Bird agreed to do so.

But even as the trading began, a violent argument took place between Nathaniel Wyeth and William Sublette. Locked in a dog-eat-dog conflict with the American Fur Company, the Rocky Mountain Fur Company was being driven to the wall. Milton Sublette, who had signed the contract with Wyeth for three thousand dollars' worth of trade goods, had turned back short of Green River because of an increasingly painful leg injury. Now William Sublette refused to honor the contract, taking only a small part of the trade goods at bargain-basement prices.

Wyeth was furious. "By heaven, gentlemen!" he told the two scientists in the party, "I'll roll a stone into the garden of the Rocky Mountain Fur Company that they can never dislodge!"

Leaving rendezvous and crossing over to the Snake River watershed, he chose a site in the low, rich bottom of the valley formed by the confluence of Portneuf River with the Snake, which it entered about nine miles below, and commenced building a trading post July 15, 1834. Among the interested observers, Tall Bird noted, was the leader of the Hudson's Bay Company brigade, Thomas McKay.

Though the Reverend Jason Lee planned to travel on to the Willamette Valley and establish a mission there, he did consent to preach a sermon Sunday afternoon, July 27, to the Indians, whites, half bloods, Americans, British, and combinations thereof assembled near Wyeth's still-being-built fort. The listeners were most attentive. Afterward the Sabbath was broken by a series of horse races, in the last of which a French-Canadian named Kaniseau was tragically thrown and killed.

Next day Jason Lee participated in a three-denominational burial service, reading the Ninth Psalm, which begins, "I will praise thee, O Lord, with my whole heart."

Wyeth wrote: "Services for him were performed by the Canadians in the Catholic form, by Mr. Lee in the Protestant form, and by the Indians in their form, as he had an Indian family. He at least was well buried."

Accompanied by the Hudson's Bay Company brigade, which had offered to see it through to the lower Columbia, the Lee party set out shortly thereafter. Building of the post, which Wyeth named after his principal backer, Henry Hall, went on. The morning of August 5, 1834, a homemade American flag was raised over Fort Hall. One of the three barrels of alcohol Wyeth had brought along was tapped, and the day was spent in celebration.

Leaving eleven men to take care of the post and initiate trade with the Indians, Wyeth and the remainder of his party moved northwest by way of Godin's River and Malade River, detaching small groups to trap these streams. It was ironic, Tall Bird mused, that Antoine Godin—the son of the trapper after whom Godin's River had been named and the man who had instigated the Battle of Pierre's Hole two summers ago by killing the Gros Ventre chief who had murdered his father—should be one of the men left to trap the area.

On September 2 Wyeth caught up with the Jason Lee party, which had traveled more slowly, at Fort Walla Walla. He noted with puzzlement that the leader and several men of the Hudson's Bay Company brigade were missing.

"Thomas McKay and half a dozen men seem to have stayed in the mountains," he told Tall Bird. "I wonder why?"

The reason soon became clear. After seeing Wyeth start to build Fort Hall, Thomas McKay decided that the Hudson's Bay Company should have a post in the area, too. Divulging his plans to no one, he and a few of his men lingered behind the brigade, chose a site on the Boise River just upstream from its juncture with the Snake, and began building a fort whose flagstaff would bear the British banner.

It would be called Fort Boise.

As the crow flew, it was located some two hundred and fifty miles west of Fort Hall—just good "neighboring" distance in this country. But exchanging neighborly visits was not its intended function. In the game of rolling stones into gardens, any number could play, and the Hudson's Bay Company was adept at bowling on the green . . .

Because of his friendship with Wyeth and his hope that the Americans would establish a permanent post on the lower Columbia, Tall Bird stayed with the party all the way to Fort Vancouver. The supply ship *May Dacre* was anchored in plain sight of the British post, her empty holds waiting to be filled with fish and furs. But try as he would, Wyeth could obtain neither commodity in any quantity.

The British were still polite, but they still would not trade. The Indians had furs, but not for him. The river was full of fat, gleaming salmon which the Indians caught, cured, stored, and sold to the British in great numbers, but would not catch for Wyeth. Work though they would, his own men lacked the equipment and know-how to obtain a substantial number of fish themselves. Growing disgusted, some of them quit him to seek their fortunes in other fields for other employers.

Hearing that trade was going badly at Fort Hall, Wyeth hired thirteen Sandwich Islanders, whom he called "Kanakas," and sent them inland with Captain Joseph Thing and a load of fresh supplies. Traveling with the party as far as Fort Walla Walla, where he left them to go home, Tall Bird later heard that the Hawaiians—who loved water but feared mountains—had taken such a dislike to the looks of the interior country that they had deserted their landlocked commander at the foot of the Blues and returned to the lower Columbia.

Continuing inland to Fort Hall, Captain Thing spent a brutal, frustrating winter there, competing with the Hudson's Bay Company and fighting Blackfeet. When he at last gave up and went back to his employer's fishery just across the river from Fort Vancouver in July 1835, Wyeth was shocked to find him " . . . emaciated, pale, and apparently seven years older than the season before."

Reluctantly, Wyeth sent the *May Dacre* back to Boston with half a cargo of salmon and furs. Recognizing the fact that he was facing financial ruin, he headed overland to Fort Hall to do what he could there. Again his best efforts failed, and he returned to Boston to consult with his backers. They could give him no more help, they said; he must carry on alone . . .

Captain Bonneville's efforts to compete with the British on the lower Columbia also failed, just as John Crane had feared they would. Competent a military leader as he was, jolly and generous as he was when it came to sharing a keg of rum or an Indian woman, he had no head for business and was too softhearted to lie, cheat, steal, and cut throats the way a trader must do in this country if he were to show a profit.

From Bear River, the Bonneville party had crossed a high ridge to the watershed of the Snake, then followed along the left bank of that river over bleak, sagebrush-covered, lava-strewn desert to the foot of the Blue Mountains just south of where the Snake entered the Big Canyon. More familiar with the country now, Bonneville shunned the river route this time, leaving the Snake and ascending Burnt River to the upper valley of the Grande Ronde. Late August had come after a hot, rainless summer, and the carelessness of man or bolts of lightning during thunderstorms had set the countryside afire.

In every direction, the plains and valleys were ablaze, fire sweeping over the long grass in billows of flame, shooting up every bush and tree, rising in great columns from the thicker stands of fir, tamarack, and pine, sending up clouds of smoke that darkened the atmosphere and choked throats and lungs.

Even at high noon, the smoke was so thick that men separated from the party could find their companions only by shouting. For days they wandered aimlessly through the eye-smarting haze, until at last encountering a group of friendly Cayuses, who led them on across the Blues and down onto the Columbia River plain. But their troubles were not ended.

"Out of the fire and into the frying pan," Bonneville muttered wearily, after being frustrated time and again by employees and Indians friendly to the Hudson's Bay Company, whose unbending policy of stifling competition by any means short of violence continued to be brutally effective.

At Celilo Falls, a hundred miles upriver from Fort Vancouver, Captain Bonneville surrendered to the inevitable.

"It's pointless to fight the British in their own backyard," he said grimly. "Tomorrow I'm heading east to the mountains, where I'll spend one more winter trying to gather enough furs to pay off my debts. Meanwhile, I'll honor my people's contracts with letters of credit."

Which are as worthless as wind, John Crane mused sardonically, *just as William Sublette predicted. But what the hell! I've seen a lot of country and had myself a high old time. Gotta thank Old Bonny for that.*

"If it's all the same to you, Captain, I'll part company with you here, 'cause my stick floats the other way. Far as I'm concerned, you've got no obligation to me."

"That's mighty decent of you, John. What are your plans?"

"Well, I got me a notion to follow the trail my pa blazed with the Lewis and Clark party years ago. Which means going on down the Columbia to the sea. Two of my trapping buddies, Joe Meek and Doc Newell, tell me the Willamette Valley is a great place. I've a mind to see it. Another friend, William Craig, says he'd like me to winter with him in the Nez Perce country. Seems he's got him a woman in the Lapwai band who he claims is all the woman a man could want. And there's lots more like her, he says, ripe to be plucked."

"And you're just the young stud that can pluck them," Bonneville said with a smile. "Well, power to you, John. But take fair warning from a man who knows. When they've been plucked, you'll find they all have sixteen real friendly hungry brothers and cousins eager to move in with you."

Later, John Crane heard that Captain Bonneville's final winter in the mountains had been as unprofitable as the ones that preceded it. But that did not seem to matter to his backers. Going east, he was reinstated in the Army by President Andrew Jackson, was dined and feted by John Jacob Astor, who introduced him to the most famous writer of the day, Washington Irving. Charmed by the chubby, bald-headed captain, Irving appropriated his notes, maps, and journals, which, with a number of interviews, he incorporated into a book entitled *Adventures of Captain Bonneville in the Rocky Mountains*.

Where fact ended and fiction began seemed immaterial to Washington Irving and the thousands of people who read the extremely popular book. But to John Crane, who had been there "when the guns went off," so to speak, the book contained several eyebrow-raisers. For example, Irving claimed it was Captain Bonneville's opinion that all the intermountain country was worthless:

> An immense belt of rocky mountains and volcanic plains several hundred miles in width must ever remain an irreclaimable wilderness, intervening between the abodes of civilization, and affording a last refuge to the Indians. Here, in time, the Indians and white men of every nation will produce hybrid races like the mountain Tatars of the Caucasus, who will become a scourge to the civilized frontiers . . .

Like Sir George Simpson, Washington Irving seemed to be laboring under the delusion that fur was the only thing of value in the Pacific Northwest. That altruistic men intent on saving a few thousand heathen Indian souls for their church might end up saving an empire for their country never entered either man's mind.

But it happened.

At rendezvous in the valley of Green River, the summer of 1835, two more American missionaries appeared, seeking information regarding the willingness of the Nez Perces and Flatheads to receive men of the cloth.

Tall Bird was there to meet them . . .

7

Why Lucien Fontenelle, who was not a very religious man, should have been chosen to escort the Book of Heaven delegation east in 1831, and the missionaries who responded west in 1835, was a thing the exasperated brigade leader never was able to understand. He certainly was not happy with the chore. Like the rough-hewn men in his employ, he equated men of the cloth with a loss of freedom and sensed that a cherished way of life was coming to an end.

While in St. Louis, which was where the Reverend Samuel Parker and Dr. Marcus Whitman joined his party, he dared not violate company policy of friendship to the missionaries. But once the brigade left Liberty, Missouri, and headed out across the open plains, he did his best to discourage the two men from tagging along.

Sponsored by the American Board of Commissioners for Foreign Missions, which was a joint venture of the Presbyterian and Congregational churches, Parker and Whitman were an ill-matched pair. Both came from the Burnt District of upstate New York and Massachusetts. Fifty-six years of age, overweight, bookish, and pompous of manner, Samuel Parker was far more at home in a pulpit than he was aboard a horse in the western wilderness. Marcus Whitman, thirty-three, big-boned and muscular, could carry his share of the work load when it came to bridging streams, prying wagons out of mudholes, or other tasks of camp and trail. Because the Reverend Parker's official title was "Missionary," while Whitman's was "Assistant Missionary," it was Whitman's lot to saddle and unsaddle, pack and unpack, pitch and strike the tent, cook the meals, wash the dishes, and do everything else that had to be done, while Parker observed the scenery, enjoyed the ride, and made entries in his journal.

In an effort to get rid of the two men, Fontenelle refused to carry their baggage in his wagons, forcing Whitman, a rank greenhorn at packing, to tie and attempt to keep all their provisions and gear on the bony back of one "poor old mule." When the two missionaries declined to travel on the Sabbath, Fontenelle and the brigade continued without them. At river fords, members of the brigade attempted to destroy a raft, constructed to float their own gear across the stream, so that Parker and Whitman could not use it. On one occasion some of the more boisterous members of the party threw rotten eggs at Marcus Whitman; others attempted to force Samuel Parker to break his temperance vows and take a drink of whiskey.

How long the hostility between the trapping brigade and the missionaries might have lasted became a moot question when the caravan reached Bellevue, two weeks out from Liberty, and an epidemic of Asian cholera struck the party.

"At this place the Lord had a great change for us," Marcus Whitman wrote. "For the Cholera appearing in camp, my aid was greatly sought. Mr. Fontenelle himself being one of the subjects of the disease and recovering (as also most of his men), he showed his gratitude, as well as all other persons in the company, by bestowing upon us every favor in his power."

Since it was not unusual for a cholera epidemic to kill half the community through which it raged, the fact that they lost only three members of the brigade—which numbered more than fifty—said a great deal for the skill with which Dr. Whitman treated the sick men.

At rendezvous, which the caravan reached August 12, 1835, word of Dr. Whitman's skills had preceded him. His first patient was Jim Bridger, who three years earlier had caught a Blackfoot arrow in his back. The three-inch head, which still was imbedded there, was "bothering him some," and he would be obliged if the doctor would cut it out.

"It was a difficult operation," Samuel Parker wrote, "because the arrow was hooked at the point by striking a large bone and a cartilaginous substance had grown up around it. The Doctor pursued the operation with great self-possession and perseverance; and his patient manifested equal firmness."

To the Nez Perces and Flatheads who had come to meet the missionaries, this was great medicine indeed. *In-sa-la,* a Flathead chief, and *Tack-en-su-a-tis,* the Nez Perce leader called "Rotten Belly" because of the long-festering wound he had received at the Battle of Pierre's Hole, both urged the two men to come immediately to their country and begin religious teaching. But establishing a mission among the Indians was not to be done that simply.

"Our primary purpose in making this trip was to ascertain whether or not your people really wanted missionaries," Samuel Parker told the Indians, with Tall Bird translating for him. "From the warmth of the reception you've given us, I'm convinced that you do. The next question to be settled is where the mission should be located."

"We would like to know if it is possible to take wagons into your country," Marcus Whitman said. "If we settle there, we'll have household goods and wives to transport across the continent. We can't ask women to ride horseback for such a great distance."

If the Indians wondered why white wives could not do something as simple as riding a horse, which Indian wives did all the time, they were too polite to voice their questions. Knowing the country as he did, Tall Bird said he was sure that wagons could be taken from Green River across the Snake River desert to the foot of the Blue Mountains, though beyond that point a good deal of axwork might have to be done to clear the trail.

"It seems to me our prospects for establishing a mission are very good," Samuel Parker said. "Shall we plan to return with the brigade, Marcus, and find out if your promised bride really is willing to marry a frontier doctor and devote the rest of her life to Christian work among the heathen?"

"She'll be willing, I'm sure. But it occurs to me, sir, that we could save time and effort if we divided our tasks."

"In what manner?"

"If you were to go with the Indians to their country, while I return to St. Louis with the brigade, you could select a site for the mission while I inform the American Board of our plans. After Narcissa Prentiss and I are married, we'll find another couple to share in the work. During the winter, we'll put together the supplies we'll need, and head west next spring. This way, we can save a full year."

"An excellent idea!" Parker exclaimed. "Let's do it!"

When informed of the decision, *Tack-en-su-a-tis* was delighted. Because his band lived at Lapwai—"Place of the Butterflies"—twelve miles east up the Clearwater, above its junction with the Snake, he immediately declared that the mission would be established there.

"Anything the *Tam-tai-nat* wants, I will give him," he told Tall Bird. "He need only name it and it is his."

"Your generosity is commendable," Tall Bird said dryly. "But you should not give away anything in the Lapwai Valley until you make sure that *Hin-mah-tute-ke-kaikt* agrees."

"What do I care for the wishes of Thunder Strikes? He is only a *tewat*."

"True. But there are those who think his medicine is strong."

"Compared to that of the missionaries, his medicine is nothing. Can he cure cholera? Can he cut an arrowhead out of a man's back without killing him? No! He is a man of little magic."

Tall Bird did not argue the matter. Truth was, he hoped that the mission would be established in the domain of Lawyer, *Ta-moot-sin*, or *Tu-eka-kas*, none of whom had come to the Green River rendezvous this year. They were men of great piety and intelligence, whose bands were not riddled by controversy between leaders, as was the Lapwai band. Further complicating the Lapwai area as a site was the fact that the white trapper William Craig often wintered there with his Nez Perce wife, whom he called Isabel. Since Thunder Strikes was her father, the two men were on good terms. Having observed the riotous behavior of American trappers at fur rendezvous, Tall Bird doubted that William Craig would be any more inclined to welcome a missionary than his father-in-law would.

In any event, the decision would be made by the Reverend Samuel Parker, who despite his age and not very rugged physical condition was eagerly looking forward to the trip. But after talking to some of the American mountain men who knew the nature of the country lying between Green River and the lower Clearwater, Marcus Whitman began to have serious misgivings about leaving Parker in the care of the Indians.

"I would never forgive myself, sir, if an accident should befall you," he told Parker. "The Christian public would condemn me severely, I'm sure."

"Oh, Marcus, where is your faith!" Parker exclaimed. "We could not go safely together without divine protection. With it, I can go alone."

Before the breakup of rendezvous, Tall Bird told the missionaries the full story of the Book of Heaven quest, which they had not heard before. Intrigued by his account of Spokane Garry's being sent to eastern Canada to be schooled and instructed in religion, Whitman said, "What an impression that must have made on the church people! If only I could do that!"

"Perhaps it would be possible," Tall Bird said. "I will ask my people."

Discussing the matter in the Nez Perce section of camp that evening, Tall Bird found two fathers who were willing to let their ten-year-old sons make the long trip east with the doctor-missionary. Pleased that they had shown so much faith in him, Whitman gave one of the boys the Christian name Richard, the other the name John.

"I'll take good care of them," he assured Tall Bird. "Tell their parents that I'll be a father to them and will bring them safely back next summer."

8

As a matter of pride, Matt Crane could not bring himself to write more than a brief, curt note to his son each year, reminding John of the promise he had made and violated to return to St. Louis, of the girl he had impregnated and deserted, and of the child he had fathered, which now was a member of the Crane family. These notes sent to rendezvous with westward-bound brigade leaders were stern reminders to John of obligations owed his parents, his child, and its mother, unsoftened by any expression of sympathy, affection, or understanding. But in her warm, loving, lengthy letters, Lydia, Matt's wife, more than made up for that.

Ever since Susan and baby Luke had moved into the Crane home, Lydia had insisted on treating them exactly as she would have done if John had married the girl in a legal church ceremony and fathered the baby within the bonds of wedlock. Indeed, if Matt had not pointed out how shocked his father and church members who knew the truth would be at the lie, Lydia would have promulgated the fiction that her son, John, and her daughter-in-law, Susan, had married before their child was conceived, keeping the ceremony a secret only because John wanted to go west with Captain Bonneville, who might frown upon signing a newly married man to a two-year contract.

"I will take the mother and child in, Lydia," Matt said gently, "loving and caring for them as if they were my own. But I will not lie about them."

Reluctantly, Lydia settled for that.

Far-flung as the fur trade was, brigade leaders and trappers wintering in St. Louis brought back news of the deeds, misdeeds, adventures, misadventures, and travels of all the men in the field. Exasperated though he was with John's actions, Matt could not simply condemn and forget him, for each autumn as the brigades returned, Lydia gave him no peace until he had extracted every shred of information he could acquire from men who had seen John at rendezvous. In early spring each year, Lydia would begin writing a long letter to John, describing how well Susan was looking and feeling, how wonderful it was to have her in the household, and what a healthy, handsome, lively little boy Luke was turning out to be.

From his talks with brigade leaders, Matt knew that John was making a name for himself as a free trapper and was living the kind of life Matt himself had lived for two and a half years during his travels with the Lewis and Clark party. He knew that John had received the long letters from his mother and the short notes from his father, but had chosen to answer neither in writing. His only response each year had been the laconic verbal statement to brigade leaders, "Tell my folks I'm all right. But I ain't sure when I'll be coming home . . ."

Ever since the Book of Heaven delegation of Indians from the Pacific Northwest had come to St. Louis in the autumn of 1831, the winds of change in that area had been stirring with increasing velocity. Captain Bonneville's mysterious venture had lengthened from two to four years, with provocative expeditions into territories claimed by the suspicious Spaniards and the commercially aggressive British. Nathaniel Wyeth, after two trips west, now was in Boston desperately seeking financial help that he likely would not get. In the Snake River country, the Americans had built Fort

Hall and the British Fort Boise—posts outwardly competing for fur, though it was becoming more and more apparent to expansion-minded leaders of both nations that the real prize was territory.

Jason Lee and his group of Methodist missionaries, which had gone west in 1833, now were well established in the Willamette Valley, building a congregation of white settlers rather than of Indians. The Reverend Samuel Parker and Dr. Marcus Whitman, representing the Presbyterian and Congregational churches, had made an exploratory trip west in 1835, with Parker going on into Flathead and Nez Perce country to select a mission site while Whitman returned to the East to put together the mission's staff and supplies, taking with him as tokens of Nez Perce sincerity the two bright-eyed, intelligent boys Richard and John.

Now, in the spring of 1836, Marcus Whitman, his new bride, Narcissa, the two Indian boys, and the austere, colorless, but no doubt sincere couple the Reverend Henry Spalding and his wife, Eliza, had passed through St. Louis on their way west. Meeting them at a special service held in the Presbyterian Church to express support for their mission, Matt was convinced that these people meant it when they said that they were prepared to dedicate their lives to carrying the Word of God to far-western Indians.

Tall, gaunt, and solemn, Henry Spalding impressed Matt as something of a zealot, unwavering in his faith and unbending in his lack of tolerance for those whose beliefs differed from his. When Matt said that he had found the Nez Perces to be a people with a rich spiritual life when he met them thirty years ago with the Lewis and Clark party, Spalding's reaction was caustically skeptical.

"How can they lead a rich spiritual life when they have not heard the Word of God?"

Eliza Spalding, a quiet, dark-haired, mousy-looking woman totally dominated by her husband, struck Matt as being far better educated than he, for she had an excellent grasp of Latin, Hebrew, and Greek, while Henry Spalding's education had been barely enough to qualify him as an ordained minister. When Matt suggested that her mastery of languages would be very useful to her in learning the Nez Perce tongue, she showed a flash of animation.

"Oh, yes, Mr. Crane! Learning their language is a first priority to me. As a matter of fact, I've already begun to learn it from Richard and John."

Dr. Marcus Whitman, of course, Matt had met a year ago when he and the Reverend Samuel Parker had traveled to rendezvous with Lucien Fontenelle and the fur brigade. Because of the doctor's yeoman work during the outbreak of cholera, he was highly respected by all the fur company people, and his surgery on Jim Bridger had made them both part of beaver-country legend. Knowing that maintaining a successful mission among the Indians would require him to look after their physical as well as spiritual health, Whitman asked Matt about the medical aspects of the Lewis and Clark expedition.

"In the *Journals,* which I've read many times, eye troubles and digestive complaints seem to have been the principal ailments of the Indians then. Is that still true?"

"So I've been told. Make sure you're well supplied with eyewash ingredients and purgatives. Be careful you don't arouse the jealousy of the medicine men—the *tewats.* When deprived of fees, they can become quite vindictive."

"Well, I'm certainly not going to compete with them!" Whitman said with a booming laugh. "But as a matter of professional curiosity, what would a Nez Perce *tewat* charge for curing a case of mumps?"

"To a man of average resources—a horse. Perhaps five horses, if he was treating a well-off chief. But before taking the case, he would make reasonably sure he *could* cure it. For if the patient died, a surviving relative might take it upon himself to kill the *tewat.*"

"That sort of thing would eliminate a lot of inept doctors, wouldn't it? I'll try to be careful."

Outshining all the others with her natural warmth and brilliance was Narcissa Whitman, who at twenty-eight was blond, beautiful, outgoing, and enjoying every minute of every day. Married only two months ago in the upstate New York church where her father, Judge Stephen Prentiss, was an elder, she considered the trip west a prolonged honeymoon. Blessed with radiant health and deeply in love with her husband, she reminded Matt a great deal of his own wife, Lydia, for both women were warm, cheerful, unable to see evil in any situation or person, and eager to make molehills of whatever mountains of adversity were in their path.

"We'll be traveling west with Mr. Thomas Fitzpatrick and his American Fur Company brigade," Narcissa Whitman told Matt. "Do you know him?"

"Yes. You'll be in the best of hands with him."

"My husband and Mr. Spalding both have wagons, but if I have my way, I won't ride a mile in a wagon. My husband has bought me a sidesaddle. When we set out across the plains, I expect to ride horseback all the way." Her musical laughter filled the room. "Won't it surprise the Indian ladies when they see me come galloping into their camp riding sidesaddle on a spirited horse? Their eyes will pop out of their heads!"

"When you get to rendezvous, Mrs. Whitman, trappers who haven't seen a white woman in years will be watching you, too. I can guarantee their eyes will pop."

"Oh, that will be fun!"

Much alike as they were, Lydia and Narcissa became fast friends soon after meeting each other at the church special service. Proudly, Lydia showed Narcissa a miniature she had had done on vellum, that she was sending with Thomas Fitzpatrick "to our son John at rendezvous."

"It's from a portrait painted by a St. Louis artist," Lydia said. "We liked it so well we had three miniatures made— one for the mother, one for the father, and one for the grandparents."

"What a beautiful child!" Narcissa exclaimed. "What is her name?"

"*His* name is Luke," Lydia answered. "He's a boy."

"Well, I still say he's beautiful. I've never seen such stunning red hair. And curly, too. How old is he?"

"Three and a half. His father went west before he was born, so hasn't yet seen him. That's why we're sending him the miniature."

"He certainly should treasure it. Seeing it ought to make him hurry home and take his flesh-and-blood son in his arms."

Her eyes suddenly misting, Lydia turned away. "Yes—we're hoping that will happen."

Matt hoped fervently it would happen, too, for he knew that Lydia's generous, loving heart would break if she ever were forced to accept the fact that their son would never come home again. Better than John could guess, Matt knew why their son did not want to come home. At John's age, the West was freedom, St. Louis a prison. Until the crippling illness incapacitated him, Matt himself had been on the point of rejecting family, security, money, a solid position in the business world, and the love of a good white woman, in exchange for an uncertain life in a wilderness land with an Indian woman and their mixed-blood son.

There was no way he could force John to return to St. Louis, he knew. Only when the young man tired of the life he was leading and decided that a wife, home, children, and a less colorful but more solid existence meant more to him than what he was giving up would he come back. In sending him the miniature of his son—who truly was a beautiful child—Lydia was using the most potent argument that could be devised to reach John.

For the past year or so, Matt had worried increasingly about Susan and Luke's future. Both Lydia's father and mother were dead now, with all the wealth John Bower had accumulated willed to Lydia in Matt's name. Matt's mother had passed away six months ago, and the health of the Reverend Peter Crane was frail. Though Matt had promised Lydia that he would love and care for Susan and

Luke as if they were his own, legally they were not. So long as he or Lydia lived, Susan and Luke would be cared for as members of the family. But life was uncertain—as witnessed by the epidemics that from time to time swept through cities like New Orleans and St. Louis with stunning suddenness and terrible mortality rates.

Unless John came home, married Susan, and acknowledged Luke as his son, how could mother and child be protected in the event something happened to Matt and Lydia? In his will, Matt had provided for them generously, but he had done nothing to affect John's inheritance rights to half of the Crane estate; that had come to Lydia from her father's fortune, though like all property under current law it was in Matt's name and under his control. The question troubling Matt was: Would John be satisfied with half the estate after his parents were gone? In highly moral St. Louis, an unmarried mother and her bastard child could expect little sympathy in the courts. If John repudiated them and sued for their half of the estate in addition to his own, he would stand a good chance of winning and making them paupers.

The only sure way to provide for Susan and Luke, Matt's attorney had told him, would be to disinherit John and will all the estate to Susan, specifying that she hold it in trust for her son until he came of age. But cutting John out of his will was too final and brutal an act to be done without Lydia's consent—which he knew she would never give. So the best he had been able to do for the present was split the estate, with the St. Louis bank at which he now was a director named as executor. If John did contest the will, the bank at least would give him a good fight . . .

9

Where time had gone to, John Crane couldn't say. Not that it mattered much when there was new country to see, game to be killed, whiskey drunk, fun had, and Injun wenches to be chased. *But hell's fire, no man in his right mind would want to go after them Injun gals of the lower Columbia River tribes, 'cause if you screw one she'll be bound to give you six kinds of disease. Course, most of 'em smell as bad as they look, are greasy, dirty, and infested with fleas and lice.*

What he should have done, John told himself, was accept William Craig's invite and gone up to Lapwai in Nez Perce country. One thing about Nez Perce women—they were clean. Like the men in their tribe, they didn't feel right unless they bathed every day, winter and summer, in some kind of water, whether it be an ice-cold mountain stream, a lake, a river, or a hot-steam sweat lodge. And some of them were real lookers.

But time had gotten away on him. Oh, hell, face the truth! What with Joe Meek, Doc Newell, and their sport-loving, whiskey-swilling, independent-minded friends down Willamette Valley way, he'd just been having himself too much of a good time to haul ass upriver and visit Bill Craig, who with that Nez Perce woman of his was acting more and more like a settled old married man, these days.

Wanting to see what the country west of the Cascades was like when it wasn't raining, he'd skipped going to rendezvous the summer of '35, exploring the southern Oregon Siskiyou Mountains and the rugged Pacific Coast as far down as the California border. But Joe Meek, who had gone to rendezvous, had brought him back the usual packet of letters from St. Louis carried west by Lucien Fontenelle—a curt note from his father, a long letter from his mother, and a short, shy note from Susan, which he was sure his mother had encouraged her to write, telling him what a fine son they had and how well she and the child were being treated by his father and mother.

Damn it to hell! With his parents taking Susan in and publicly acknowledging that he was the child's father, he surely would have to marry her if he went back to St. Louis. Not that she was repulsive to him; fact, of all the girls he'd fooled around with back home, she'd been the liveliest, the most fun, and the one he'd liked best. But it was that "have to" that stuck in his throat. Once he'd cut his ties with home and become his own man, damned if he ever again intended to do anything just because somebody in authority said he had to.

After wintering in the Rogue River country with Joe Meek, Robert "Doc" Newell, and half a dozen other mountain men, he'd drifted east with them during the spring and early summer of '36, finding good trapping along the Klamath, the John Day, the Malheur, the Owyhee, and the Snake and its headwaters up toward Jackson Hole. By rendezvous time in early July, they all had acquired enough furs to assure them of credit for a couple of weeks of drinking, with some left over for powder, lead, and possibles for the coming year.

Talk circulating around the campfires in the upper Green River valley was that this was to be the biggest and best fur rendezvous ever held in the West. The American Fur Company brigade led by Thomas Fitzpatrick contained seventy men, four hundred animals, and seven wagons heavily loaded with supplies, each pulled by a six-mule team. Close to five hundred trappers were there, coming in from all points of the compass to view a sight not seen by many of them for years—two white women, the first ever to cross the Continental Divide. Hudson's Bay Company parties led by Thomas McKay and John McCleod were there, no doubt with instructions to do everything possible to persuade the American missionaries to emulate the Reverend Jason Lee and establish their mission in the Willamette Valley rather than in the upriver country. But the Flatheads, the Nez Perces, and the Cayuses also were there, determined that this time the cherished religious teachers were going to settle in their homeland.

By custom, serious drinking took precedence over reading letters from home, so John Crane was more than a little mellow by the time he opened the packet of mail given him by the brigade clerk. As expected, the envelope addressed to him in his mother's handwriting was thick, appearing to contain at least a dozen neatly penned pages of warm, loving details of home, Luke, and Susan. She never criticized him in any way, assuming in her generous, openhearted fashion that when the time came for him to do the right thing by Luke and Susan, he would do it. Loving his mother as he did, he got such a good feeling from her letters that he always saved reading them until the last. Susan's letter, which usually was reserved and brief, he always read second. His father's, which usually was short and curt, he always read first.

But this time the envelopes addressed to him by both Susan and his father were much bulkier than usual. Hefting them as he lounged in the shade of the brush shelter he had rigged to break off the wind and sun, he took another swallow of the alky-and-water drink in the tin cup in his right hand, muttering, "Now, you mean ole son of a bitch. What kind of nasty names you gonna call me this time?"

Open the shitty thing an' find out. Swallow the bad-tastin' pill first. Then see what sweet Susan has put in her package for you. What a sweet package she is, come to think about it. Sweet and hotter'n six hundred dollars! An' wouldn't I like to have 'er with me now! He pawed open the letter from his father. *Okay, ole man! What 'ya got to say?*

"Since it has now been four years since you left home," his father wrote, and continued:

and you have made no effort to return to St. Louis and assume your responsibilities to the family business, your child, or its mother, I have been forced to take legal steps that will assure that those obligations are cared for in a proper manner. After discussing the matter with your mother and with Susan, I have instructed my attorney to draw up a new will, which secures the future welfare of Susan and her son after your mother and I are gone.

In that revised will, a copy of which is enclosed, I have recognized Luke as your natural son and as my grandson, with the same inheritance rights he would have if you and Susan were married. Half of my estate is willed to him, to be held in trust by the executors until he comes of age, with his mother receiving whatever funds she may need for his care and hers as long as they live.

My own preference would be to eliminate you completely from any chance of inheriting any portion of the considerable substance which your mother and I have accumulated during our lifetimes of hard work and sound business judgment; but your mother feels that you should be given an opportunity to come home and repair the hurt you have caused and the damage you have done by marrying Susan and accepting your responsibilities. Reluctantly, I have agreed to give you one last chance to redeem yourself.

For the time being, you remain in my will as the recipient of one half of my estate, which is essentially a sum of the assets inherited from John Bower by your mother, and by law put into my name as head of the household. Until December 31, 1836, I will not alter your status, giving you an opportunity to come back to St. Louis and accept your responsibilities. If you do not, I shall in all probability rewrite my will, cutting you off completely despite the feelings of your mother.

Not bothering to read the copy of the will, which was seven pages long, John Crane stuffed it and his father's letter back into the envelope, took another long drink, and raised the tin cup in a sardonic toast.

"Up yours, you ole bastard!"

"Bad news?" Joe Meek asked, pouring himself a drink from the alky-and-water cask and then sprawling out in the shade of the brush lean-to.

"My ole man just disinherited me—in a half-ass sort of way."

"Why'd he do a thing like that?"

"Like I tole you, I knocked up a gal 'fore I left home. When the baby came, she run to my ma, who's soft on kids 'cause after havin' me she didn't have no more. Make a long story short, my folks taken Susan an' Luke in as their own. Now Pa says if I don't come home, git married, and act like a real father by the end of the year, he'll disinherit me."

"He got much money?"

"Hell, he's rich! Got a bank, a fur company, a bunch of mercantile stores, a lot of property, a steamboat line—he's into every business in St. Louis."

"This gal you knocked up. She ugly?"

"Lord, no! She's a ravin' beauty. Got the purtiest face an' figger and the shinin'est red hair you ever seen. Top it out, she's sweeter'n wild honey."

"How about the baby? It ugly like you, er purty like her?"

"I ain't never seen it, Joe. But way she describes it, it looks a lot like her. Which'd be purty. Here, I just got her letter. Let's see what she says about it this year."

Opening the envelope from Susan, John Crane exposed a four-by-five-inch leather-bound case that, when unfolded, disclosed a color portrait on vellum protected by glass. He stared down at it in amazement. The face looking out at him bore a striking resemblance to Susan and to himself: the green eyes, the milk-white skin, the stunningly brilliant red hair curling in thick ringlets, the devilish glint of mischief in the corners of the mouth.

"My God!" John exclaimed. "She's had his portrait painted! Look at the little rascal!"

"Hey! He's a purty young-un!"

"Ain't he, though!"

"John, are you gittin' rich trappin'?"

"Not to notice."

"Been in the mountains four years, ain't you?"

"Yeah."

"Seen about all there is to see. Raised about all the hell you want to raise. Screwed your share of Injun squaws."

"About the size of it, Joe."

"Then what in eternal tarnation is keepin' you out hyar, you damn fool? If I had waitin' fer me what's waitin' fer you, I wouldn't hesitate fer a minute. I'd haul ass fer St. Looie."

"Happen you could be right, Joe. I'll shorely give it some thought."

Because he was mighty drunk in the Green River valley during the next week, John Crane's thoughts were a tad disconnected for a while. But as his incoherent periods became fewer and his sober periods more frequent, he began to string his thoughts together in a more logical sequence. Face it, he wasn't a green peckerwood kid no more. He was twenty-eight years old. He'd seen a lot of country and done a lot of damn-fool things. He'd learned a lot of ways a man could get killed out here. Maybe the time had come for him to go home and settle down.

Sure be nice to see his mother again. Be great to see Susan, too. And Luke. Say, wouldn't it be fine to have that bright-eyed little tyke tagging along at his heels, learning to ride a pony, learning to hunt and trap, listening to his father tell all the things he'd done? Bet your sweet life it would! Aw, hell, it would even feel good to make up with the old man, who under the surface crustiness really wasn't a bad guy.

That afternoon, he went to Tom Fitzpatrick and told him he'd like to go back to St. Louis with the returning brigade.

"Fine," Fitzpatrick said. "You'll be welcome to travel with us. By the way, an express has just arrived from St. Louis. Check with the clerk. He has a couple of letters for you."

Dated three weeks after the ones brought out by the main brigade, one of the letters was from his father, the other from his father's attorney. Taking them to the brush shelter where he could read them in private, he opened the one from his father first.

Dear Son: With a great deal of pain in my heart, I must write you sad news. Ten days ago, an epidemic of Asian cholera swept over St. Louis and a large number of people took sick and died. Among the first to go were your mother and your grandfather. At least God was merciful in that their suffering was brief.

Susan and I both were taken ill. Her condition still is grave and I am so weak I can hardly find strength to hold a pen. Fortunately, at the first indication of the disease, we got Luke out of the house and into the home of my attorney, Samuel Wellington, whose estate is several miles out of St. Louis, on higher grounds whose air is unpolluted by poisoned city vapors. Last word is that his health remains good.

By now you should have received my letter stating my deadline for your return home and your acceptance of your responsibilities by the end of the year. Because of radically changed circumstances—i.e., your mother's death—I rescinded that deadline and committed an act that I know will strike you as outrageous. To assure Susan that she and her son will be members of the Crane family, I married her a week after your mother died. I am sure your mother's spirit blesses the marriage.

I have asked my attorney, Samuel Wellington, to write and explain to you how my marriage to Susan will affect your status as an heir and as Luke's father. My intent was to place control of their welfare in my hands, rather than yours, because you have amply demonstrated that you have no concern for them. In the event that Susan, I, or both of us should die, the bank will become Luke's legal guardian and will control any relations you might have with your son.

My hand is so weak I can write no more . . .

Stunned, John Crane dropped the letter to the ground. With a feeling of foreboding, he opened the other envelope.

"It is with deep regret," Samuel Wellington wrote, and went on:

that I inform you of the deaths of your father, Matthew Crane, and of Susan, the mother of your child, two days after your father wrote informing you of their marriage. Your son, Luke, who is being cared for in my home, remains in good health.

While your father's marriage to the mother of your child no doubt will strike you as most unusual, I assure you that it is legal and cannot be negated by any action you may choose to initiate. Henceforward the child, Luke Crane, will be a ward of the executors of your father's estate—namely, the Bower & Crane Mercantile Bank. Any contact you may wish to have with him must be arranged through me.

With deepest sympathy, I remain . . .

His head aching with the worst hangover he'd suffered in years, after getting blind drunk and staying that way for

SPECIAL PREVIEW!

Award-winning author Bill Gulick presents his epic trilogy of the American West, the magnificent story of two
brothers, Indian and white man, bound by blood and
divided by destiny . . .

NORTHWEST DESTINY

This classic saga includes *Distant Trails*,
Gathering Storm, and *River's End*.

---

*Here is a special excerpt
from Volume two, GATHERING STORM
—available from Jove books . . .*

Hearing that his half brother, John Crane, had come to the Green River rendezvous, Tall Bird went to William Craig; because of Craig's long association with the *Nimipu*, Tall Bird trusted him more than any other *Suyapo*. He asked Craig to point out the man without revealing Tall Bird's relationship to him. Because it was common knowledge among the Nez Perces that a number of persons about Tall Bird's age had been sired by members of the Lewis and Clark party, William Craig had long been aware of the relationship.

"Sure, I'll show him to you," Craig said genially. "But if I was you I wouldn't go near the booger till he sobers up. When he's on a toot the first week of rendezvous, John ain't very civilized."

Watching the long-haired, shaggy, unshaven white man swagger drunkenly about the camp for the next few days and nights, Tall Bird was glad he had not disclosed himself. So far as he could observe, his half brother was a lecher, a loud mouthed braggart, and a fool.

Tall Bird noted that, after a week of heavy drinking and debauchery, John Crane did begin to act more sensibly, sobering up, shaving, getting his hair trimmed, and donning decent-looking clothes. Still, Tall Bird did not approach him, deciding to wait until just before the breakup of rendezvous, so that if he were rebuffed or insulted he would not have to endure his half brother's presence for long.

But when he did seek the man out the day before leaving with his family and the party of white missionaries, he found John Crane so drunk and disheveled that it would have been impossible to communicate with him, even if he had wanted to. So, with loathing and disgust, Tall Bird left the man lying in his own vomit and filth in the shade of his brush lean-to, vowing never to attempt to talk to him again.

Soon after meeting the two missionary couples, Tall Bird had sensed that friction existed between them. Friendly and outgoing, Marcus and Narcissa Whitman liked the Indians and the mountain men, relished the excitement of rendezvous, and were inclined to overlook the rowdiness of this brief annual carnival as a relatively harmless expression of high spirits.

On the other hand, Henry and Eliza Spalding were horrified and repelled by the excesses of the trappers; they kept to themselves, and showed by their stern faces and dour looks that they disapproved of everything that was happening around them. While Narcissa Whitman was radiantly healthy and full of energy and high spirits, Eliza Spalding could not tolerate a diet of buffalo, antelope, elk, and dried salmon; languishing for days ill in her tent, she spent a great deal of her time writing in her diary, reading her Bible, and praying. Even so, she persisted in her quest of a working knowledge of the Nez Perce language, spending several hours each afternoon talking to the Indian women whom she insisted Tall Bird bring to her.

Between the Cayuses and the Nez Perces, an intense competition developed as to which tribe would play host to the white missionaries. Always an aggressive, quarrelsome tribe despite their relatively small numbers, the Cayuses insisted that the first mission be established in their homeland, the Walla Walla Valley.

Even more insistent was the Lapwai chief, *Tack-en-su-a-tis*, who declared that the mission must be established in his

part of the country. It had been the Nez Perces and Flatheads
who organized and carried out the journey in search of the
Book of Heaven, he said, so it was only simple justice that
the white religious teachers build their first mission in the
heart of Nez Perce and Flathead land. Furthermore, had he
not proved his loyalty to the Americans by fighting with
them against the Gros Ventres at Pierre's Hole, suffering
the grievous wound which had given him his name?

"Indeed, this is true, Rotten Belly," Tall Bird said dryly.
"But the *Tai-tam-nats* are men of peace, not of war. They
do not approve of killing."

"Just as you do not?"

"I obey my *Wy-a-kin*, as a man must."

When rendezvous broke up, the small band of Cayuses
and the large party of Nez Perces accompanying the white
missionaries toward Fort Hall argued so vociferously over
where the first mission should be located that the usually
cheerful Narcissa Whitman became alarmed.

"The Nez Perce women say we are going to live with
them," she wrote, "and the Cayuse say we are going to live
with them. The contradiction is so sharp they nearly come
to blows."

So far as the Indians were concerned, the dispute was
settled amicably enough after a few days on the trail, when
the Reverend Spalding pompously announced, with Dr.
Whitman nodding silent agreement, "We have reached an
important decision. Two missions will be established—one
among the Cayuses, with the Whitmans in charge; the other
among the Nez Perces, with myself and my wife in charge."

While the joy on the faces of the listening Indians of both
tribes was unrestrained, Tall Bird noted that the expression
on Narcissa Whitman's face was one of quiet relief. Though
she seemed to genuinely like Eliza Spalding and sympathize
with her physical frailties, it was obvious she had no use
for her dour, unbending husband. Nor did Marcus Whitman
treat Spalding with anything more than cold politeness. In
fact, the two men were increasingly at odds over the light

Dearborn wagon which the Reverend Spalding had insisted on bringing along, but whose management he was leaving more and more to Dr. Whitman.

As the summer days turned hot, dusty, and dry, the terrain became rougher and more difficult to negotiate. When Spalding suggested that the baggage be transferred to packhorses and the wagon left behind, Whitman became so exasperated he could not contain his anger.

"Leave it, you say? If I had known you were going to give up so easily, Henry, I would not have sold *my* wagon—which was heavier and better suited to rough trails—in St. Louis, and put our baggage in *your* wagon—which is too lightly built for this kind of country."

"You had seen the country, Doctor," Spalding said testily, "while I had not. You should have known the difficulties of taking a wagon across it. In fact, it is my firm belief that Mr. McKay is right when he says that taking a wagon through to Oregon is impossible."

"Thomas McKay is a Hudson's Bay Company man, with good reasons for discouraging our taking a wagon through. But I say it can be done. With a bit of perseverance, some shovel and ax work, and a lot of sweat and muscle power, we'll take the wagon through. Damned if we won't!"

"Profanity ill becomes your calling, Doctor."

"Then pray for me, Reverend. But while you're praying, I'd be obliged if you'd put a shoulder to the wheel."

Despite Narcissa's concern that her husband's strenuous efforts to take the wagon through by sheer brute force would injure his health, he refused to give up, no matter how many times the wagon mired down at stream crossings, upset on sidling slopes, or careened down steep pitches with frightening speed. To him, taking a wagon through to Oregon was a symbolic act, Tall Bird realized, which would demonstrate dramatically that the continent could be spanned by a wheeled vehicle.

"The Bible, the wheel, and the plow," Tall Bird heard him say to his wife one evening, after an especially exhausting day. "Where they go, civilization follows."

Though she sympathized with his goal, Narcissa secretly rejoiced when the wagon took a particularly bad fall on a steep slope near Fort Hall and shattered its front axle on a rock. Because no hardwood from which to fashion a replacement was available, she was sure the vehicle that had become such an obsession and burden to her husband would now be abandoned, with the baggage it carried transferred to packhorses. But she underestimated her husband's stubbornness.

"I'll cut it down to a two-wheeled cart," he declared. "I'd be obliged, Mr. McKay, if you'd loan me a saw."

But at Fort Boise the ungainly, battered, weathered cart was abandoned, for the long journey west had become a race against time. Giving the forlorn-looking, empty cart a last yearning glance, Dr. Whitman shook his head wearily.

"I've not given up yet," he told Tall Bird. "Next summer, after we've built the missions and gotten ourselves settled, I'm coming back to Fort Boise for the cart. Mark my word, I will take wheels through to the Columbia."

Reaching Fort Vancouver in mid-September, the men of the missionary party enjoyed Dr. John McLoughlin's hospitality for a week before heading back upriver to select sites and start building shelters. Though McLoughlin questioned the wisdom of establishing separate missions, and urged them to leave the two women at Fort Vancouver until next spring, neither Marcus Whitman nor Henry Spalding would change his mind.

"We told the Cayuses and the Nez Perces we would establish separate missions," Spalding said dogmatically. "That is what we intend to do."

"Our wives want to be with us," Whitman said. "In four or five weeks, we'll have some sort of shelter thrown up and will come for them."

At Fort Walla Walla, *Tack-en-su-a-tis*, Tall Bird, and a large band of Nez Perces were waiting for the missionaries, as were a number of Cayuses. Whitman and Spalding wasted no time selecting sites.

The spot chosen by Dr. Whitman in Cayuse country was on a flat, open, grassy plain between a clear-flowing creek and the Walla Walla River, with the two streams joining a short distance to the west. Because of the tall, grainlike grass growing in marshy areas along the stream, the Cayuses had called the flat *Waiilatpu*—"Place of the Rye Grass." Located twenty-two miles east of Fort Walla Walla, it was midway between the bone-dry, sagebrush-covered, sandy desert country flanking the Columbia River and the lush, tree-covered, much moister western slope of the Blue Mountains.

"Here we'll have the best of two worlds," Whitman told Tall Bird. "The sunshine, good soil, and mildness of the low country, and the timber, dependable water supply, and cooling night breezes of the high country. The site is ideal for a productive, self-sustaining mission."

Assisted by William H. Gray—an opinionated and contentious but highly skilled craftsman who had been employed by the American Board to help the missionaries—Whitman drew up plans for a house, a gristmill, fenced fields in which to keep the cattle he had brought along, and a large area to be plowed and planted with vegetables and grain. Meanwhile, the impatient *Tack-en-su-a-tis* and the Lapwai Nez Perces urged the Reverend Spalding to ride on with them and select the site for the mission he would build in their country.

Lapwai meant "Place of the Butterflies," Tall Bird explained as he rode with and interpreted for the missionary. By white man's measurement, it was 120 miles from the Cayuse mission site to the place where this band of Nez Perces wanted him to settle.

"But our country is big and has many beautiful valleys," Tall Bird said. "You should not choose a site until you have seen it all."

"Are the other leaders of your tribe as eager to hear God's word as *Tack-en-su-a-tis*?"

"Lawyer, of the Kamiah band, whose father cared for the Lewis and Clark horses, is most anxious to welcome religious teachers. *Ta-moot-sin*, of the Alpowa band, has heard God-talk from Spokane Garry, and is eager to join the church. *Tu-eka-kas*, head chief of my own Wallowa band and my cousin, has said that wherever the *Tai-tam-nat* establishes his mission in Nez Perce country, he will go there to live and listen until he has become a Christian."

"That is gratifying to hear. But since *Tack-en-su-a-tis* has made such a great effort to welcome me, I feel a site in his country must be given first consideration."

Because of the hot and rainless summer, the steep, barren brown hills of the Clearwater Valley offered a bleak visual prospect in early October as the party rode eastward. Tall Bird could see that Spalding was depressed by the look of the country.

"It's so mountainous and broken," he complained to Tall Bird. "There's no good soil or flat areas for crops and pasturage. We could never subsist our people in this kind of country, let alone a large band of Indians. Is it all like this?"

Before Tall Bird could answer, *Tack-en-su-a-tis*, who had guessed what Spalding was feeling, dropped back and rode beside them. Signing for Tall Bird to interpret truly, he spoke to the minister.

"We are now near the place where there is good land, if anywhere in the Nez Perce country. Perhaps it will not answer, but if it does I am happy. This is all my country, and where you settle, I shall settle. And you need not think you will work by yourself. Only let us know what you want done, and it will be done."

Ten miles above the juncture of the Clearwater with the Snake, *Tack-en-su-a-tis* and the band of Nez Perces turned south up the valley of Lapwai Creek. Here Spalding's spirits lifted visibly, for this valley contained good soil, was over half a mile wide, and supported a growth of small trees. Two and a half miles up the creek, the missionary halted and nodded.

"This will do fine. This site meets all my requirements."

"I am full of joy," *Tack-en-su-a-tis* said fervently. "Now tell me what you want us to do."

Selecting a building site at the foot of Thunder Mountain near a good spring, the Reverend Spalding told the Nez Perces, on October 12, 1836, that he intended to leave at once for Fort Vancouver. There he would pick up Mrs. Spalding and Mrs. Whitman, along with a large quantity of supplies and tools that the American Board was obtaining from the stores of the Hudson's Bay Company.

"Can your people meet me with plenty of horses in five weeks at Fort Walla Walla?"

"We can."

"Uncomfortable though it may be, Mrs. Spalding and I can endure living in a tent until our house is finished. When we come back, we will set one up near the site."

"A tepee will be warmer and drier. We will have one waiting for you."

Whatever Henry Spalding's faults as a person may have been, lack of energy was not one of them. Six days after leaving Lapwai, on October 18, he arrived at Fort Vancouver and began assembling the baggage and supplies to be taken upriver. Heading up the Columbia on November 3, he and his party reached Fort Walla Walla ten days later. There they were met by 125 Nez Perces, with a large herd of spare horses. The efficiency of the Nez Perces amazed Spalding.

"They took entire direction of everything," he later wrote, "pitched and struck our tent, saddled our horses, and gladly would have put victuals to our mouths, had we wished it, so eager were they to do all they could to make us comfortable. I was astonished at the ease with which they handled and packed our heavy bags and cases, the latter sixteen inches square, thirty inches long, and weighing usually 125 pounds. Our effects loaded twenty horses."

It was clear to Tall Bird that the missionaries had come to stay. In addition to the five thousand pounds of farming tools, provisions, clothing, books, and building materials the horses were carrying, Spalding took five cows, one bull, and two calves out of the herd that had been driven west from the States.

At first, relationships between the Spaldings and the Nez Perces at Lapwai were good. *Hin-mah-tute-ke-kaikt*, the *tewat*, accepted the missionaries cordially enough, joined the church, and was given the Christian name James. *Ta-moot-sin*, who moved his lodge from the Alpowa country to Lapwai, and *Tu-eka-kas*, who moved from the winter home of the Wallowa band at the mouth of the Grande Ronde to the vicinity of the mission, were Christianized and given the names Timothy and Joseph. Piqued by the way the three Indians had ingratiated themselves with his prize, *Tack-en-su-a-tis* refused to join the church or accept a Christian name for the time being; while Lawyer, of the Kamiah band, shrewd politician that he was, decided that he, too, would stay out of the church until he saw which direction it was taking his people.

Working together, Spalding and Gray designed a house eighteen feet wide by forty-two feet long that could be used both as living quarters and as a meeting place. With considerable help from the Indians, they completed the principal work on the structure in three and a half weeks. Logs for the building, which had been cut some distance upriver and then floated down the Clearwater, were carried on the shoulders of the Indians more than two miles from the river to the site. Boards were whipsawed for the floor. The roof was made of timbers covered with a layer of grass and then a layer of clay—a not very satisfactory covering, for when it rained, mud oozed through cracks between the timbers and into the rooms below.

Skilled though William Gray was as a carpenter, he was bitter and discontent with the role he was playing at the missions. Fanatically religious, he wanted to serve God as a minister, doctor, or both, he told Tall Bird, though he was not qualified for either profession.

"If they'd just let me go back East next summer, I'd spend the winter studying medicine and reading the Bible. Come spring, I'd be as qualified to doctor as Whitman and as fit to preach as Spalding. Which ain't very fit. He's a bastard, you know."

"You mean, he had no father?" Tall Bird asked.

"Oh, he had one all right, like every bastard does," Gray said with a shrill laugh. "Trouble was, nobody except his mother knew who he was—and she never told. In fact, she thought so little of Spalding she gave him away to another woman when he was only fourteen months old, and never saw him again."

"How did he become a minister?"

"Plain bullheadedness and guts. At twenty-one, he could barely read and write. But he kept going to school till he finished Franklin Academy and Western Reserve College at the age of thirty. His wife, Eliza, who is a lot better educated than he is, ran a boardinghouse to help him through college. He don't like Narcissa Whitman because years ago he asked her to marry him and she turned him down."

Despite his contempt for Spalding's background, Gray was eager to enlist his aid in setting in motion a plan which would give Gray the mission of his own that he so deeply desired.

"What you Indians need are milk cows, beef cattle, and white teachers. You've got thousands of horses. If I could persuade your chiefs and Whitman and Spalding to let me have a few dozen good horses, I'd take them to fur rendezvous next summer, go to St. Louis with a brigade, trade the horses for cattle in the settlements, spend the winter in the East studying and recruiting people and funds, then the next year I'd come back and set up a mission of my own. Among the Flatheads, maybe. Or in the Spokane country. What do you think of the idea?"

"Such important matters can be decided only by chiefs," Tall Bird said cautiously. "But I am sure that the cattle and the teachers would be welcomed."

Though Tall Bird had returned to the winter village at the mouth of the Grande Ronde by then, he heard that William Gray and the Reverend Henry Spalding went in March 1837 to the Spokane country, where Spalding preached a sermon to the Indians, with Chief Garry interpreting. Afterward, they worked out a deal by which Spokane, Nez Perce, and Flathead leaders supplied Gray with a number of horses to be taken East next summer and traded for cattle. If the American Board approved his request, he would return in the summer of 1838 with the cattle, substantial reinforcements for the two missionaries already in the field, and authorization to inaugurate a new mission of his own. Accompanying him would be half a dozen Nez Perce and Flathead Indians.

Exactly what happened during the eastbound trip would forever remain in the realm of speculation, so far as the Nez Perces and mountain men friendly to them were concerned. Reaching rendezvous grounds several weeks before the caravan from St. Louis was due to arrive, Gray abandoned his plan to cross the plains under the protection of the returning fur brigade, impatiently deciding to proceed without it.

"It was a damn fool thing to do," William Craig later told Tall Bird grimly. "Jim Bridger advised him agin it, saying the Sioux would be bound to attack such a small party, kill the Injuns in it, and steal the horses. But he was bound and determined to go."

Near Ash Hollow, in Sioux country, Bridger's prediction came true. The Indians who were with Gray were killed and the horses stolen, Gray himself barely managing to escape with his life. Despite his later self-justification of his behavior, the verdict among Indians and mountain men was that he had cravenly deserted his Indian friends in a tight spot, trading their horses and lives to the Sioux for his own.

Though the American Board was displeased with Gray's unauthorized trip east, and horrified by his account of the killing of his Indian friends, they did come up with the funds and personnel to supply a substantial reinforcement to the missions in the Oregon Country.

Because he wanted to build a gristmill and needed Gray's assistance as a carpenter and millwright, Spalding reluctantly accepted him at Lapwai upon his return in late summer 1838. But after hearing what had happened on the way east, Spalding was deeply concerned about the reaction of the Nez Perces to the killings.

"It is said," he wrote, "they will demand my head or all my property."

No violence was done him by the Indians, but he was obliged to give cows to the chiefs who had lost horses. From that time on, Tall Bird knew, *Tack-en-su-a-tis*, who had lost a relative, and the white mountain men living near Lapwai, who had taken Indian wives, had little use for missionaries . . .